DROWNING IN SAND

Drowning in Sand

J. Marc Harding

www.JMarcHarding.com

Library of Congress Control Number:		2016910137
ISBN:	Hardcover	978-1-5245-1167-8
	Softcover	978-1-5245-1166-1
	eBook	978-1-5245-1168-5

Print information available on the last page.

Rev. date: 06/17/2016

To order additional copies of this book, contact:
Xlibris
1-888-795-4274
www.Xlibris.com
Orders@Xlibris.com
742560

CONTENTS

There once was an ocean,
Clear and peaceful,
With blue sky and clean sand for the people.

But the wave's motions,
Constant and thrashful,
Carried chemicals and trash: 'twas crassful.

Soon the State set in motion
A healthy chore:
Have sickies convalesce at the ailing shore.

With almost no commotion,
The sick and crazy,
The thick and hazy, went to live by the sea.

She's sick, the ocean,
And so are we all,
But that polluted tide shall be my pall.

**Handsome Kelly (a.k.a. "Northern Wrecks")
Sickie Shoals, NC**

CHAPTER ONE

the Convalescents by the Sea

This is it: Old, bleached beer cans jingle in the dying dune grass; if it shines, it is shattered glass. The sand blown against crab shells and the sea oats' orgy are a percussive hypnotic; the stench of death is enough to bring you down from any prescribed narcotic.

Mere yards away, the grinding breakers moan constantly, taunting the nauseated convalescents. The wind thrashes through vacant ocean-front dwellings and makes a mournful sound, not unlike members of a pod searching for their beached brethren, left unfound. A rot riot.

"The Shoals."

Yes, that sweet sea breeze that lulled so many people to sleep is now gag-inducing to the resident insomniacs.

This is it: Plastics overstay their welcome and are scattered by the ghastly gales, some blown in to tangle among the sparse vegetation, while some just float on those poor, overdosed waves.

The laughing gulls hang over head, constantly screeching, like mocking a tortured child.

There's the occasional aggressive wasp, a dwindling herd of skinny island deer, a random dead fox at the side of the sandy road, a skittish sanderling, a rare healthy sandpiper, but mostly it's just the gulls and the convalescents.

"Welcome to the Shoals," says the resident insomniac, sick from prescribed narcotics, listening to the percussive hypnotics. One never feels fine this close to the trashline.

1

There was no welcome station to embrace him when he got here. There is no reason for tourists to visit, no desire to come down to the shore anymore. The Barrier Islands have become the Burial Islands.

He's talking to himself and getting sand in his teeth from the rank winds; the mad winds turn the most stoic among them into amenomaniacs. His tongue will feel swollen shortly; it will feel covered in an ashy film from the dirty wind, momentarily. Soon. Soon. Now.

When the sun rises the first thing it shines on is the floating junk, the omnipresent trashline trespassing just past the breakers from the derelict houses, discarded medical devices, and beached dolphins. The rot riot; the rot race.

"Sickie Shoals." He's gotten used to talking to himself and almost accustomed to the grinding of sand in his mouth. Gritty utterances. Sandy spit.

Yes, this is it: There are no surfers here anymore, not even when the storms roll in great waves, as no one wants to surf the trash. The lifeguard stands are rotting where they were deserted, some have become gull havens, some have become splinter palaces, some have been torn apart, their wood used for beach funeral pyres. Salt water fishermen have all driven inland to the fresh mountain streams; they abandoned their surf rods on the littered dunes.

He spits out ash-gray sand. A gull laughs from somewhere, hovering nearby, fighting the winds above the quisquilian shore. If he's had enough pills, he will answer himself. But he's not to that point tonight; not yet. Not yet. Maybe sooner, maybe later. Probably sooner.

The waves crash onto the trashed shoreline in front of him; no one has played in these breakers for years, at least not intentionally. A body is found occasionally, crashing in and washing out, crashing in and washing out, over and over and over, a Sisyphean drowning.

When he sits at this spot on a clear day, as clear as it gets here at least, and watches the sun rise up, he see little midnight-black specks and spots shoot across the glare: sometimes the specks are gulls flying by, more often it is airborne trash.

Different waves have different voices, and now they sounds like an angry mob, calling for a captive, him, if but as a scapegoat, yelling from there and from over there, yelling, chanting, taunting, for him, for him. The gulls shriek siren blasts. He wouldn't be the first dragged out by this patient yet persistent tidal force, those ripping tides, if he could get close enough for it to grab him. But he can't. Not without help; he's gotten used to it by now.

He sits at an open sliding glass door, rubbing his oily fingers onto his jeans; the grease and oil is from his wheelchair. The front wheels are as far as they can go without going over a bump and out onto the wet, warped deck. He stares out at the surf, at the waves, at the trash in the water, the floating trashline, bleach bottles and milk jugs; feathers and more feathers, endless floating feathers. When the wind is blowing just right, in the direction of their house, it smells like a mismanaged seafood restaurant in an under-populated strip mall during an extended power outage.

There are few footprints on the sand; though there's the random soul wandering, dazed from a dosage. The beach patrol has been disbanded; it's been 'at your own risk' for a while now. The trashcans are still there, somewhere under that pile of trash and sand and shells and fishing lines and hooks and feathers, but they are the end of the line now, the landfills are on the beach, and the beach is a landfill. Now there's a great difference between being sea sick and being a sea sickie.

Feathers are spread around like a mad man slashed his way through a Las Vegas show girls' dressing room.

There hasn't been a child in a sandy bathing suit making sand castles here for years; no parent, responsible or not, would allow their child to play in such a vile and foul dump. The only children here are the ones who are too sick to make it, the ones for whom there is no hope, no cure, nothing but chemical comfort until, until…

His feet are sticking out over the deck and getting wet from the rain, but the eave shelters most of him. He's still in the socks he was given in the hospital, short socks with rubber grips on the bottom so he won't slip when he walks, if he walks. He can walk a little, but it hurts a lot. He doesn't mind his feet getting a little wet in the cold rain; he can't feel his left one right now anyway. The left one: swollen, inflamed, rebellious, and odious. Brimstone and fire reign under his skin.

Out there, beyond the polluted breakers, beyond the trashline, but before the smoggy horizon, is that smoldering ship. It looks like a toy from this distance; like a toy that's been set on aflame and set adrift. It has been slowly burning out there for weeks; at first it was said that it should burn itself out after ten days, and then after the next rain, and then next week or so. But it's been out there, floating and smoking, filling the sky with an ebony tattoo of smoke that smells like burning truck tires and burning pubic hair and burning plastic dolls. Percussive hypnotics; prescribed narcotics; resident insomniacs; indolent hypochondriacs. The Barrier Islands have become the Burial Islands. The rot race; see the rat rot by the sea.

He tries to move his left toes; he thinks he sees them move, slightly. Two toes feel crushed and he expects to look down and see them swollen or bruised, but they look fine. He can't feel the other three toes on that foot, which is fine, at least they don't hurt. He does the same to the toes on his right foot, the one that can feel the rain land on it, even thru his socks. He sees that as a small victory, but a victory none the less. He can see the big toe move, and he can feel it move, too, and he can feel a jolt of hate run up his leg and stab him in the buttocks before it wrenches him in the spine, and then shocks him in the neck. He forgets about the small victory.

The state agencies who would protect the sea turtles nests have long disbanded. The sea turtles have stopped laying their eggs for a simple reason: near extinction. One is found dead, washed up and half eaten, every couple of years.

He winces in pain and accidently takes a deep breath and inhales the rancid combination of the trashy sea smell and the burning ship. The ship's fumes keep burning off, and the sucker just seems to float in one place, in front of their oceanfront unit, their convalescent house. When he takes a deep breath, his hip stings as if from a dozen wasps, his left leg burns as if covered in kerosene and lit.

There is no sweet odor of suntan lotion in the air; sour disinfectants are in excess.

He coughs, it burns, and when he coughs the burn goes up his throat while the pain spills down his legs and he feels like he's going to jump out of his chair, and then he feels like he's going to cry. He holds his breath and waits for it to pass, waits for his nerves to settle, and he holds it in, and tries not to cough, and tries not to breath, but he coughs again, and he hurts all over, and sometimes he thinks that if he could get out of this chair, and if he could get over the dunes, and walk on that trashcan beach, avoiding all of the dead sea gulls, and even worse the sick gulls, and get to the water, he'd wade right in and swim past the waves, past the trashline, and just swim out to that burning ship, and not bother to take in air, and he'd get tired, but soon at least he wouldn't have to be putting up with this, this constant burning sensation, the lightning legs, the spinal stabbings.

A volley ball net, torn in places, traps careless gulls where they stay stuck until they die, looking like demented Christmas tree ornaments, looking like warnings to other gulls: disregarded warnings.

Being like this, being in this wheelchair with this atomic explosion of pain in his raped nerves is considered a success: keep him in the hospital for a week, then another week (ammonia smells; hacking sounds; buzzers and beepers; stretchers and walkers), and then they realize that all he does is vomit from the pain when he tries to walk. It used to be easy, walking, standing, but that seems so far away, so far in the past.

So they put him onto one of the public transports and send him and his wheelchair down to one of the beachfront convalescence units, so he can moan and throw up there, out of the way; so that they can go ahead and open up space for the people who can actually be helped, easier, cheaper. So, he's been here, not getting better, just puking into his lap. Trying unsuccessfully to sleep; turning in bed and waking screaming, trying unsuccessfully to concentrate on anything, anything but the pain, the spasms, the stomach bile in his lap. He watches the waves get bigger and the dunes get smaller. Week after week, and the trashline gets wider, and that ship keeps on burning and burning, but won't sink or smother, and the whole waterfront stinks like a neglected paper mill, like an unmanned landfill in July, like downwind from a pod of bloated, beached whales.

So, now he sits, and the bad air goes in again, and he bends over and throws up on his lap, legs, and feet. He can feel it on his socked right foot, but he can't on his left foot. Pins and needles; lightning pain: he dreams that his leg bones have been replaced with lightning rods which are continually struck by bolts.

And he gags, and coughs again, and he feels like he's going to die, wishes he would actually. Once he stops coughing, he wonders if he's pissed himself as he hears his name being called; he's afraid he might crap cobwebs his intestines feel so upside-down from the pills, from the cure.

Gag. Cough. Piss.

Repeat.

Then repeat again with the occasional vomit and persistent depression.

Percussive hypnotics; prescribed narcotics; resident insomniacs; indolent hypochondriacs. He's gotten used to it by now, being sick at the sea, sick on the Burial Island. The rot race; see the rat rot by the sea.

"Map?"

He looks over at her. He thought that she was asleep in her trough.

She's so big that a special tub, resembling an industrial trough, was installed in the living room. It's a huge tub, it's the largest that Map has ever seen and her flesh spills out of it, as if it is trying to escape from her, as if trying to retreat.

He looks over at her, at all of her, spilling out of it. He stares her way for an instant; his medicine improves his eyesight (the only benefit from all of this) and he gets lost focusing in on a cool grayish drop of water, the size of a pencil eraser; he watches that gray droplet slowly roll over her rolls, leaving an oily trail on her skin.

He rubs his fingers together at the sight, instinctively; he hates this oil on his fingers. He smells of vomit; he hates it.

"Map?"

"..."

"Excuse me, Map?"

"Yes, Ms. Nevershe?"

"Map, would you be a dear and roll into the kitchen and grab Pistachio a snack? And maybe close that door; that smell is making me hungry for fast food; and I'll catch a cold here in this tub."

"Yes, Ms. Nevershe; I'll get Pist something. Let me go change first."

He sits there in his chair, not moving, staring at the charcoal-gray glob of dirty water dripping down off her fat, and she's in that water, the same stale water that she's been in since yesterday, maybe the day before that actually, her whale-sized private parts covered by stained beach towels.

And on her mountainous left tit sits Pistachio, her fur dyed cotton candy pink. Huge prune hands pet Pistachio as the dog stares at Map, and he reaches down and turns his chair around and wheels over into the kitchen.

The staff usually won't allow the patients to have pets; but Ms. Nevershe made such a fuss, and she stirred up such a stink that they allowed her to have her piggy-pink poodle Pistachio. Recently, Ms. Nevershe mumbled to Map, through her bloated and chapped five-pound lips, that Pistachio was twenty-three years old. 'And it looks like it,' Map thought to himself. But, perhaps he misunderstood, he wonders about that: twenty-three? Is that possible?

Now, he rolls himself into the kitchen, and grabs a can of expired baby food, drops it into his lap, where it lands in his throw-up. He wheels himself down the hall, past the other closed bedroom doors, and when he rolls past the second one he hears a hacking cough, but he keeps on going; he's gotten used to it by now.

He wheels into his assigned room, and gets some clean pants and a shirt out of the sandy chest-of-drawers. He positions himself next to his bed, and he readies himself to stand up and deal with putting on the clean clothes.

He takes a deep breath, and at least it smells cleaner in here, away from the beach stench. He holds the air in; this beach house has a mild hospital smell to it, and it burns his lungs. Ammonia. Bleach. Urine. He rubs his eyes, rolling his greasy fingers in slow counterclockwise circles.

Headaches haunt him. Lethargy lingers.

Toes throb. Seditious spine.

Never-ending nausea. Piss and vinegar.

He's gotten used to it by now.

He puts his hands on the side of the chair, and he thinks about getting up for a minute or two. And then he starts, and he gets halfway up and he sits down again. Or, rather, he drops himself down. But he smells the vomit, and that's enough for him. He does it, he stands up. Fire and brimstone jump up and down his legs, and the corners of his eyes darken, and he gets dizzy, but he stands up and reaches out for a desk to hold onto, and he stands, and he smiles, a sweaty, pale smile.

Sweet, sweet dizziness. Dizzy, dizzy sweetness.

Sweaty dizziness. Sweaty shivers.

He's gotten used to it by now.

After he struggles through changing his clothes, he wheels himself back down the uneven hallway with its piss and vinegar reek. Map pauses between two closed bedroom doors. One is quiet; but he expects that one to be quiet until after dark, at least. In the other, he doesn't hear a hack again, but hears the medical-television change channels a few times, so he knows that Ehab is in there and alive.

He wheels himself into the great room, the main room, the communal area.

"Here, Pist."

The dog wags her decades-old, balding tail and raises one paw, just a little, and waits for Map to feed her. She's gotten used to him by now.

He wheels over and positions himself next to Ms. Nevershe, who is snoring like a drunken foghorn in her mid-bath nap. Map opens the jar, mashed peas that expired three years ago, and uses a spoon to get some of the web-like mold off the top of the now rot-brown colored green peas, and holds the jar near the dog's mouth, who gingerly starts licking the rancid mush.

The dog eats, and Map sits there, in his wheelchair, rubbing his greasy fingers onto the dog's thinning fur, and he watches out the window as the sky darkens into night, and the dark plume from the smoking ship is now barely visible on the darkened horizon, but the trashline out there glows a dying-neon-green hue, and Map feels the wind picking up again, like it does all the time, and then he smells the salty trash and rot of the beach. That abandoned seafood market smell. The rotting sea turtle cologne. The severed dolphin tail perfume. The decapitated stray dog-head aftershave. He's gotten used to it by now, somehow. The rot race; see the rat rot by the sea, sickie.

The med-t.v. behind him changes channels, and he looks back, turns painfully and sees nobody else there in the room with them. Ms. Nevershe wakes for a moment, looks over towards Map, and mouths a blubbery 'Thank you' before she returns to sawing redwood logs in her insipid soup. The dog, exhausted from eating, closes her ancient eyes and falls asleep with her senior snout inside the peas, so Map gently lowers the jar and holds the dog's aged face with his other hand and lowers it onto the fatty pillow that is her owner's left breast.

He wheels himself back to the sliding glass door, and positions himself there, watching those waves get bigger and bigger and those dunes get smaller and smaller. After a second he needs some fresh house-air, so he throws the half-eaten jar of rotten peas out over the deck; the tide will come up and grab it and take it back out to the trashline, the ever growing, glowing trashline.

The sun finally goes down behind them, west of the house. The medical-television changes channels seemingly by itself again; and as the last rays of sunlight disappear and the ocean and the sky are dying black, Map hears a bedroom door open and then hears light footsteps in the piss and vinegar sprayed hallway. Map hears the refrigerator door open and close, and the footsteps come into the room he's in, near the sleeping Ms. Nevershe and the digesting Pistachio.

He reaches down and turns his wheelchair around.

She waves to him.

"Hello, Tonya," he says.

She walks around the room, closing the blinds in all of the windows, and then, when they are all closed, she looks over at Map and smiles and says, "Hey, Map, how are you?"

The med-t.v. across the room changes channels; the dog burps in its sleep.

Neither of them says anything, but they stare at the med-t.v. across the room, until she yells, "Turn the channel, Ehab, this is a re-run!"

There's a cough in reply from behind the wall.

The channel on the medical-television changes again, from a heart transplant to a breast enlargement, and Tonya shouts, "Not this, Ehab, perv!" and the channel changes and the cough from behind the wall has a laugh in it. The next show is a knee transplant, and Tonya yells, "Wait!" and there's a cough from behind the wall.

Map turns his chair to face the far wall, where the medical-television is, and he stares at the screen and begins to lose focus for a second when a cough from behind the wall wakes him and Tonya shouts, "Ehab, you alright?", and then the coughing stops, and Tonya goes back to watching the operation on the screen.

She glances over at Map and says, "I'm going to go grab some applesauce; do you need anything?"

Map shakes his head 'no', and wishes he could smell the vomit from his old shirt, as a new rancid whiff of outside air makes it way inside and into Map's nostrils. It is horrid. He grimaces from the smell and then shakes and shivers as small pains make their way around his legs and spine, stabbing him here and there with little piranha teeth.

Devil's daggers. Satan's spears. Lucifer's lances.

Craps of fate, he's gotten used to it by now.

Ms. Nevershe and Pistachio snore and burp in their watery and pissy bed.

The med-t.v. changes channels; a cough emits from Ehab's side of the wall. Tonya comes in carrying a bowl of applesauce; to Map, the cinnamon on top looks a little too sandy. She's holding her finger to one of her teeth, and moaning; she looks around at the windows in the room, they are all shut and the blinds are drawn, so she speaks towards Map: "Is she okay over there, in her slosh?"

"Well, she's been asleep a whale."

"A while."

"Right; huh?"

"Not a whale."

"What?"

"You said 'whale'."

"No, I didn't; are you sure?"

She nods. He looks over towards the snoring mass.

Tonya smiles and holds a tooth; "I think another one of these is going to fall out soon."

Map looks over to her from his position in his chair; Pistachio moans in her sleep; the water softly splashes about in the tub nearby; Ehab changes the channels in his room and the med-t.v. in front of Map and Tonya flips from an elbow surgery to a dental surgery; Tonya keeps on holding her rotting tooth with one hand. She shouts: "Ehab, wait!"

After a minute of watching the procedure on the med-t.v., Tonya looks over at Ms. Nevershe and Pistachio, who is still asleep on her owner's swollen teat, with her leg dangling down, tucked between the oversized tub and the oily flesh of her supersized owner.

Tonya says, "Is it just me, or is she bigger than she was earlier?"

Map looks away from the med-t.v. and looks at Tonya, and says, "Come on, that's not nice."

"No. Look at her." He does; she continues, "And I don't mean that she's gotten bigger since I was sent here, because, believe me, she has; but I mean, doesn't she look like she's gotten bigger recently, like, since the breast augmentation operation we were watching a little while ago, after Ehab changed it from the heart transplant?"

Map keeps looking at Ms. Nevershe; she does looks to be spilling over the side a little more than she was earlier; but then he lies to Tonya, "No."

He looks away; she looks away; then she looks back and says, "Are you sure, Map?"

He looks back; the dog moves her geriatric bones in her sleep, but her rear left leg is stuck now, stuck between the tub and the blub.

"Hmm. I'll watch her some more."

There's a cough from behind the wall, and the channel changes once more, to a genitalia reconstruction operation. Tonya hiccups, burps, and then shouts "Ehab!" until a cancerous cough comes from behind the wall and the channel changes again, and the hack continues. Map looks over towards Tonya, who's watching molars being extracted on the sandy screen, and Map sits in his chair, getting tired from his pills he took after dinner, and the pills he took later because he was bored.

He might need more soon, will need more soon. Sooner than later. So soon it is almost now.

He closes his eyes for a minute; Tonya is quietly watching the operation on the med-television. And in the quietness, Map can hear the wind picking up outside, the wind is whipping the rank air around the house, and the waves outside are getting bigger, and the manmade dunes, made from old Christmas trees and some broken horse skulls and old canvas bags, are getting smaller, and smaller.

His eyelids are getting heavier now.

"Ahh!"

"Wooooof!"

"Ahh!"

"Aarp! Aarf! Aarp!"

"Ahh!"

Ms. Nevershe and Pistachio are exchanging screams of pain; Tonya is asleep on the sofa, a program on corpse embalmment is on the screen, the volume is off, no coughs are coming from Ehab's side of the wall. Tonya jerks awake and sits up; hears the screaming giant in the tub and says, "Map! Wake up!"

Map opens his eyes and hears Ms. Nevershe's "Ahh!" and the cherry blossom pink poodle is screaming in her own canine dialect and starts to pee; the old dog's urine rolls down the huge fat rolls into the oily tub water with the dust floating on top; "Ahh!"

Map tries to get up, out of instinct, and that's when an invisible spirit appears to hit him in the spine with a tire iron, or at least that's what it feels like to him.

He aborts trying to stand, and he wheels his chair around and he finally gets a good look at her, at Ms. Nevershe, at all of her, and he says, "Ahh!"

Map glances from the tub, which appears to have bags of leaves in it, but the bags are made of flesh, the pulled pinkish flesh that covers all of the acreage that is Ms. Nevershe; he looks over at Tonya, shakes his head, and says, "She's huge. Huger."

"That's not even a word; and I told you earlier that she was."

11

Then there is another scream of tormented agony from the tub, and the senile canine barks and barks and then passes out, as her owner expands further.

From the other side of the wall, there's an inquisitive cough, and Tonya answers, "We don't know, Ehab, we just don't know."

"Ahh!" And then she, Ms. Nevershe, passes out in the tub, light gray water running out from where her expanding doughy flesh overgrew its welcome in the tub.

Map says from his wheelchair: "Where's a phone? I need to call Dr. de Gouge!"

There's some fumbling around between the sofa cushions, and Tonya hands Map his phone, and he enters a number, and sweats while the phone is ringing, and he looks over at Ms. Nevershe, and she's gotten even larger, he imagines folds of fat will be touching the floor soon if she keeps on growing.

The doctor's phone rings; the wind blows harder outside; the waves keep getting bigger, and the dunes keep getting smaller, and the trashline out beyond the breakers is glowing mint green; there's a cough from the other side of the wall, and then the television changes channels to a show informing the units about trichomoniasis. He's gotten used to it by now.

It is later now, well past midnight:

Doctor de Gouge is standing in the living room, it's dark outside, but the first thing he does is open the blinds and look out over the ocean; Tonya quietly takes her old bowl of applesauce and leaves the room, Map hears her door shut a moment later, and then he hears a cough from the other side of the wall; the medical-television goes back to a breast enlargement surgery; and the doctor asks Map, "Is she still out there? Burning?"

"She? The ship?"

"Yes. Is she still out there burning up? I would think you could see a glow out there..."

"No; the only glow out there is the trashline. On the first handful of nights, you could see a burnt-orange glow over there, near the horizon, it was deliciously weird. But then, I guess with all of the smoke and all, it just stopped glowing."

"Well, what can you do?"

"Right. And, hey, what can you do, about this, about her?"

"Who?"

"Ms. Nevershe."

"Who?"

"Ms. Nevershe."

"The whale?"

"Yes: Ms. Nevershe."

"Oh," the doctor rubs his dreadlocked red beard, "oh," and he looks at the folds of flesh before him, and bends over and feels the humidity coming from the enormous nostrils, and he looks for toes, but realizes that he can't see any, "oh," and he reaches down to move one of the mildewed beach towels covering the metes and bounds of private parts, but then pulls his hand back, quickly as if he'd been burned, and he rubs his nappy beard, and finally sighs and says, "Nothing."

"Nothing?"

"Craps of fate, nothing."

"…"

"This woman has been one of the more difficult, er, interesting cases I've seen in all my years working down here at the convalescent units."

"Oh?"

"Well, young man, I mean, have you seen her?"

"I called you about her; I've seen her, yes."

"Then you know."

"I guess."

"In all my years, with the difficult cases, the sick, the dying, most of those cases I at least understand, I at least have some idea… Not just me, either, no one. This one, er, it's been a whale since I've seen something like this."

"You said it, too. Whale."

"Er, huh, ah."

"…"

"As I was saying, that's why she's here, convalescing by the sea, because, well, you know, what's to be done?"

"I don't know. I have no idea."

"Most people don't. Myself included in that statement."

"…"

Map is silent; the baby-pale pink poodle whines in its slumber; the mass in the tub grows; the doctor gets his finger caught in his beard and then removes it, and says, "Well, maybe," and he turns and walks across the room to where he dropped his medical bag, grabs it, and swiftly crosses back across the room with his index finger extended up in the air, "Maybe, if," and he plops the bag down into Map's seated lap, gracefully unzips it, and reaches in and pulls out a container of pills. "Hmm...." He opens it, peers in; the pill container is the same color as his knotted facial bush, "If... oh," and he pours a handful of shamrock green pills into his palm, looks at Map, and says, "There's not much hope here, at all," and he tosses three of the pills into his mouth, and then signals for Map to open his mouth and then he drops two of the pills into Map's mouth. The poodle wakes at this point and looks over at Dr. de Gouge, and the doctor responds to the dog with a gentle, "Oh, dear lord, old lady, you're going to need more of these than anyone."

He slowly feeds a handful to her, as the old dog slowly chews each pill one by one, and begins to wag her tail after the second pill, burps after the fifth, and by the seventh she is out cold again, her tail wagging in a narcotics-induced doggy dream.

The doctor feeds himself two more pills, and then gives Map one more and says through his thicket of scarlet beard, "This is where it gets unpleasant."

"..."

"Craps of fate, this is when it gets hideously unpleasant. For all of us, yes. Brilliantly unpleasant, yes indeed."

And the whale in the tub snores, and the wind outside screams, and dog in the tub howls as the doctor slowly saws off her rear, left leg, as it was mercilessly being pressed against the enormous tub and the continental-shelf sized flesh that lives day-in and day-out in that filthy, tepid tub water. Percussive hypnotics; prescribed narcotics; resident insomniacs; indolent hypochondriacs. He's gotten used to it all by now.

When the doctor is done there is a puddle of poodle blood on the floor, a smell of cauterized flesh and burnt hot pink fur. The whale of a woman in the tub is still asleep, larger yet, and the dog is passed out in pain and from pills. The doctor sits on the floor and takes two more pills out from his pocket and tosses them into his mouth, swallowing one reflexively and crushing the other between his filling-dotted molars. The sound makes Map flinch, and he moves the wrong way and as he does hits a nerve wrong and then all of a sudden he's shot by Satan in the spine, and he wishes that he had some more of those pills that the doctor has in his bag.

But it passes in a moment, his pain. Like two kicks in each gonad, and a kick in the chest, all at once. It floods over him, kicks him in the butt, and then stops just as quickly. He's gotten used to it by now.

The doctor sits on the floor, and picks up pieces of dog flesh and fur, and gets his stout body back up and walks over to the sliding glass door, opens it, tosses the bits of poodle out over the deck to the trashed shore and says, "Those filth-flocking gulls will love this," and then the wind carries in the smell of the shore, of the pollution and the trash, and the gusts bring the burning plastic and burning rubber and burning hair smell from the ship that's ghost-floating out there, burning in the wind, and he says, "Ah, there she is, ugh," and then he closes the door, gags a little, and looks over to Map and says, "Nothing like convalescing by the sea, eh, is there now?" And he smiles a fake smile; and Ms. Nevershe gains six pounds; Map smiles nervously and looks back over towards the med-t.v. where the breast enlargement is still going on, and he picks up a spoon (with hardened and sandy applesauce on it) from the table and throws it against the wall, and there's a damp cough and then the channel changes and the cough continues for a minute and then stops.

"..."

"Well said, er, ah, Map, well said."

"Hey, doctor?"

"Er?"

"Was that absolutely necessary?"

"Well, you saw how that leg was being strangled per se in that tub of blub, blubber, huh? No, no, that leg would have been no good to her after that; it was already dead. Circulation. Or, rather, lack thereof, you know?"

"Oh. Okay."

"But, as you ask, was there something else that could have been done? Oh, I don't know. Maybe. But this got the job done."

"The dog has one less leg now."

"Oh, that would have happened anyway, if not five minutes ago, sometime in the future. And in the near future, look at that old thing, like a 'ye olde colonial bitch', ha, that pox-plagued crust."

"..."

"Well. Can't look back now, can we, no?"

"No, can't go back now."

"..."

"..."

"It just seems like maybe there was something else that we could have done."

"Well, don't you worry, Map. We're here to help. We know what's best."

"…"

"We know what's best for you, for all of you. We're here to help; don't worry."

"…"

"Don't worry."

Craps of fate, craps of fate indeed.

"Aarp! Aarf!"

The pink poodle opens her bloodshot eyes and looks over at the doctor and at Map in his wheelchair, and then at her slumbering owner, and then to where her left leg used to be, and then again, "Aarp! Aarf!", and the dog stands up, drugged and dazed, and looks back at her master and then jumps down onto the floor, "Aarp!" and then after looking at Dr. de Gouge and Map, she lets out one last "Aarf!" and then the dog chokes for a second, closes her eyes, and the three-legged pastel pink pooch rapidly and violently expands to three times her previous size.

Stunned, the double-decades old dog is silent.

Dr. de Gouge looks from the dog to Map, and then asks, "You see that, too, er, right?"

Map nods his head; the doctor shoves his fingers into his dreadlocked beard and says, "Er, you and I are going to need more, um, medicine."

"…"

"Soon. Now, actually, hmm."

The prissy pink furry balloon wallows on the floor, rolls herself around for a minute before she gets upright, walks over to the windows, looks out and barks, no doubt at one of those mad gulls, and then she starts walking in circles, seemingly somewhat comfortable.

Map watches her from his wheel chair; the dreadlocked doctor turns and watches a spinal operation on the med-television; no one hears any coughs from the other side of the wall, but Tonya's thin voice comes through, "How is she?"

"Who?"

"Pistachio."

Map hesitates, "Fine; but different."

"And how about the other one?"

"Who?"

"The other one?"

"Ms. Nevershe?"

"Ms. Nevershe."

Map looks over to the doctor, who's still entranced with the blood and tubes on the television; Map looks over at the lady asleep in the tub, gaining ounces with every snore, and then coughs (and there's a reply cough from behind the wall) and he says, "Different; but fine."

The sky outside is getting lighter; the wind is howling and throwing sand against the house, chipping away what was left of the exterior paint; Map gets a random shock of pain down his leg and his eyes get watery; the television channel changes. A close-up video of vaginal thrush fills the screen; Map looks away; the doctor looks closer.

Through the walls, Tonya says: "Well, good night then."

Map: "Good night, Tonya."

"Good night, Ehab," she says from her room to his, there is a cough in reply, the channel changes again, to a burn victim being rehabilitated.

The doctor, sitting on the sofa among piles of sand and fidgeting with his beard's dreadlocks peers down to the table in front of him, and says aloud, towards Map, "There seems to be a tooth here, on this table."

Map keeps his eye on the sleeping pink fur, and says back to the doctor, "That's Tonya's."

"Maybe I should look at her, too."

"She doesn't seem to mind."

The doctor is silent; the medical-television stays on the same channel; no one coughs; the woman in the tub snores; the dog sneezes, and appears to lose a little weight, a few pounds maybe.

"Doc, look at Pist."

The dog coughs again, and quickly loses five pounds; meanwhile, her slumbering mermaid of a master in the tub takes in a cooler-sized gulp of air and gains ten pounds, the seams of the tub are starting to stress, folds of flesh are escaping.

"Hmm; okay, ah."

The sky out the window is private-parts pink, except for the plume of dark filth ruining the sky above the simmering ship out there; and the wind howls and the waves get bigger; and dead Christmas trees from the last four years are the most beautiful thing at the shore.

The dog gets smaller; the pounds seem to be jumping from the dog to her master.

The dog gets up, seemingly fine except for the missing rear left leg, and she hobbles over to Map, who sits in his chair watching the predawn sky being desecrated by the sour sight of the ship, and he scowls a little when the dog licks his hand, and then smiles and says, "Oh, alright," and he pets the disturbingly-pink poodle, who is now back to her normal size, give or take a leg.

The doctor gets tired of themed-television; he stands and maneuvers his barrel-like body over towards the transplanted tub in the middle of the room, and he stares at the flesh of Ms. Nevershe, and she burps in her exhausted sleep, but she doesn't lose a pound, quite the contrary actually, and he watches another olive-sized droplet of silver-gray water slowly climb down the massive body, between the stained beach towels, and the droplet slides its way down in the reservoir of stale dirt and sweat in the stressed tub; and the doctor turns away.

"Well, there's nothing more we can do for her now."

"Okay."

"Just watch her; let me know if she gets smaller."

"And what if she gets bigger?"

The doctor turns and looks back at the woman, who has gained three pounds since he last contemplated her a minute ago; "I don't think it's going to matter at this point."

"Nothing you can do?"

"Well, Map, ah, that's why she's here," and he stares out of the window now, towards the brightening horizon, towards the abandoned ship, "convalescing by the sea." He holds his lips closed tightly, he's staring out over the sea. "But let me know of the dog, let me know how she does; I think she'll be fine; but different. Significantly different indeed."

"So, uh, what's wrong with her? Any diagnoses?"

"Er, uh," he fiddles with his scarlet and dreaded beard, "Who?"

Map points over towards the giant tub.

"Ah, yes, yes. No. No idea. Not for sure at least. I imagine just due to nature. Or what's become of it."

"Sorry?"

"Just the price to pay to be alive in twenty-first century America, son."

"..."

"All the crap we put in ourselves, the stuff we keep our food in. We have to make a decision, eat and live how we want to, some of it is good for us, some of it is bad for us; all of it is bad for the world around us, and that's the choice we as a society have made."

"Hmm."

"Craps of fate, just look at my Santa Claus figure... it was from my choices, I chose to eat the flockin' crud they sold me, I could have made better choices, but I made the choices I wanted to, not necessarily the choices which were best for me, or best for the world as a whole."

"And?"

"I don't know what's wrong with her, Map, it appears no one does; but I assume it was from her lifestyle. We take advantage of the bad and it does us no good, er, right?"

"Right, I guess. I guess."

"So, however she lived her life, I'd advise you to do the opposite, if you care to."

Map is silent.

The doctor's dreaded beard giggles as continues: "I mean, just look at what she ate. And look at how much she ate of that crass crap. I've seen the, ah, er, the itemizeds; I know what comes and goes into these units. All the reports, they go by me. Some first, some last, but all of them eventually. That's part of our job. Part of, er, my job. But I've seen those reports; I thought that there was a mistake at first, of course."

"..."

"And think of all those pastries, her sweet breads..."

"Okay."

"Do you see what I'm getting at? The azodicarbonamide. Too much. She's been ingesting way, way too much. Way too much."

"I see."

"Do you? I mean, you're asking what's wrong with her, and the answer is exactly what I'm telling you. She did it to herself. That one poison itself is in everything from her hot dog buns to her tennis shoes, back when she could find some she could fit into. Those years are long gone, long gone now. And if we're not careful, ha, we'll end up like her."

"..."

"I mean, uh, craps of fate but I can't rule out some kind of zoonosis, not with all those gullpoxed bastard birds flocking everywhere. Gadfly dung, there's no way to name all the flocking poxes pestering down in this landfill, floating in the trashline. Gullpox. Dolphinpox. Tunapox. Skunkpox, they're down here, those sick little stinkers. Foxpox, a personal favorite of mine. Foxes, that is, not poxes. Sparrowpox. Toadpox. And, orf, mustn't forget orf, no, no. God, orf can be nasty... I mean, it could be worse, she could have the old scabby mouth. Makes me shiver every time." He shivers; his dreadlocks dance, sand falls like snow from his thick facial hair.

"If Ms. Nevershe was poxed that would make her contagious."

"Well, that dog, you know, so, seems to be so, yes, yes... But, I like to think she's an extreme case. An extreme."

"..."

"We like to keep quiet about her. Hush, hush now."

"Why?"

"Not good for the reputation, no. For the good reputation of the Shoals. Of the units. Or for morale."

"Ha. Reputation. Morale. It's like sand in a milkshake."

"Oh, no. No, no. No joke."

"Oh. I see."

"..."

"Well, nothing to do?"

"Nothing to do, no, yes."

"Well, we're too late now, is that what you're saying. What about Tonya?"

"The pale one?"

"Yeah."

"I think it's all in her head."

"Look at her; she's pale, skinny, and her teeth are falling out, and she looks way too young to be like that."

"Maybe a combination of lifestyle and thoughts, eh? Thoughts manifest themselves, I'm sure of it, I am."

"You think she wants to be here, like this?"

"Map," he squints at Map through his bushy, vermilion eyebrows, "think about it. She's in the system, living off the system's food, tossing back the system's pills, living in a free waterfront convalescent unit. What could be easier? Seriously? What could be easier than living off the system, living the convalescent life?"

"Hmm."

"I mean, think of the alternative, will you? You're older than she is, but younger than I am. You've lived an adult life, you know how it is. Bills, exhaustion, meaningless work…"

"…"

"…not that I find my work meaningless, sometimes I like helping people; need another pill? Taxes. Stress. Failed relationships. Mortality. Death. Death of love, death of pets, death of family. I could go on and on."

"And you think she made herself sick just to get in the system, to get away from it all, to live an easy life?"

"Oh, er, craps of fate I never said it was the easy life; Lord knows I wouldn't want to be living in this fusty, sandy hell, er, no offense."

"None taken."

"And, no, no, I don't think she's faking it; I think there's something legitimately wrong with her, some chemical imbalance, and I think it is making her body sicker and sicker, but there's no operation or physical therapy that's going to be able to fix that. There might be some pills, but we haven't figured it out yet, and as I said, I think she likes living in the system."

"…"

"And, I guess, there's a good chance she's got a bit of mouth cancer; that would be my guess. But she won't let us check. Oddest thing."

"Mouth cancer?"

"Most likely. Perhaps with a bit of cachexia, she's gotten awfully thin recently. But that just might be a sign of a cancer. Usually is."

"I see."

"Map?"

"Yes?"

"Don't go making friends down here. It's just not a good idea."

"…"

"Okay?"

"Oh. I see."

"Good."

"…"

The doctor looks down and taps on the keyboard of his tablet, taps some more, looks over at Map, looks down to read, and looks back at Map again.

"Well, Matt, er, Map, it appears that you know exactly what I'm talking about."

"..."

"About coming down here. About being down here."

"Right."

"There are two types; the types that have to come, and those who chose to come."

"..."

"Well, I don't know what to say. It's just... Well, I don't know. I mean, I know your problems aren't in your head, flockin' hell I'd hate to be you, you seem like you feel like hell all of the time. No, I know you've got issues, that why you're in that chair all the time."

"I'm sick of it; tired of it."

"Right, right. I know there was nothing else that they could have done; they tried all they could, and I know they botched the last operation with the slip of a scalpel. Scar tissue. Bad discs. Spinal stenosis. I know it about it. I've skimmed your file."

"Yeah."

"But I also know you could have gone back home to convalesce."

"..."

"But that you chose to come here."

"..."

"Is that right? You chose to come here?"

"In a way."

"What way? Doesn't make much sense to me. I don't care; I get paid either way, as do the rest of the staff."

"You're welcome."

"But, Map, there are two types of hopeless cases."

"Okay."

"Yours and hers." He tilts his head towards Ms. Nevershe's tub. "We can't do much for either one of ya'll, but with her, flock it, we both know she's come here to die, as our friend Ehab did, too. Nothing we can do for them."

"..."

"But with you, you are a different case; you could have gone home to be in pain all the time. Your problems aren't going to kill you; they just feel like they might."

"Yeah."

"So, Map, why would you decide to go into the system like this? I don't think you're crazy or lazy like Tonya, you're not suffocating to death like Ehab, drowning to death in his above-water bed, and you're not some hopeless case like that whale over there, whatever the flock might be wrong with her..."

"I had my reasons."

"Well, they are yours to own and to live up to. But, and this is off the record, most people come here to die, we just lie and tell them that they are here to convalesce, but they all know better, we all know better."

"..."

"Map, you and I both know that these convalescent units are just the modern hospices. You're not going to die, unless you decide to. I hope your reasons are good ones, and I hope you go home, someday, sometime, but sometimes once you're in the system, well, you're in the system for good."

"Okay."

"I just hope you know what you are doing."

"Like I said, I had my reasons."

"I hope they were good ones, though it seems you won't be telling me what they were."

"Yeah, doc, I hope they were good reasons, too, I really do."

"..."

"..."

"But it makes me wonder..."

"What's that?"

"It makes me wonder about her, about the lady in the giant germ bath over there."

"Ms. Nevershe."

"Yes, yes. It's just so curious, don't you see?"

"I've seen alright, oh, yes, I've seen. I don't know whether curious is the word."

"But it makes me wonder about her blood."

"Her blood?"

"Makes me wonder if it is something in there that is transferable to you, well not you, rather to others."

"If she's contagious?"

"Yes, yes, something like that. Well, of course, we know she's not contagious from being around her..."

"What about the dog?"

"The bitch? Well, you see how much she licked her master all the time, made me sick just hearing that licking sound. And that whale of a woman always had open sores, you've seen them, I've ignored them."

"Yeah, I have seen them, sure."

"The dog maybe licked as open sore, or ate a scab, or both."

"Nasty."

"Well, that's what makes me wonder. Just about her, her blood. About what would happen, if, say, you got some in your bloodstream?"

"Me?"

"Well, not necessarily you. Any of you down here."

"Oh?"

"It's just me thinking out loud. Never mind me. It's just things that we think after we're down here long enough."

"..."

"Well, Map, good chat, good chat."

Both men are silent for a minute; the doctor stands at the door, his dreadlocks getting salty and dirty from the ocean breeze, his lips getting chapped in the cool, dusty air.

"Well," the doctor says, "I guess I should be getting home: more appointments in the, er, morning you know, which isn't too far off now, no."

"No, it's not."

The doctor walks over to his bag and reaches in and finds two pill containers, opens each of them, and drops two from one bottle into his hand, and promptly tosses them into his mouth and starts to munch them, and then takes three from the other bottle, hesitates, and then takes two more and puts those into his pants pocket, and then hands the containers over to Map, who put them into his lap, between quick shots of pain down his legs, which he pretends to ignore, but the pain is obvious. He's gotten used to it by now.

"Those are for you, and the dog, and the woman, whatever, whoever," the pale-hot-pink poodle hobbles over on her three legs and starts to lick his hand, the doctor smiles down at the dog and looks back to Map, and continues, "whatever you want to do with them actually."

He walks over to Map, then smacks himself on the forehead, "Ah, yes, I must," and he reaches into his bag and pulls out a handheld scanner, "I must scan your bracelet for those."

Map holds out his arm; the doctor leans in with the scanner, it beeps and chimes in acceptance; the doctor squints and then asks Map, "Matt?"

"No, it's a typo. They never can get things right."

"No, ah," the dreadlocks chuckle, "no, they can't, can they?" He laughs jovially, spit flies from his mouth, sand falls from his dreads.

"No offense."

"None taken." He laughs again, the dreadlocks seemingly smile. He has his bag in his hand, he takes a final look out the window and said, "Ah, I used to love it here," and then he looks back to the woman in the tub, and then to Map, "but now, I don't mind a visit, but I wouldn't live here. Er, no offense."

"None taken."

"You know, Map, and I must be leaving; I can only be here for so long according to the regs. But I'm glad you're here to take advantage of the units."

"Yeah?"

"Well, yes, of course. That's why they are here. To help people like you."

"I thought that they were just here because the shoreline was so messed up that no one else wanted to come here anymore, that there was just no more use for it."

"Oh, we found a perfect use for it now, haven't we?"

"..."

"Speechless? I don't see how. We, and I say we literally, not only do I work down here, daily, helping, but I was one of the doctors nominated to be on the committee to get the ball rolling."

"Really?"

"But of course; I couldn't say it if it wasn't true. And I wouldn't lie to you. What would be the point of that? Don't answer, there would be no point. But, er, yes, yes. You can all thank me and my colleagues. We saw a problem, we saw a need, and then, well, and then, do you know what we saw?"

"What's that?"

"A solution. I'm nothing if not pragmatic."

"If you say so."

"We saw a ruined, empty shoreline, deserted for a handful of years, a once thriving place where we all used to love to go, but no more, no, no more. The people turned and left. And why?"

"The trashline?"

"Well, that's one reason. But who goes in the ocean anymore? I wouldn't. But if you're down here recovering, convalescing, well, you wouldn't be able to get in there even if it was clean enough to go in."

"I see, I think."

"I mean, why have all these people dying in hospitals and hospices in the cities, with nothing to look at, no morning sunrise over the ocean, no evening sunset over the sound, and the stars, craps of fate, you just can't see the stars in the cities anymore..."

"Well, doc, you can't see them here either anymore."

"Eh?"

"The smog."

"But it's still better than in the cities."

"Maybe, okay. Maybe."

"No, I've seen the data, I've seen the research. Remember, I was on the committee that helped set this all up back then."

"But it's gotten worse, every year, noticeable worse."

"I don't know about that."

"..."

"But, as I was saying... It's best for everyone. Best for the patients, best for the staff, and the highest and best use of the land here and there."

"Here and there?"

"The vacation houses here are used for the hospices, and the hospices in the cities are being torn down and nice new houses are being built in their places. The money is moving from the vacation houses at the shore back to the cities."

"Hospices? I thought this was just supposed to be convalescent homes."

"Did I say hospices?"

"Yes."

"Are you sure? I'm not supposed to use that word with the patients in the units ... must be those pills we took, loose lips sink ships, don't they now, Map, ha."

"Hmm."

"But we found it was the best use of land, and resources, and we know best, yes, yes, that's why we do what we do, to help out those who don't know, who don't know best. And we put you all in a place I personally loved as a child."

"But that was a long time ago, when you were a child; heck, it was a long time ago when I was a child and you're old enough to be my father."

"Well, a fact is a fact, and a shoreline is a shoreline. There are a lot of worse places to be."

"..."

"I'm glad we can get all of you together, out of those cities, and into these units. As I said, we've thought for a while now that it is the best for everyone, everyone, sick and well, patients and doctors, nurses and family, healing and dying."

"I see."

"It's nice to have you down here, Map; I hope you feel better soon, somehow."

"Yeah, yeah; so do I."

The sour smell comes in through the cracked door again; the rising sun illuminates the trashline.

The doctor starts to walk out from the room, "Well, good luck to you, take some of those pills, but save some for the dog," he puts his hat on his head, "and call me if you need me." And he spins, slowly, and walks out of the room, and Map can hear the heavy footsteps going down the sandy piss and ammonia reeking hallway, passing the two closed bedrooms doors and the two open bedroom doors, and then the front door of the unit opens, and then slams shut.

It is quiet now, save for the wind and a shriek of a gull here and there. He's gotten used to it by now.

He wheels his chair back over to the door and watches the sun come up; his head is exhausted, but his heart is still pumping too fast from the doctor's pills. He opens the door as far as it will go, letting in some of the grime in the wind, particles of dirt and smoke are landing on Ms. Nevershe, giving her a slightly grayer complexion, almost a corpselike hue, except for her burps and snores and ongoing constant expansion.

His feet are now sticking out of the door, hovering over the deck a couple of inches below his feet, where they rest in the wheelchair's foot rests. The rain from last night has stopped, but puddles are on the deck; the puddles are brownish orange in the early morning light. He looks down onto the beach, some buckets and trash bags have washed up overnight; there's a rusting truck that appears to have been left on the beach a couple of years ago; sick gulls are picking at the carcasses of dead cousin gulls on the blood and oil stained sand. The trashline lingers just beyond the waves, the white capped waves, with floating junk and dying fish, and the beach is empty now, like it always is, and Map sits and stares out onto the horizon, at the burning freighter. He turns his head south, and he thinks he sees, yes it is, it is another one; it'll be on the news later, these deserted ships always make a headline for a week or less, but not like they did at first.

The dog has fallen asleep again, next to the tub; its master is snoring and gaining weight; the rancid wind blows and blows, the waves are getting bigger, the dunes are getting smaller, and the trashline is getting wider.

Map looks away from the new ship out there, towards the other ship, their ship almost as it is, as it just sits there in front of their house, stalled and simmering. And the new ship is empty, too, of course, and fuel is coming out into the water nearby, and the dead fish just end up rotting on the shore or being trapped in the trashline limbo; and the currents are pulling the ship this way.

Map breathes in some air, and coughs, and tried to stop it, but ends up sneezing, and that's when he wants to die because the pain is going everywhere over his body now, his legs, down his left arm and into his fingers, his private part even hurts. He holds his breath; his chest hurts. He ends up coughing, hacking up some brown goo, which he spits out onto the wet deck; there is a cough in reply from Ehab's wall. He's gotten used to it by now, it seems.

After a minute or so the coughing stops; Map wheels himself back in, closes the door, looks over at the slumbering giant in her cesspool, and then at the unnaturally pink poodle, both snoring. Then he wheels himself out of the room, past a knee reconstruction surgery on the medical-television, and down the hall past Ehab's room, where he hears another dry cough, and then past Tonya's room, where he hears nothing, and into his own room.

He stops his wheelchair next to his bed, places the pill containers the doctor gave him onto the institutional bedside table, and then he prepares himself, mentally, for the agonizing process of getting up from the chair and into his bed. He sits there for five minutes, six minutes, and he's getting ready to get into bed, getting ready to maybe throw up on himself again, and he hears the morning wind whipping around the corner of the house. He starts to stand up, to get in bed to dream about convalescing by the sea, and in his dreams, it is only sometimes painless. Sometimes, but not always, not usually.

And outside of the unit, the wind is screaming and howling; the wind is shrieking and spitting; the wind is laughing as it rapes the beach, and the rebel waves are encouraging it, waiting for their turn.

Waiting. Waiting, but not patiently. Spitting blood; spewing hate; aggressive rhetoric; flexed muscles. Brooding, like a drunk and well-armed mutinous militia waiting to topple an aloof leader, unconcerned about consequences, sure of success.

This is now, and this is how it is: Percussive hypnotics; prescribed narcotics; resident insomniacs; indolent hypochondriacs. The rot race; see the rat rot by the sea, sickie. He's gotten used to it by now, and there's no going back.

CHAPTER TWO

---

the Sickies on the Barrier Islands

This is how it is at the ruined shoreline: Map wakes up a handful of hours later, not enough for him, and he rubs his crusty eyes and grinds his gritty teeth. The gulls outside are shrieking sickly. He spits onto the floor; his tongue is sandy, heavy. He rolls over onto his side and does it too quickly and his whole left side is engulfed in invisible flames of torture, but he falls back onto his back, like he was, and the torture subsides, slowly.

He rolls a little slower onto his side, rests for a minute and listens to the waterfowl outside scavenging the beach and eating foul trash for breakfast. He rolls a little more and grabs onto the headboard of his bed, and prepares himself, and lowers his legs slowly to the ground while maneuvering himself up by pushing against the headboard. He is sitting now: his head aches, he feels like he's going to throw-up, and this won't be the last time today he feels this way, not by a long shot.

His heart hurts some, from all of the pills and the pain, too; maybe he should have mentioned that to the doctor, maybe another time. Maybe never. Whatever.

He closes his eyes and he lets his body relax a little, he tries to will away what pain is still stubbornly clinging to his nerve ends; he wants to cry.

For breakfast, he washes down a few of the pills he got last night; they should help in a little while, but they never work fast enough. He swallows two, and keeps one under his tongue.

Slowly, he stands, and just as he's almost all the way up, his left leg changes its mind and goes limps and Map awkwardly tumbles back onto his rumpled bed with the cheap, stained sheets. He gets that sick feeling again, and he tries harder to ignore it as he doesn't want to throw up and waste the pills.

His chest hurts again, a quick spasm of pain. It starts in the top left of his chest, and then explodes into all directions. He thinks he feels his heart miss a beat, but he's not sure.

He closes his eyes for a few minutes to build up his determination and some energy, and the will to just get out of bed; his will is smaller and smaller each day, it diminishes with each pill he takes, every day that is filled with constant-pain and nerve-mutinies makes him think about how long he can put up with it, and how easy it would be to not feel it, to not feel anything anymore to no longer swallow his pills with bits of dirty, gritty sand that blow constantly into the house through the old windows with the wretched wind.

The eight inch scar on his back still burns on the inside and itches on the outside; he is afraid of scratching it in his sleep and maybe ripping it open. But he hasn't, yet.

That panic fills his few dreams. No sex dreams, just scar dreams.

He lies on the bed with his eyes closed, and listens to the wind and gets a whiff of the trashline through the closed window as he waits for the pain to stop, to go away. The wind screams, the waves bring in trash and then drag it out again to the trashline, and the dunes get smaller and smaller. The sand kamikazes against the house and rips paint from the wood. Sand is everywhere in this house, and it's all a ghastly-gray hue; the beach is no longer a nice tan color.

He finally has to go to the bathroom; so he opens his eyes, ignores the trashline smell, and starts to get himself upright. Slowly, he lowers his legs together, as a pair, over the side of the bed; and winces in pain as he does it. He's pushing himself up with his elbow now, and closing his eyes once again. He stands up slowly, keeping his eyes closed the whole time; his knees are feeling weak.

He's doing it: he is standing.

He smiles a little and opens his brown eyes and scratches his skull under his thick brown hair. He's not as strong as he used to be; he's tired a lot. He's lost weight. But being here convalescing by the sea is good, or so the doctor says.

He rotates his body so that he is standing in front of his wheelchair, and then he feels blindly behind him, and finds one arm of the chair, and then the other, and lowers himself down, slowly, but painfully. When he's in the chair he rests again for a little while; he closes his eyes and listens to those crazy gulls out there, sick and screaming. He hears the ocean, mighty and dirty, and the wind blows and the dunes get smaller and smaller and he slouches over in his chair asleep, exhausted.

He awakes to a sonic stew of Ehab's cancerous coughing, Pist's confused barking, and Ms. Nevershe's gigantic snores. He opens his eyes and stares out his window at the gulls seemingly frozen in mid-air, all squawking thru beaks holding trash or rotting pieces of fish; sand grits in his teeth and is always in his hair.

He stops looking out the window, and wheels his just-under two-hundred pound body to the bathroom, where pain accompanies nature's call, as usual.

After he struggles himself back into his sandy wheelchair, he maneuvers himself down the piss and vinegar hallway. He pauses at Tonya's door, as much out of curiosity as out of exhaustion, but he hears nothing and no light is coming from under the door.

He rolls a little more down the hall and Ehab's television is off, which means he's either asleep or trying to fall asleep; Map hears two hacking coughs, which means nothing, as the man coughs whether asleep or awake.

He rolls past Ms. Nevershe's opened door to her unused room with the twin sized bed which cannot contain the entirety of her girth. He wheels himself into the kitchen, avoiding the piles of sand which seems to be perpetually piled against the floorboards.

The punk-pink poodle is in the kitchen on the tile floor, and is, once again, an extra-large basketball with three legs, a crooked tail with skin showing thru the thin once-hot-pink fur, and a bark that is half confused and half insulted. The dog has rolled herself to its empty food bowl and is looking from her bowl to her expanded, sleeping owner, and then to Map, sitting spaced-out from pills in his wheelchair. Ms. Nevershe, in her watery sleep, yawns so hard that the curtains on the window nearby move; or was that from the wind sneaking through the neglected windows?

The dog stops looking at Map, and seems to forget about her hunger, and she waddles over towards her mistress, and begins to lovingly lick folds of fat. The dog, tired from carrying her massiveness from the kitchen to Ms. Nevershe's industrial-sized tub, falls asleep on a fold of fat, as if it were a mattress made for her; her massiveness somehow fits onto the skin. Map looks over and thinks that Ms. Nevershe is larger than she was last night, or rather early this morning, when Map and the doctor were watching her expand in her slumber.

The television across the room turns on by itself, and changes the channel from a routine teeth cleaning to an operation that is slowly separating a pair of conjoined twins; Map looks away, but says to the wall, "Morning, Ehab."

Ehab coughs up some gunk in response; Map sits in his chair. Ehab's cough wakes the passed-out pink poodle's mistress from her watery snoozing. Her gigantic eyelids open, slowly. While looking out at the trashline and scanning the horizon for more smoking ghost ships, she says: "Map, will you bring me a handful of my doughnuts; I'm starved."

She keeps looking out the window; she hasn't looked down at Pist yet; Map answers her: "I'll bring you the whole box; I think there are only five or six left."

Ms. Nevershe licks her blubbery lips and says with a sigh, "Oh, I guess that'll have to do until they get here; I'll ask them to bring me some more." She continues looking out of the window that's in front of her industrial tub. She's drooling a little on the right side, anticipating the doughnuts that Map has on his lap as he wheels his chair back across the room. She goes on: "Those dunes just keep getting smaller; and it would be okay if the waves were still beautiful, but they're all trash."

Map speaks as he wheels over to Ms. Nevershe, with his feet almost touching the snoozing, bloated poodle, "I used to love the smell of the ocean," he sets the box of doughnuts on the moist beach towels on her torso, "but now I can't stand it."

She's already finishing up her second doughnut with a third in her left hand, ready to be eaten. Map continues, staring at a marble-sized crumb hanging from her lips like a mountain climber in danger of plunging into a ravine. "And, uh, have you noticed your dog? Pist?"

"Pistachio?"

"Right, Pistachio. But, the point is, have you seen her recently?"

"Isn't she sleeping on the floor? I can hear her breathing," she turns her monumental head, slowly, and starts to sweat while doing so. She tries to look over her massiveness to view her slumbering canine, but she cannot see past her expanding fat. "I can't actually see her, Map. Would you lift her up, so that I can see her?"

Map looks down at the sleeping poodle, he hesitates for a moment, and then says, "Well, Ms. Nevershe, that's the problem; I can't lift her right now."

Neither one of them speaks for a minute; Ms. Nevershe closes her eyes and takes a cat-nap. Map reaches over and takes the last doughnut from the box. The gulls fly in circles outside of the window, chasing each other, screaming sick profanities at each other, and Map watches the birds as they fly around the house, shrieking, and then one rams head-on against the closed window in front of Ms. Nevershe's tub. The bird smacks against the window at full speed, cracking the pane and breaking the bird's neck, and it falls with a thump against the deck, leaving nothing but a crack in the window and some mystery goo rolling down the cracked pane; the other gulls continue unbothered as they shriek and caw above the trashline. Later, they will return to peck at the brethren's feathery, salty corpse.

The crack and the thud awakes Ms. Nevershe from her sleep; "Oh, Map, now what were you saying about Pistachio?"

"She's huge."

"I don't understand; what did you say?"

"She's huge; there's no better way to say it; she's ballooned up to the size of a medicine ball."

"And you can't pick her up to show me?"

"Well, being in this chair doesn't help, but I couldn't lift her right now anyway, with my back and all." And as he says this, as if on cue, those wretched legs of his start to feel like they are on fire, and he burns in his left leg from the knee up, and in the right leg he burns from the toes up, and he's in so much pain that he's afraid he's going to wet himself. He closed his eyes, and his grips the edge of his chair, and he holds on tight until the pain subsides. When the stabbing sensation stops, he keeps his eyes closed and he wipes the sweat from his brow, and looks down at the dog. The queen-pink dog is awake and licking herself in her pale-pink private area but now she is back to her standard size. Map rubs his eyes, wipes sweat from his brow again, and says to Ms. Nevershe: "Nevermind, Ms. Nevershe; it looks like she's back to normal. It happened last night, too, when the doctor was here."

"Doctor de Gouge?"

"Doctor de Gouge."

"He was here last night?"

"Filthiness and all," Map reaches into his shirt pocket and pulls out some pills. He throws one pill into his mouth, drops one in front of Pistachio, and hands two over to Ms. Nevershe, "He left some of these for you."

"What are they?"

"Hmm? Oh, I'm not sure, but I've taken a handful of them and feel better. A little, I think."

She puts the two pills into her mouth and crushes them with her colossus coffee-stained molars: "Thank you." She turns her head back towards the window and continues to stare out at the angry waves, the shrinking dunes, and the aggressive gulls, and she says once more, "Thank you," and then she shuts her eyes, and within a minute begins to snore; Pist is still licking herself, and continues to lick and lick and lick.

Map wheels his way past the dog and the tub over to the cracked window. He looks down and sees the dead gull lying there, on the deck, and he hears one gull crying out, and then another, and less than a minute later, three, then four gulls swoop down and land on the deck and begin to hack into the stomach and eyes of the dead gull with their beaks. Map watches this for a minute, and then backs away and looks over at the television; the channel changes again to a program about shigellosis, and a hacking cough comes from behind the wall.

And outside, the wind blows stronger, and the waves are getting bigger, and the gulls are getting full from eating their cousin on the wet deck, as nasty bits of ocean spray land on them and on the windows, leaving a slate gray residue on the grimy window panes.

Now, he's sitting in his chair in the kitchen: he can smell them from here, Ms. Nevershe and Pist; it smells as if they have both wet themselves. He makes a mental note to himself not to put Pist in his lap today (but he forgets most of his mental notes). The drooping skin, which looks rubbery but smells like new plastic, sickens him; he threw up a little while ago, again, but can't know for sure if it was the pitching of pills down his gullet or seeing the seventy-year old flesh trying to evacuate from its swollen master, or a combination of everything.

The television changes channels and the screen is filled with an eyeball. There's a knock on the front door; a cough come from Ehab's room; silence emits from Tonya's darkness; the front door opens without a second knock.

Footsteps enter the foyer; Map calls out, "Oh, come on in," and they do.

The next cough from Ehab's room sounds as if it may be his last, it finally stops, and Map asks, "Are you alright in there?"

The only reply is a smaller cough, and then the channel on the living room med-television changes to an inner-ear operation. Map looks over at them and says, without a smile, "He's fine, I guess."

They don't smile; they look at each other with ennui; one of them spits sand from her mouth onto the threadbare carpet.

She says to her co-worker, "Let's get on with this; two more units, and then we can get away from this stinking hellhole."

Her co-worker nods, and reaches her small, pale hands into a bag she's carrying and takes out an electronic notebook. She holds the device cradled in her left arm; she types into it with her right hand.

The one with the computer in her arms types a bit more, and then says, without eye contact, "Matt? Matt Baron?"

He corrects her: "Map. My name is Map Barons."

She just stares at him.

He says, "Map; not Matt."

She shrugs. She makes no movement with her typing hand to change to error; the other one, the smaller of the two, says, under her breath, "Whatever; let's just do what we need to do and get on to the next unit." She's carrying a handbag identical to the other nurse's.

The one with the electronic notebook, the taller one, says, "Alright, Matt, Map, I mean; you're first today. I'm Princess."

"I can't wait," Map says as he wheels his chair down the hall and towards his room.

Princess, as she passes Ehab's room, says through the door: "I'll be in there in a few minutes, Ahab."

There's a slight cough of reply.

"It's Ehab," Map informs her.

"Rehab?"

"Ehab."

"Is he looking any better? Mr. Ehab?"

"Is he what?"

"Is he looking any better?"

"I've never so much as seen a glimpse of the man."

"Oh, yeah," Princess the nurse says, walking slowly behind his wheelchair, "you're the green one here; I never expected that he would be here so long, 'convalescing by the sea' as the doctor says."

Map says, "The doctor was here last night."

"Last night?"

"Well, early this morning."

"What for?"

Before he could respond, the other nurse, who had by this time found her way to the living room, has spotted the colossal Ms. Nevershe in her immense tub. As the shorter nurse (who never introduces herself) is entranced by the howling snores coming from the seemingly comatose woman, the senile pink poodle stands up, looks around, pees on the floor and immediately expands again to the size of a medicine ball.

The shorter nurse runs down the hall and grabs Princess by the back of her sandy uniform and says, "Holy country seed! Have you seen what's happened to that old bitch in there?"

"Which one?"

"What?"

"Which bitch?"

"The ancient pink one!"

Map interrupts the two nurses with: "She won't bite you."

"Which one?"

"The pink one."

"What about the other one?"

"Ms. Nevershe?"

"Ms. Nevershe."

"She might bite you, I'd be careful."

The short nurse stands in the vinegar-stench hallway, the piss-stained corridor, Map has stopped his chair and Princess is stuck between the two of them. The short one says, "Maybe I'll deal with that one next. Where's the nutcase, the one with her teeth falling out? Tanya?"

"Tonya. Tonya, not Tanya. If the sun is up, she's in her room."

"Doing what?"

"I don't know; I don't go in there." He begins to wheel himself into his room, Princess follows behind him, and he hears something mumbled under the breath of the small nurse.

They wheel on into his room; Princess closes the door behind them. She asks Map, "How long have you been here? You weren't here last time I was here. Let me see your wrist and get your pulse."

He extends his arm to her, "Oh, I guess about two weeks, give or take; the meds make me a little off sometimes, you know?"

She's looking at her small wristwatch and counting to herself as she takes his pulse, so she doesn't answer him, but does nod, expressionlessly. After a minute, she drops his hand, and picks up her electronic notebook that she placed on his bed, and types into it. She reaches into her bag and wrestles around and finally extracts a digital thermometer. She holds it in her left hand and rummages around more with her right hand.

As she doesn't say anything, Map breaks the silence (the verbal silence that is, the wind has picked up outside and the waves are noisily crashing down on the trashed beach) and asks her: "What happened to Ehab? Why's he here?"

"Open wide," she says, and he does and she sticks the thermometer into Map's mouth, and continues, "Ahab, I mean Ehab, well, you haven't seen him?" Map shakes his head 'no' and she says, "He's burned from head to toe. A house fire, I think, maybe. I don't know; I don't care. Open up." He does and she takes the thermometer out and looks at it, and then types into her notebook.

"Oh, I didn't realize; I thought maybe it was lung cancer or something like that."

"I think he inhaled enough smoke to kill an elephant. I hadn't expected him to last this long, actually. The last time he was on my route, he looked horrible, he sounded horrible."

"He spoke to you?"

"No, has he spoken to you?"

"I've never seen him."

"But you've heard him, right, through the walls? They're paper thin."

"I've heard him cough."

"That's all he can do now. Take off your shirt and stand up."

"Pardon?"

"Take off your shirt and turn around."

He hesitates; she waits. He begins to pull himself up, but sits back down after the pain moves through his entire being. He begins to sweat; she waits. He tries again, and feels as if he will throw up. He doesn't.

She says to him, "Here," and she extends her right hand towards him.

He laughs a little, smiles for the first time in too long. She understands and holds out both of her hands.

She says, "Let me try to help you."

"No offense, but you're what, twenty-one years old and one-hundred-twenty pounds?"

"Twenty-three, and one-ten, thank you very much. Here." She's still holding out her hands, steadily, "Are you ready?"

"I'm ready; is this going to hurt?"

"I understand that it does; but it'll help. I just need you on the bed, on your stomach, with your shirt off."

"Needles?"

"Needle. One."

"I used to hate needles; now, they're old hat."

"Ready?"

"Ready."

She grips his hands and pulls him up; he hurts and fights down the vomit; his vision tunnels; and then he's standing on his feet, half supporting himself, half being supported by Princess. He closes his eyes for thirty seconds or so, dizzy, and when he reopens them, his tunnel vision is gone. He removes his left hand from Princess' firm grip and wipes beads of sweat from his forehead; he smiles a little, looks down at her, at her blue eyes, and says, "You're stronger than you look."

"I've been told that before, by larger men, bigger people. You ready?"

She lets go of him, he sits on the bed, removes his long sleeved shirt and then his t-shirt and he maneuvers, with a pained yelp, onto his stomach. She reaches into her bag and removes a packet of alcohol swabs, tears it open, and puts it down on his back. She takes a pre-prepared syringe from her bag, takes the protective cap off, and holds it in her mouth as she wipes the alcohol swab onto Map's lower spine; he shivers from the cold sensation.

"Alright; are you ready?"

"I guess so."

She inserts the needle into his back; she's off by a little bit and she hits a nerve and his legs involuntarily kick. She apologizes slightly and then she steps across the room and drops the used needle into a bright red wastebasket; she reaches into her bag and pulls out another needle.

"Let's try this again."

"Why not?"

She hesitates, and spits a little on the floor and says, "God, I hate that sooty sand. I don't see how you live here." She spits again, digs around her teeth with her tongue. Spits again.

Map starts, "Well," but he never finishes his thought; she wipes a cold alcohol swab on his spine again.

"Hold on."

"I'm not going anywhere."

She plunges the second needle in, into the right place maybe by skill, maybe by luck, and Map tries to keep his composure and he makes fists so tight that his fingernails dig into his skin, and his left palm begins to bleed a little. It seems to him that she leaves the needle in there for a minute, but it's probably only there for a second or three. She pulls it out; the cool sensation from the alcohol wipe has disappeared, and the initial sting from the needle biting through his skin is gone, but he feels waves of pain rippling away, and then he releases his fists. He hears her drop the needle into the wastebasket; he unclenches his teeth; she's zipping up her bag; he's closing his eyes.

"You might find yourself a little tired for a while; stay still," she looks down at him; his eyes are already closed, "I'm going to go check on Mr. Ahab …"

He dreamily corrects hers, "…Ehab…"

"…and when I'm done with him I'll peek back in on you."

Map is asleep from the medicine before she leaves the room, snoring to himself, a bit of drool, pebbles of sand...

He awakes a little later; the nurses are gone. The unit is quiet.

He's face down on the bed still. He feels like he's been stung in the spine by a stingray; he burns and itches. He feels disoriented, groggy; the gulls outside sound like they're screeching in a tunnel. He doesn't smell anything, and he knows that is not right. He closes his eyes again for five minutes, then ten. He slowly opens his eyes again; the light from the window is rust orange; he's slept the rest of the afternoon away.

He stays on his stomach, resists the temptation to scratch the burning on his spine; he rolls, as a log, onto his side, compressing a nerve too much, too easily, and his toes curl, one knee bends, the other stiffens; he sucks in air, and holds it tight. The gulls are still in a tunnel in his ears. His eyes are closed. He, with flat palms to the mattress, pushes himself upright on the bed; chills go down to his ankles; his toes are cold and numb.

He grabs a cane from next to the bedside table, and pushes himself up, standing so he can hobble to his chair. He stands up, and stands straight, and still.

Supporting himself with his cane, he takes a few jagged steps, and hobbles past the wheelchair. When he gets to the bedroom door, he grabs onto the doorframe like a drowning man's manic grasps; his tongue finds grit between every tooth, in every crevice of his mouth, his still-present tonsils have sand embedded in their soft, pale flesh. He holds himself up with both hands, leaving the cane to rest momentarily against the wall, and he looks back to the bed, and to his chair, then he grabs the cane, takes a deep breath, and gets ready to wander a painful stagger.

He hobbles first past Ms. Nevershe's empty room, he can already hear Ehab coughing in his sleep; Map slowly wanders down the dim hall, and stops at Tonya's room to catch his breath.

He's been moving slowly; he looks out a window down the hall and sees that the sun's almost down. He stops to catch his breath, and does so for a minute, and after he rubs his eyes, he's getting ready to walk to the kitchen, when he hears sounds coming from Tonya's room.

He listens closer, it sounds like scratching on the wall.

He knocks, gently, on the thin door.

No response.

He knocks again, firmer this time.

"Tonya?"

No response; the sound stops momentarily, then continues.

"Tonya?"

The sound keeps going.

Map reaches down and puts his hand on the doorknob, "I'm coming in."

"Okay, I guess."

She's on her bed, a small daybed, which is pushed up against the wall that separates Tonya's room from the unit's main living room. She has a long, metal nail file in her hand, and she's slowly turning the point in a circle into the wall; the file has gotten about half of its length into the wall.

"What are you doing?"

She starts turning the file again, and looks over at him, "What are you doing, walking?"

"I don't know; today's a good day I guess; they gave me a shot. It seems to have worked some."

"Let's hope it lasts."

"Yeah. So, uh, what are you doing?"

Tonya continues to turn the file into the wall; there's a cough from Ehab's side of the wall; she stops, leaving the nail file stuck in the drywall.

She looks at him, and says plainly, "I want to be able to watch television in bed. There are two televisions here; and I'm not getting into Ehab's bed."

"Oh."

"…"

He stares at her; she looks at him for a second, eye contact, smiles, and then looks away and goes back to the task at hand. Map watches her for a while. He looks around her room, he's never been in here before, and he finds it is blank, no pictures on the wall, no books or magazines around, nothing on the bureau, not even a shoe on the floor.

"How long have you been living here, if you don't mind me asking?"

She pauses, "A while."

"A year while, or a month while?"

"Oh, somewhere in between I guess. I'd say the former or the latter, but I always forget which of those two is which." She smiles again at him, as she absentmindedly continues to turn the file's point into the wall.

"Ah."

"The guy who had your room before you died after a week here."

"Good to know."

"I don't think it was anything contagious."

"Good again."

"But I don't know for sure."

"Ah."

"Yeah."

"Well, I'll go check on Pist and Ms. Nevershe."

"Okay, see you soon."

He turns, wordlessly; she continues to work on her peephole and says to his back, "I mean, I literally will be seeing you, soon." She smiles, showing missing teeth in her sandy grin.

"Weird." He hobbles out of the room, she calls out for him to shut her door, and he reaches back, has a lightning bolt of pain in his lower back, and pulls the thin door closed behind him.

In the kitchen, he's standing there, getting his breath again (he breathes in deeply and can smell the ocean here, and he wishes he couldn't). He's about to open the refrigerator when he hears heavenly singing.

He stands still, taking it all in, the foreign sounding singing, the nasty beach smells, Ehab's coughing almost as a rhythmic beat now, and the slight but certain sound of the wall being chiseled. He hobbles into the living room and almost loses a grip on his cane as he looks over and sees Ms. Nevershe, smaller than she was, but still huge, awake and alert and soaking in her tub, with a normal-sized but still three-legged pink poodle resting on her bloated belly and she's singing a song in a language Map doesn't know (Italian) and the poodle is licking its owner's sizeable jowls, wagging her tail in ecstasy. Ms. Nevershe happens to turn her head Map's direction, and she sees him in the kitchen, and she smiles, and Pist the poodle looks over at him, and smiles too, and Ms. Nevershe causally finishes the verse that she's singing and soothingly caresses her poodle's fluffy head, and says, "Oh, Map, honey, you do look so very, very nice when you're tall."

"Thank you, Ms. Nevershe." Now that Ms. Nevershe has stopped singing, Map can clearly hear the chiseling sound coming from Tonya's nail file.

"It's such a lovely day; so nice to be here at the beach, with my loved ones, and just enjoying the sights." She's petting her pink poodle with her pink hands as she says this.

Map looks out the front windows of the unit; he looks out to a darkened and deserted beach, with tidal pools of starving gulls, and the waves, rising just in front of the trashline, which is lingering out there, like an army gathering for an invasion: the trashline is coming!, the trashline is coming!

"Yes, Ms. Nevershe, it is." He doesn't like to lie, but he's confused.

"You do seem to be feeling better, walking around tall and all."

"Yeah, better than I was, for sure. And, if you don't mind me saying so, you, also, seem to be feeling much better." She just smiles at him and then stares back out over the empty beach; he continues, "Did you take any more of those pills I gave you?"

She keeps stroking her dog and smiles in Map's direction and says, "No, pills always make me feel a little bloated; I gave them to the girl."

"Which girl was that, one of the nurses?"

"No. No, our girl. The pale one."

"Tonya?"

She nods her less-massive head.

"..."

The chiseling sound in the wall stops; the medical-television changes channels, but Map cannot see what's on the screen. Ms. Nevershe takes a deep breath, smiles, and kisses the top of Pist's pinkness, and says, "I've always loved the smell of the beach, ever since I was a child." She looks over at Map, and like a sleepy cat, stares at him purposelessly for a while.

Map inhales and exhales and instead of thinking about the rank shore odor, he tries to make his mind think about something else, flowers, cars, mountains, but instead, he teeth feel gritty from the sand and then he glances up to the darkening horizon, and his eyes rest on the two ships, with the columns of smoke. He thinks that they look like waterspouts out over the Atlantic, perpetually stopped in place, ransacking the two ships ceaselessly, endlessly, mercilessly. He's gotten used to it by now.

"Me, too, Ms. Nevershe, me, too."

She looks away from Map, looking out over the beach, somehow enjoying the view. Map comes closer to Ms. Nevershe, and stands behind a chair, to which he was able to hold onto for support. She says to him, "How does it feel, to walk some? How do you feel, dear?"

"Oh, it's nice; it's nice to be up out of that wheelchair. They said I would be out and that it was just a matter of time. But, my legs still hurt so much I want to puke."

"And I want to thank you, Map, for helping out my baby girl. Pistachio was feeling pretty bad, but she's a lot happier now."

Maps glances down at the dog that has fallen asleep amid fleshy stroking from Ms. Nevershe's baseball mitt sized hand, and says, "Yeah, she's looking much better. And how are you feeling?"

"Oh, I'm tired. But still, it's nice to be here, in this hot tub, with everyone on the beach; I just love the sights and beach smells."

Map rubs his eyes, and says, "Ma'am, I need to go to my room for something, I'll be back."

The medical-television changes channels concurrently with a smoky cough from Ehab; Tonya's file turns slowly, working its way through the wall. The channel changes one more time, this time without a cough, and the nail file turns slowly, and the trashline outside floats, and the wind lashes out, the waves are getting bigger and closer. The gulls continue to cannibalize. Map swallows some sand that had been dislodged from between his teeth, and he slowly canes his way back through the kitchen (still hungry), stepping on a tooth (Tonya's, certainly), and hobbles down the uneven hallway, his footsteps synchronizing with coughs emitting from Ehab's musty assigned room.

As he passes Tonya's room, she says, "Hey."

He stops, rubs his back near his incision, and opens the door and peers in. "Tonya?"

"Yeah?"

"Did you say something?"

"Yeah, I did. Hey, since you're the only roommate that is mobile, kind of, can you go with me on my walk later?"

"What walk?"

"With Pist. Who did you think walked her? Ms. Nevershe? Yeah, right. And you know Ehab doesn't leave his bed."

"Hmm, I guess I never thought about it. You're going to go out tonight, in the dark?"

"When else?"

"Yeah, I see."

"So?"

"Sure. I mean, I'll try. I need to walk some, and I haven't walked outside in weeks it seems. Darn chair, bad legs."

"Good. I need you to carry the tennis racket. I think you can carry it in your left hand and hold the cane in your right hand."

"Um, what?"

"I said, I think you could hold the cane in your right hand."

"No; before that."

"Oh, I need you to carry the tennis racket."

"Oh. What tennis racket? I can barely walk, I can't play tennis now."

"You're funny, Map." She smiles; he grins.

She keeps on slowly turning the nail file into the wall and doesn't look back at him for a moment.

He says, "I'm confused, Tonya. Are you going to play tennis? In the dark? But, wouldn't we need two rackets to play tennis? Last time I checked, it took at least two people."

She keeps on making her peephole in the wall, and laughs a little, but doesn't look over to him, "No, no, no. It's in case any of those bubonic gulls get near me, us. You're taller than I am, probably stronger than I am," here she stops and glances over at Map, hunched over his cane, rubbing his back with a pained expression on his face, "maybe, that is, maybe stronger than

I am, but taller for sure. If any of those flying rats get near us, I want you to hit them with a backhand so hard they poop out their beaks."

"Hmm."

"So? Will you walk with us?"

"Oh, okay, sure."

"Great, I'll come and find you when I'm done in here and have some applesauce for dinner."

"Ok, I'll be in my room; if I'm asleep, wake me."

"Alright, Map, thanks."

"Yeah."

He starts to cane his way away from Tonya's room, and Ms. Nevershe starts to sing, loudly, and then Ehab starts to cough and Map hears the channels on the television changing with each cough and then Ehab stops coughing and the channels stop changing. Ms. Nevershe sings a little softer, but still like an angel, and Map reaches into pockets and pulls out one of the pills the doctor gave him, and he slowly canes his way into his bedroom, and painfully lowers his battered back onto the bed, winces when he actually gets down. He props his cane up next the bed, and he closes his eyes, hearing Ms. Nevershe getting softer in her singing, or maybe the wind is picking up more: he can hear the wind whipping around the corner of the house, and he hears the waves crashing onto the filthy sand just in front of the unit. He rubs his eyes and finds sand in his eyelashes, and he grinds his teeth for no reason, they are gritty. He's gotten used to it by now.

The waves seemingly get quiet, and the wind surprisingly dies down, and all he hears is Ms. Nevershe's angelic voice and then he doesn't hear anything else. But, moments later, Tonya hears his snores through the wall. Percussive hypnotics; prescribed narcotics; indolent insomniacs. The rot race; see the rat rot by the sea, sickie.

Chapter Three

the Sandy-Hell Stenchers

This is what's going down at the place no one wants to be: Map wakes to a tapping sound, along with the wind screaming and the ocean crashing and the trashline stinking and stenching.

"Map."

"…"

"Map?"

"Yeah?"

"Wake up; it's me."

"Tonya? What time is it?"

"About one o'clock, or so, maybe. Does it matter? Do you have a date or something?"

He looks towards the windows and all he sees is darkness outside. "Huh? What's going on?"

"Map, it's one in the morning, it's time to take Pist out for her walk. And I have the tennis racket for you. You've been asleep; you're foggy because of your pills. Get on up, okay?"

"Okay."

"I'll see you in the great room. Soon, okay. Stay awake, you hear me?"

"Okay."

"…"

He stays in bed for a minute or three, slowly making sure his legs will work. Each time he moves one, especially his left one, he shouts, as muted as he can, in pain; Ehab hears and coughs twice in solidarity. Map rolls onto his left side, which is a mistake as it makes him feel like he's going to throw up, so he rolls, slowly, onto his back, where his incision scar alternates between burning and itching. He stays put another minute or two; Ehab has not coughed again. Then, slower than before, Map rolls his way onto his right side, easy does it, and he does it, easy, and doesn't feel like vomiting, not yet. He slowly drops his right leg down, letting his socked foot rest on the sandy floor, and he slowly drags his left leg (tugging on his pants with his hands) until the leg is close to the edge, and then he drops it down as he is sitting up, and there it is, that familiar old friend nausea; but he fights it, and he wins, and he's in pain, but he's not getting sick.

He sits up; he's burning from the waist down and aching in his lower back. He sits still for a minute, then two more, and he hears, from the living room, "Map, come on, this dog needs to go out. I mean, her bladder may be older than I am."

He reaches over and gets his cane; he just holds onto it for a few minutes, like an old man staring at a chess board trying to determine his next move but knowing all is lost. Then Map grasps onto the handle, inhales a lungful of the sordid sea breeze, coughs, (Ehab coughs in reply) and with all of his atrophied muscles, Map shoves his weight down on the cane to lift himself up from his thin mattress. His legs have been napalmed; his knees buckle and then regain their composure, and then buckle again; his left hip feels as if an arrow has been shot and lodged there with infection spreading. A cold flame enters into his scar on his back, and then nips his nerves, just enough to make him vomit, for the first time today, only an hour past midnight as it is.

In the process of getting sick, he drops his cane, which falls to the floor with a smack so loud it momentarily drowns out the filthy waves crashing onto the beach. He sits on the twin mattress; he holds his head in his hands, he closes his eyes, his mouth tastes like vomit and his throat is sore and hot. Raw. He's gotten used to it by now.

"Map?" His bedroom door was open a little already, but is now opened all the way; a concerned cough comes from Ehab's wall.

"Hmm."

"Map, you okay?"

"Mmh. Sure. Maybe."

"It smells like the dog died in here, but it is hard to tell down here with the sickly sea air, right? Hold on, just sit there for a second and I'll be back to clean this up and then to clean you up or whatev."

"Okay."

Tonya turns and leaves the room, walking down the hall quickly.

Ehab coughs curiously.

"Yeah," Map replies, "I'm okay."

Tonya returns with some rags in one hand, a jar of disinfectant under her arm, and a ceramic bowl in the other hand. She places the bowl onto Map's chest of drawers, slightly above eye level for him. He doesn't look up. He sighs. She ignores him, pleasantly enough, and bends down onto one knee, places the bottle of powder-blue liquid on the floor, and pulls handfuls of brown paper towels off of the roll and begins to clean up. She throws the used paper towels into the waste basket, next to the one marked for used bandages, syringes, and vials. He watches, with his head in his hands still, and he thanks her: "…hhrmmfff…", and she smiles and looks up to him and replies: "…mmm…" and keeps on working.

She finishes and stands up; she hands him the cereal bowl: "Here you go."

Map places his cane against his lap; he uses his right hand to spoon, and his left to hold the bowl. Three spoonfuls in, he pauses and says, "Why am I not surprised?" He smiles, they both laugh. "And I'm not trying to be sarcastic or anything, thanks, good idea."

"Yeah, well, applesauce always seems to take the nasty taste out of my mouth when I get sick."

"I'll keep that in mind; I get sick a lot, and usually suck on a mint. And fewer cavities this way, with applesauce, I guess."

"Well," she smiles a semi-hollow smile, "How are you? Are you feeling any better?"

"I'll be okay."

"You still want to go with us, with me and Pist?"

"Yeah, I could use some fresh air I guess."

"Well, where are you going to get that?" She smiles, dark hollows show where teeth are absent.

"Good point. I'll go with you; besides being sick and all, I feel okay, I mean, with my leg, my legs."

"Alright, here, let me help you up, take my hand."

"Thanks."

"Whatev."

A sigh.

"Hurts, huh? Oh, guess what? Never mind, don't guess, but I finished my peephole today; I watched midnight surgical specials from my bed tonight, while you were snoring and Ehab was coughing. Ms. Nevershe must have fallen asleep, because she stopped singing earlier. She doesn't know about my little peephole, I don't think. You haven't told her, have you?"

"No."

"Good. But anyway, when I went into the kitchen, to get some applesauce and some water, I looked around the corner at her, and guess what?"

"..."

"She's smaller, now. I mean a lot smaller, it's weird, at first I thought it wasn't her."

"Really?"

"..."

"Was she sleeping? Was she alive? The doctor told me to call him if there were any changes."

"I guess this would be a change, huh?"

"I guess."

"Ready?"

"Ready."

"Here."

"Ah!"

And he's up, on his feet, with biting pain from his ankles up to his thigh, and then deep in his side it tears at him. He stands still; he holds onto his cane with his right hand and has his left hand on Tonya's shoulder. The liquored-up passed-out black-blinders are creeping around the sides of his eyes, around the perimeter of his vision; tiny white lightning strikes appear on his eyelids; the pains ebbs and flows up and down his legs like the tides outside, his heart jumps a beat and shocks him. Map feels more sand in his teeth, he swallows some. Gritty teeth, gritty tongue, gritty tonsils. He's gotten used to it by now, somehow.

"Thanks."

"Okay, you ready to go, slowly, of course?"

"Yeah, well, maybe first I should go and see Ms. Nevershe."

"Sure."

He walks slowly down the hall leaning heavily against his cane; she follows closely behind him, with her hand gently holding his left elbow, being as much mental as physical encouragement to Map. They walk past her empty room, and Map pauses at Ehab's door and listens. Nothing. Dead quiet. He remains there and keeps listening. After another minute with no coughs, Map whispers to Tonya, "Do you think he's okay?"

She pauses, listens for a minute more, still holding onto Map lightly, "Yeah, I guess he's just sleeping; it is after one in the morning."

"Have you always been a night-owl?"

"It seems."

"Have you ever seen him?"

"Who? Ehab?"

"Yeah, Ehab."

"No. Have you?"

"No. How long has he been here?"

"I don't know; I've never talked with him. I mean, I've spoken towards him, but never actually conversed with him. Like this."

"Was he here when you got here?"

"Hmm." She ponders this.

"I know, if you're like me, I've been on so many meds recently that I can't think straight sometimes, most of the time."

"I think he was here when I got here. And your room was occupied, but then that guy died..."

"You've mentioned that."

"And then you showed up, and you haven't died yet."

"Yet, nice."

"Sorry. Neither have I. Yet."

"Let's go look at her, at Ms. Nevershe."

"Okay, whatev."

He turns around, slowly on the slick floor, and limps on his cane down the Pist-pissed hallway; Tonya follows him.

When they enter the living room, Map gets a whiff of the trashline as the sliding glass door is partially open. Pist wakes up and lifts her dated head and looks through cataract damaged eyes at the two figures in the kitchen. The dog's delicate tail begins to thump against the floor.

Map and Tonya slowly walk across the room and make their way to Ms. Nevershe's trough. The bath water is a death gray, with particles of sand floating on top and what appears to be an oil spill lingering above where her thumb-sized toes are submerged.

Map and Tonya walk up to her, the sleeping woman, and ignore the paradise-pink poodle that licks at their feet.

"Well, what do you think?" Tonya asks Map.

"..."

"Yeah, me too."

"I mean, she's not small, she's got to be four hundred pounds if she's an ounce, but she's not nearly as, as, as bloated as she was this morning. Or last night, or whatever. I get thrown off by your schedule. Night and all, you know."

"You'll get used to it; I have. But she looks okay, right? I mean, she's breathing, and she's not small enough to drown in there. I guess I'll just let her sleep."

"Yeah, I guess, let her sleep. I better text the doctor. Let him know what's going on. The dog looks fine, though, huh?"

"Yeah. I mean, a leg is missing, but besides that, whatev."

He pulls his phone from his left pocket, and types with his thumb as he holds himself up with his right hand.

"Alright, done."

"Good."

"You get the leash, and I'll get the tennis racket."

Tonya smiles, says, "Oh, Map, silly, we don't need a leash. Look at her, this dog is like one hundred years old or whatev, she's not going to go anywhere but right next to me. And, jeez, I end up carrying her more than half the time, that's why I need you to carry the tennis racket."

Map nods his head, "Oh, yeah, I see."

Tonya smiles, "Yeah," and she bends over and reaches down and pets the decrepit dog behind its ears, and then picks it up like a baby, and says, "Let's go."

As they walk through the kitchen, Map picks up the tennis racket that Tonya had left on the counter. Tonya is walking down the hall towards the front door, by now the poodle's head is resting on Tonya's shoulder looking backwards at Map. As she opens the front door, a cough emits from Ehab's room; Tonya smiles back at Map, "See. He's okay."

"Well, he's alive, at least."

"For now, yes." Her smile has gaps.

She holds the door open and a brisk breeze enters the unit. Map can smell the trashline as if it were a hot summer day, with all that crud baking out under the hot sun. The smell just never seems to get any better; it does not get any more pleasant to the nose.

Tonya closes the door after Map limps out, slowly, and she asks him, "Did you hear about the leukemia unit? The one that got hit?"

"No. No, I don't know what you're referring to. What are you talking about?"

"Oh, I'll show you; we'll walk past it," and then she glances over at Map and his cane and his limp, "if we make it that far, that is."

The wind whips Tonya's hair; she reaches into her pocket and pulls out a hair band. "Sometimes I think I'll get little bits of crud in my hair; sometimes the sand is the more pleasant of the options. I'd rather have some sand in my nose and teeth, than some windblown bits from the trashline."

"Yeah."

"You know what I miss most?"

"What's that?"

"Just being a kid on the beach and picking up sea gull feathers."

"Hmm."

"Now, holy flock, no way. Nasty." She gags at the thought.

"..."

"Nasty."

"..."

The dog squats on the sidewalk; Map's leaning against his orthopedic cane; Tonya fidgets with a loose tooth. She wiggles it back and forth; Map watches, bewildered; the dog finishes and wiggles its hindquarters; Map looks over, disgusted.

Tonya stops wiggling her browning tooth; "I taught her that."

"What?"

"The peeing and all on the sidewalk."

"Oh?"

"Yeah."

"Why?"

"Well, the patients in the units nearby all got upset when the dog was pooping on their lawns."

"Well, sure, I can see that."

"I mean, because now she's doing it on the sidewalk; the public sidewalk. I own some of this. So do you."

"Shouldn't we keep it clean, then, maybe?"

"But I'm keeping my neighbors' yards clean. Even better. Karmically, I mean."

"Ah."

"Yeah."

The dog walks slowly in the dark. Ash gray gulls on the dunes between the beach front units are staring at them as they walk. The ocean hisses on the other side of the dune line, and out past the trashline the two beacons of smoke rise up into the air, penetrating the clouds, as galactic distress signals: S.O.S. He's gotten used to it by now. S.O.S.: Silence Our Sickies, or Save Our Sickies?

"The dog likes her walk, huh?"

Tonya: "Well, last couple of days she's been acting a little off."

"Yeah, I would, too, I guess. I mean, she's lost a quarter of limbs recently."

"Yeah, yeah."

"Hmm."

"Do you like it out here, at night?"

Map: "Smells a little better than in the day."

"Yeah, it does, the sun is baking all that rubbish and rot. The early, early morning is my fav."

"Why?"

"No one else is out there, usually; and those leper gulls are finally asleep."

"Why are we on the sidewalk then?"

Tonya: "Oh, you wouldn't want Pistachio to walk on that nasty beach, would you? She's too old for that."

"I guess not."

All of the houses that they walk past are dark. Map wishes that he, too, were back in his bed, lying still, not aching, his weak arms not having to hold his cane all the time. Better than the wheelchair though, he concludes.

His legs are weak and slow; the wind from out east over the trashy Atlantic is enough resistance on his legs to slow him down; standing still, the wind makes him sway sideways. Map feels as unsteady now as the first time he drank, more than two decades ago now. He stands still, a bit of rest for screaming muscles and angry nerves; his ankles throb, the toes on his left foot feel crushed, broken, and his ankle feels bloated (he's sure that if he looks down at it, it will be a blue-black) while the toes on right foot feel swollen and sting like a bloom of jellyfish attacked it. He expects that his toenails might be falling off. But the strangest thing, for him, is the difference in the feeling and the reality. His toes feel crushed, damaged and deranged, and whenever one of his socks are off, he glances down and feels like he's going to shudder, but then it turns out that nothing is wrong, on the outside at least. His toes look fine.

But now, after Tonya's help moments ago, the toes are covered by socks and shoes, sheltering his nerve damaged toes from the acrid air, from the smoke which is rubbery smelling tonight from those two wasting vessels and the permanent stench of water logged gull corpses. He's gotten used to it by now.

He scratches his ear; sand is lodged within. He grinds his teeth: gritty. He spits a gooey gray glob onto the sidewalk; the old three-legged dog wags its pale-rose-pink tail.

"I might need to carry her soon," Tonya says, looking down at the withered, weathered canine, which is mimicking Map and scratching her ear with her remaining hind paw, losing her balance like a pink furry three legged wino.

"You might need to carry me next," Map smiles, but turns a little too quickly in Tonya's direction and his smile quickly morphs into a wince.

"Yeah, maybe a block or two."

"Yeah."

"You ready? To walk some more?"

Map: "Yeah, why not?"

As he's about to turn and walk down the sidewalk, letting the wind fill his ear canal with sand, his phone vibrates in his pocket and beeps a moment later; he pulls it out and glances at it, "It's the doctor; he's going to be over soon. In an hour or less."

"I like a doctor that keeps night hours."

"Yeah, well, I don't know when, or if, he sleeps; he seems to be, uh, artificially stimulated at times, you know?"

"Ah; I see."

"But, I don't care."

"Yeah, does it really matter anyway?"

"Huh?"

"Nothing."

"..."

When the dog decides to smell an area of sidewalk, to see if it's a proper enough spot to leave waste on, it takes an eternity for it to turn and then lower its arthritic neck. When she sniffs the ground, the neurons aren't firing as fast as they should or as they used to: those old neurons are taking naps on the way to the old brain, and once they get there, to the brain, the dog's epicenter, they must rouse it, wake the ever-sleeping nerve headquarters. And by then, the dog has forgotten that it has even sniffed a crack in the concrete at all, and it slowly begins to move her three paws forward.

The three legged dog and the three legged Map (the third leg being his cane) follow Tonya. Map has the cane in one hand and the tennis racket in the other; if people were to have been out, like one of the sleepless geriatrics from one of the other seaside units, they may think it was to hit balls for the dog to chase and retrieve, the old, gnarly three legged pink Pist, who has teeth so old that they'd break if even softly closed around a tennis ball.

Tonya stops, lets the old dog hobble up to her, and she bends down and picks up the furry old bag of bones, and carries it in her arms as if it were a three-legged pink-furred infant human.

Map says, "I've never liked small dogs like that. I've always thought they smelled weird, no matter how clean or dirty they were."

"I've never owned a dog; I've never even lived with a dog until I moved into this unit."

"But you like this one?"

"Well, there's no one else around to talk to, you know?"

"..."

"I mean, I'm not trying to be rude and say I can't talk to you, but, you know, you basically just moved in here. And, besides, you're always asleep at night."

"It's been an old habit of mine, sleeping at night."

"Well, you're missing the best time of the day. The dark part. My fav."

"Oh?"

"Yeah, I can stand out there, on the rotting deck, and not have to close my eyes, and I can hear the waves crash, but can't see all of the junk on the beach, or the trashline, although there is that weird glow that hovers over the water, but I can imagine, kind of, that it's how it used to be."

"Yeah?"

"You know, clean. Fun. Pretty."

"Yeah, I remember."

"Now, don't hurt yourself; I can't carry this dog and you, too."

"I'll try to be careful, sure."

"Hey."

"Hmm?"

"Why do they call you Map? I mean, is that a nickname? Short for something?"

"No. My parents named me. They named me Map."

"Why?"

"Why did they name me Map?"

"Yeah."

"They were lost. Young and lost. I mean, not like starving lost, just like, I don't know, aimless, soullessly lost."

"Is that what they said? That they named you Map because they were lost?"

"No."

"No?"

"No. It was obvious. It was obvious to everyone that they were lost. It was even obvious to me when I was a kid."

"Ahh. I see."

"And that's why I've always been able to see it."

"To see what?"

"That I am lost, too. It is so obvious to me. Now. Not always. But recently."

"Hmm."

"Good times, yeah?"

"Yeah, well, any day is a good day at the shore."

"Day?"

"Night."

"That sounds right."

"Yeah. So, Map, how old are you anyway?"

"Old enough."

"No, come on …"

"Let's just say I'm around forty, give or take."

"Old man, huh?"

"…"

"…"

"Well, how old are you?"

"Does it matter?"

"No, I guess not."

"Wrong answers; if it doesn't matter, then I don't need to answer."

"Fair enough."

"But I'll follow your example: I'll just say I'm in my mid-twenties. Give or take."

"Ah..."

"Yeah, I've been in my mid-twenties for a decade or so, whatev..."

"..."

A few blocks from home, they're walking down the deserted sidewalk east of the quiet two-lane road; most of the houses to the east of them are dark, with only a light here and there, probably someone up getting sick, or taking a dosage of something or other. Beyond the old houses is the dune line, which is even lower here where they are walking than where their unit is located. The dunes here are so low that in some places there isn't even a dune line. Under the house currently right next to them, to compensate for the lack of dune line, the county workers have dumped piles of dug-up highway concrete, with its rebar intact, to create a rugged, harsh border between the houses and the hissing pissed-off tides.

A few houses in a row have false dunes like this. Then they walk past a gap in houses, with a driveway and a broken piling or two that held the now-missing oceanfront house up off of the ground. At one point, these houses were prized for their views of the beautiful beaches and the murder-blue sea. But now the best views are in the darkness and the wind whips even more, and the ocean hisses and rises more and more every day, and the dunes die down until they are replaced by these nasty manmade trash piles, protecting the units from the powerful waves that are reaching out more and more every day to drag the houses out to be part of the growing trashline for eternity.

At the second driveway to nowhere, Tonya stops and spits some sand onto the cracked sidewalk, turns, and peers down the driveway to a line of trash and house bits, a door frame, a window, some shingles, and then out to where the ocean is laughing mockingly and threatening the shore and the residents.

"What? What are you looking at?"

"This."

"Yeah?"

"This is where it used to be, this is where it was."

"Huh? What now again?"

"That unit."

"Which one?"

"This is where that leukemia unit was. For boys. Four boys."

"..."

"It happened at night. I was awake; it was real late or early maybe, and they were probably all in bed asleep. Sound asleep. Dreaming. Dreaming of toys, hair, parents, play dates."

"..."

"But I guess someone noticed the noise or something. I was up, of course, watching some surgery on the television ... Ehab must've been asleep because the channel never changed the whole night ... I got worried he was dead, maybe; because I didn't hear him wheeze at all. I was getting worried that he was a doornail, dead as one as they say. It was so quiet. Silent, actually, silence: no wind, no flockin' gulls mad as hatters, no coughs, no hacks, no moans, no pukes. Serene, for a moment, a fleeting moment, just for one fleeing moment. And then I heard some sirens; I heard them coming from a few miles off, and I went out and walked down the street, I had nothing better to do, and when I got here, there were all these firemen just smoking cigarettes with the EMTs and just staring at where the house used to be."

"..."

"It was just gone. I mean, there was a piece of piping here, some wires there, and some wood, here, but the boys were gone. The patients were gone. Just gone."

"..."

"Gone. Just like the planners planned it. Just like they wanted it. Like they want it for all of these units. You know that's what the dreadlocked looney doc de Gouge wants. I bet his old man boxers get wet just thinking of it all, just thinking of those units being cleared and swept out to sea. I bet he'll brag about it to his superiors, if he has any, who knows, seems to be in anarchy down here, and he likes it that way, but I bet he brags about how the sick kids are gone and no funds were used. Or, wasted. I'm sure some see us convalescents here as just wasted funds, funds that could be used for defense, or political perks. Whatev, you know, whatev."

"Yeah, yeah, I know."

"I got the impression that the people there weren't there to save the house, or rescue those sick bald kids, but to figure out why that house was torn from its pilings and dragged out to sea so easily."

"..."

"And how they can get it to happen to the rest of the houses here, you know?"

"Hmm."

"Yeah, right?"

The wind whips where the old house used to be, where the dying kids played donated video games and ate stale potato chips. The dune is dead here, and the gross ocean is laughing, and growing, and spitting salty spews of insults towards Map and Tonya and Pist, who is now asleep in Tonya's arms.

"Come on, limpy, let's turn around and get on back to the unit before the doctor gets there."

"Ah, yes, the doctor. I'd almost forgotten; damned pills."

"Plus, I'm starving. I could use some applesauce. Apple yogurt. Apple ice cream, mmm. Maybe some nice soft, super soft, cooked apples. And of course with cinnamon. Mmm."

"I guess an apple a day doesn't keep de Gouge away."

The dog wags her tail in its sleep; Map grips the tennis racket and the cane; Tonya takes one more look at the empty lot and she starts to walk, with Map following a few paces behind her.

"While we head back, Map, let's play a word game. About this place, about the Shoals."

"Sickie Shoals?"

"That's what it's been called for a little while now, yes."

"Uh, okay, Tonya. But what kind of game did you have in mind?"

"I say a word and tell you me if you feel it. Down here."

"Down here, at the Shoals. The Shitty Shoals."

"In Sickie Shoals, yes."

"Okay, sure."

"Okay, ready? Pain?"

"Duh."

"Competence?"

"From who? The staff?"

"Yeah."

"No."

"Compassion?"

"Nope."

"Hope?"

"Try again."

"Self-loathing?"

"A bit like 'Beer and Self-Loathing in Sickie Shoals'."

"Nice one, except that's there no beer allowed here."

"I take too many pills to worry about something as weak as beer."

"Self-destruction?"

"Pass the beer and all of the pills, please."

"Anger?"

"Don't make me hold back a slap."

"Okay."

"..."

"Community?"

"I don't think so."

"No, the only community I've found is fleeting and between unit mates. Hence, the fleeting nature of the feeling of a community, yeah. There are no long termers here. No. Well, except for me."

"De Gouge advised me not make friends down here."

"Well, he doesn't want us forming bonds, or a community."

"..."

"Pleasure?"

"Ha."

"Suffering?"

"Of course."

"Sorrow?"

"No."

"No?"

"Too many pills to feel sorrow."

"I see, I hear you. Sickness?"

"Too many pills not to feel sick."

"Constantly?"

"Constantly."

"Bonds?"

"Not many, no."

"None?"

"Well, I wouldn't say none. Just not many, no."

"Yeah, me either, Map, me either."

"…"

"But it's nice to have you here."

"Thanks."

"I just hope you stay around longer than the others have."

"Thanks."

"And not, like, you know, croak on the way back home…"

"Yeah."

"Because you're too heavy for me to carry."

"…"

"And those nasty gulls would eat most of your flesh before I got someone back to get you."

"Are we still playing the word game?"

"I don't know, I think so."

"It's taken a pretty dark turn."

"Well, you know, that's what happens after living in Sickie Shoals too long."

"I guess."

"Most people don't know."

"Let me guess, because they don't live long enough."

"You're the one getting dark now."

"…"

"…"

"Come on, let's get me home before I die."

"And the gulls eat you."

"Right."

"…"

"Good times."

"Always good times convalescing down by the sea…"

"See the rat rot by the sea."

"What?"

"A sickie nursery rhyme: 'The rot race; see the rat rot by the sea, sickie; now it is his fate, but soon it will be me.'"

"…"

When they get to the unit, the doctor is waiting at the front door, with his big, fading black medicine bag at his feet, and his bored hands fidgeting with his sandy dreadlocked beard.

"Ah, Tonya and Matt..."

"...Map..."

"...nice to see you both, on such a nice day like this..."

"...night..."

"...and how is, ah, how is, I just forget her name, I'm sorry, but what is her name?"

"Ms. Nevershe."

"Ah, yes, how is Ms. Nevershe?"

"Well, I'm not sure how to answer that question."

Map stands leaning against his cane and lets Tonya go up and unlock the front door to the unit. Tonya goes in first, followed by the huffing and puffing doctor, and then Map follows with the cane in one hand and the tennis racket in the other.

Map walks a few paces behind the other two. He watches as the doctor stops at Ehab's door and clears his throat loudly, then waits, and Ehab coughs once in reply; then again, the doctor clears his throat two times, and after a moment comes two slightly louder coughs from inside the door. The doctor turns around, smiles at Map and then nods, and then hobbles down the hall, carrying his fading black bag in one hand, and scratching sand out of his natty beard with the other hand.

Map slows down; he's struck with a jolt of pain that keeps him wordless and breathless. Map takes the opportunity to let the unused racket fall to the floor and then he closes his eyes and leans against his cane, and stands still for a moment. Ehab coughs to him, but Map ignores him and walks down the hallway with its heavy odor of Pist's piss, towards the kitchen, and then into the great room.

As he steps into the room, he's distracted by the pungent sea smell, and then his arm starts to hurt. He pauses, and clenches his left hand into a fist, and then he lets it out, and an acute pain, a rape of fire goes up his arm and deep into his shoulder. A pain stabs his chest and into his back. He's about to say something to the dreadlocked doctor, and that's when he sees that the doctor and Tonya are staring intently and silently down at Ms. Nevershe's vast tub.

"Is she alive?"

"I'm not sure, Tanya."

"Tonya."

"..."

Map sees that Ms. Nevershe is now the same size that he is, maybe two hundred pounds. Her eyes are open; her mouth is wide, but still as a statue, just like the rest of her, still and silent.

The pink poodle walks on her creaking three legs to the tub and stares up. The dog looks from the vacant eyes of its master to the worried eyes of Tonya to the disturbed eyes of the doctor.

Map gets struck with another sharp pain and he sucks in air loudly and accidently drops his cane, and it hits the floor with a smack and the doctor and Tonya turn around quickly and the dog yelps and turns and Map blacks out, and slumps to the floor. Before the doctor can respond, Tonya takes a step forward to help Map when Pist once again balloons up to fifty and then sixty pounds. Tonya trips over the now-huge dog and falls to the floor like the cane, only when she lands she spits out a tooth, and her eyes close and she's out like a pissed-on candle.

And as the doctor is leaning over to help Tonya, glimpsing slightly over at Map (who is on the floor and drooling), and paying little to no attention to the bloated and yelping dog, Ms. Nevershe starts to sing, loudly, and she sings louder and louder and the dog yelps more and more until finally both the woman and the dog fall silent, and shut their eyes, and the hot-pink ancient dog collapses on the floor.

The doctor stands up and looks around him and sees three people and one dog passed out cold. The doctor looks over at the snoring siren in the tub, and as he looks over at her, she increases in her girth by one hundred pounds. He rubs his eyes. The woman appears to reverse burp of sorts and then gains fifty more pounds, and then she opens her eyes and shrieks and finally expands one hundred more pounds before she closes her eyes again and appears to be a statue of a whale in the tub.

"Craps of fate."

The large doctor reaches into his pocket, and pulls out two pills, and tosses them both into his mouth and chews them like candy.

There is a cough from behind the wall.

The doctor scratches his twiggy, natty beard and responds to Ehab: "I don't know, Ehab, I just don't know."

Ehab emits a dry, concerned cough in reply.

Outside, hanging in the wind, is the last of the pox-free gulls. The rot race; see the rat rot by the sea, sickie; now it is his fate, but soon it will be me.

CHAPTER FOUR

the Drugged and the Dying

It is like waking up from being beaten in a drunken daze; hung-over, scratched to hell, in a sick, sandy haze. He has carpet burns from where the doctor dragged his limp body across the living room carpet, over the sandy kitchen floor, and down the dark hallway into his room.

"Why didn't he just get my wheelchair?"

Tonya: "I don't know."

Map: "..."

Tonya: "I was on the floor."

"..."

"Out cold on the floor, swallowing a tooth, I think." She pauses and searches through her teeth with her tongue. "Yeah, at least one, I think. I blacked out. Give me a break, Map."

He's back in his chair.

Tonya is on his bed. She has a welt on her forehead.

"Did you wake up in bed?"

"I woke up on the sofa; I have a vague recollection of seeing the doctor wiping globs of sweat from his beard after he hauled you back down here. I think you wore him out and he decided just to drag me across the room, instead of across the unit."

"Hmm."

"Yeah."

"How's the dog?"

"I haven't checked."

"Did I hear people in there? In the other room?"

"Yeah."

"Well, who is here?"

"Them."

Map: "Oh."

"…"

Map: "What are they doing here?"

"I'm not sure; I woke up when they were heading to see Ms. Nevershe and I came in here to check on you. He must have called them and told them to come here."

"What time is it?"

"Well, I'm not sure exactly, but the sun's not up yet."

"Ah."

"Do you need any help with anything? Getting in bed?"

"No, I can manage. I'm pretty tired and I feel like hell."

"You look like you do. Sorry."

"It's okay."

"I'm going to my room; I'm going to watch what's going on out there through my peephole until morning. I'll talk to you tonight."

"Okay. Thanks, Tonya."

"For what?"

"Oh, I'm not sure."

They smile. She turns and leaves, shutting his door.

He decides to sleep hunched over in his chair; he doesn't want to deal with trying to get into bed and he hopes that when he wakes up, he'll be able to get up on his own. He sits and listens to the wind; he's gotten used to it by now.

Map can feel the wind coming through the cracks of the old windows. He hears those nasty gulls screaming bloody murder. Map's room begins to smell like the beach, like the rotting sea turtles, dirty diapers, and bloated sea gulls floating in the tepid surf; the discarded cancer-patient wigs with sea life living and dying in them; the washed-up chairs that were once white and are now asparagus green with algae. Tonya once told Map that she's found a human hand on the beach a few times, and on one occasion, that she found a human penis on the beach, being fought over by two one-armed crabs. She'll never get used to seeing something like that.

He's asleep again.

Sometime in the midst of his slumber he wakes up and transfers himself, painfully and fitfully, from his chair to his bed.

Then he sleeps. He sleeps the sleep of the drugged, the sleep of the dazed, the sleep of the dead.

When he wakes, it's dark outside, and he's been in such a deep sleep that he doesn't know whether he's been asleep for twelve minutes or twelve hours. The waves still crash against the soggy baby dolls and the barnacle covered boots which have washed up on shore; the winds blows a rancid smell into the room and he grinds his teeth and feels a bucket of oily sand in his mouth. He's gotten used to it by now.

"Hey."

He looks around the dark room, confused about not only what time it is, but where he is. He smells her before he can see her; she smells like applesauce. His room smells like cinnamon applesauce and rotting sea gulls, which is an improvement.

"Hey. What time is it?"

"Past dark sometime."

He looks around; he wipes sand from the corner of his eyes. "Oh; I wasn't sure if it was still before sunrise or after sunset. Did I sleep all day?"

"I guess. I did. But I don't leave my room in the day."

"Yeah, I've noticed."

"How are you doing?"

"Feeling like hell. You?"

"Been better."

Map: "How are the others?"

"Well, I've heard Ehab cough, and Pist bark, but I haven't seen them, and I haven't heard Ms. Nevershe talking or singing, which doesn't mean much, she sleeps for days at a time sometimes."

"Are they still here?"

"I heard some other female voices leave hours ago."

"How about the doctor?"

"I heard the front door shut a little while later, after the nurses left, and I haven't heard his voice since. No voices at all, actually."

Map: "Ah."

Tonya: "Yeah."

"Maybe we should go check on Ms. Nevershe."

"Okay. Do you need some help getting out of bed? Into your chair?"

"Well, no, thanks. Hmm. You know what? Yes. Yes, I do. Please."

She struggles to get him up from the bed and into his chair. She bends over and he sits himself up as much as he can and then she pulls him up and he wraps his arms around her neck, and he swings his numb legs over the side of the bed and mutters "Craps of fate indeed" and feels like he's going to throw up, but he doesn't. Then he pushes himself up off of the bed while Tonya pulls him up.

He never gets fully on his feet, and Tonya gets him to his wheelchair in a combination of a drag, a shove, and a pull. When he's in the seat, hurting, sweating, burning, he looks up at her, and between getting his breath and not throwing up, he mutters towards her, "You're strong…" and she replies, in a hush, "Apples, you know, are good for people." She sits on the floor and pulls off Map's old socks, and then tosses them under the bed, and she starts to tug a new pair onto his cold feet.

"How do they feel?"

Map: "What?"

"Your feet. Legs."

"Not as good as earlier, yesterday; and almost as bad as they felt for the rest of the time recently."

"Ah."

"Pain, numbness, cold fire, hot ice from hell."

"Yeah."

"Oh, well."

Tonya sighs, smiles, shrugs.

"Thanks."

"Hmm?"

"For helping. Me. With the socks."

"Oh, sure, whatev. No problem." She finishes getting the sock on his other foot. "I guess, sometimes, that I don't mind helping others here. I've seen people come and go. They only go one way. I guess that I feel like at least I can help a little. I feel luckier than everyone else here. Sorry, but it's true. I feel lucky that I can still walk, and see, and help."

"But, your teeth…"

She smiles: "There's always applesauce."

"Good attitude."

"A girl's got to do what a girl's got to do to get by, you know?"

"Yeah, I hear you, I hear you."

"You ready?"

Map: "Yeah."

"Can you do it yourself, or do you want me to help you?"

"Well, no, it's okay, but, you know, yeah, I mean, if you don't mind."

"I wouldn't've asked if I didn't want to."

Passing the closed door to Ehab's room, Tonya pauses while she's pushing Map down the hall, and she listens for a cough, or a wheeze. After not hearing anything for thirty seconds, she exchanges glances with Map. She lets go of Map's chair, and moves closer to Ehab's door, and puts her ear against the door.

Softly: "I don't hear anything."

Gently: "Let the man sleep; he's fine, probably."

She keeps her ear against the door a little longer, shrugs, and starts to push the chair down the piss and vinegar hallway again. She manages to get the chair to the kitchen, where they are met by the normal-sized three-legged pink poodle, Pist, who is about to squat and pee on the floor.

"Pistachio! Stop!" She lets go of the chair and looks down at Map, "Here, I'm going to park you here. I need to walk this poor dog before she gets huge again." She hops over and bends down and picks up Pistachio and walks away and disappears from Map's sight; he hears the front door slam shut seconds later.

A cough questions from Ehab's room.

"Yes, Ehab; everyone's fine. Tonya's just walking the dog."

Ehab coughs one soft cough, a goodnight wheeze, and his wall is silent again.

Map sits in his chair and looks out the grimy sliding glass door at the moon's reflection over the trashline and the stinking breakers; the wind whips into the room, and he feels sand getting into his ears and nose.

"I'm going to close my eyes for a few minutes until Tonya gets back, Ms. Nevershe, wake me if you need me, okay?" And he does, he closes his eyes, and he falls asleep in his chair, listening to the wind as it whips the trash around and erodes the sand dunes in front of their unit, where they are convalescing by the sea.

He wakes as the front door to the unit slams shut. As he opens his eyes, the curtains and mini-blinds in the room all move a little, like a tornado is about to strike. Tonya enters the hall and walks down past the empty rooms, pausing for a second for a wheeze which she never hears from Ehab's room. She slides through the applesauce kitchen, and enters the great room. She has the now-swollen pink poodle in her arms. Tonya puts the dog down and walks across the room and she looks down at Ms. Nevershe and says, "Uh, she's dead."

Map looks over, sleepily.

Map: "Hmm?"

"Did you not notice, Map?"

"Well, no, actually."

"Hmm."

"Yeah."

"You didn't smell anything weird?"

"The whole beach smells weird."

"True. Hey."

Map: "What?"

"You know my peep hole?"

"Yeah."

Tonya: "Well, last night I was watching the med-t.v. some, through the wall, and after the last nurse left, I think I saw the doctor put a needle in Ms. Nevershe and take something out of her."

"What do you mean?"

"Like blood."

"Blood?"

"Blood."

Map: "You sure he wasn't giving her a shot?"

"No, the nurses left, and he left the room for a minute, and then he came back, and took a needle and inserted it in her neck, and stuck little clear vials on it, and they filled with blood, but then I stopped watching, I was tired. And then a little bit later, I think he was the last to leave."

"Did you hear anything from Ms. Nevershe after the doctor left?"

"Uh, no."

Map: "Hmm."

"But she's definitely dead, Map. I know, I've seen a few dead people in this place, and they looked like her, just not as big, or wrinkly."

Map: "Well, it's too late to call the nurses; they've all gone home by now. Let me call the doctor."

Map wheels his way over to the phone which is sitting on a cheap table at the end of the stained sofa; when he picks up the receiver, it smells like apples. He punches in a number, then turns the speaker on and puts the hand piece down.

The phone rings, and rings, and rings, and when an automatic voicemail picks up, Map hangs up and dials again. Finally, the phone is picked up, and a scratchy voice answers, "Er, where, I mean, hello?"

Map speaks, "Dr. de Gouge?"

"Um, no, I mean, yes, maybe. Who is this?"

"Map."

"Map?"

"Map Barons, in the unit, in the chair."

"Ah, yes, Map, why are you, I mean, what can I do for you?"

"It's Ms. Nevershe."

"..."

"She's dead, it appears."

"..."

"So, we called you."

After a pause, the doctor finally speaks, "Now, Matt, Map, whatever, Ms. Nevershe: is she dead?, or does she appear to be dead? There could be a difference, quite a big difference indeed."

Tonya chirps up, "She's doornail dead."

The doctor responds, "Oh, dead, indeed. Craps of fate. Well, thank you for calling, and that's too bad, but I must run and get some sleep."

"But, doctor?"

"Er, yes, uh, Map, well here's the thing, um, are you still there?"

"Yeah."

"Well, here's the thing: the nurses are off at this time of the night, there are limited funds to go around to pay for so many hours, with the cut backs and all, I'm sure you understand ... so I won't be able to get a nurse or two over there to dispose of the body tonight, but anyway, but, well..."

"Yes?"

"Well, it could take me a half a day to find someone, some people that are on one of the contractor lists, who will come down by the sea for a body, especially a large sick one; it could take a whole day ..."

"Okay."

"Maybe even two days. Three perhaps."

"And in the meantime?"

"Well, uh, er, craps of fate, in the meantime I guess just cover her up. And if it takes more then two or three days, I'm sure five at most, tops, sure, but if it takes more, and she, well, you know, smells, just open the front door and let some of the nastiness in the breeze in and you won't smell her one bit more."

"…"

"Oh, and Map?"

"Yes, doctor?"

"Just be careful, and for craps of fate's sake, don't let that nasty pink bitch chew on that dead whale."

"Yes, sir."

"Well, I hope you're doing better, tell Tanya hello…"

"…Tonya…"

"…and I need to go, go shower and get this sand out of my beard, and er, um, get some sleep too, yes, bye bye." And the line clicks dead and Map turns his chair around and looks back and forth between Tonya and the late Ms. Nevershe.

After a minute, Tonya says, "I'll go into her room and get her bed sheets and cover her up."

She comes back with her arms full of wrinkly bed sheets. She walks over and covers the entirety of Ms. Nevershe with sheets, wordlessly.

She looks around the room a second, makes eye contact with Map and then breaks it, and says towards the wall, "Ehab?"

She waits a minute and then says a little louder, "Ehab?"

After a minute of nothing, she looks down at Map and says, "Sshhh: I'm going to make a hole into his room too, just to make sure I know what's going on around here, everywhere in here. Don't tell, okay?"

"The way you say it makes it sound like you might already have a hole into my room."

"…"

"Well, do you?"

"The guy before you, well, he may have been dying, but he was hot and he slept naked."

"…"

"He's where I got the idea from."

"I see."

"Yeah."

"…"

"Well, let me go, or whatev."

"Okay."

"What are you going to do?"

"I don't know, maybe I'll just sit here."

"Right there, with her there? Dead and all?"

"..."

"That's kind of weird, Map, kind of gross."

"Hmm, maybe."

"Just remember to do one thing."

"What's that?"

"Don't let the piggy-pink bitch chew on her."

"Ah. Yes. Sure."

"And don't pull that cover off of her, and don't let the wind blow it off."

"I guess I could just keep the door closed."

"No, no, let that nasty gale in; she might start to stink soon." She looks over at Ehab's wall, and listens for a cough or a wheeze, and after not hearing anything, she lowers her voice and bends down to whisper into Map's ear, "So, I figure that if we don't hear him, Ehab, cough for a day or so, we should smell under his door, for, you know, rot, decay."

"Hmm."

"..."

"Why not just open the door and check in on him?"

She looks down at Map, and opens her mouth but shuts it before she speaks, waits a second, and starts to speak again, "But, Map, that would be rude, so rude."

"Ah, well, if he's dead, it wouldn't be rude."

"But what if he's alive and just quiet; that would be rude then."

"Ehab's not quiet too long, ever."

"Yeah, you're right. Good point."

Map sits in his wheelchair next to the bloated and covered corpse; Tonya stands for a second, and then rubs his hair and walks away.

"Good night, Tonya, are you off to work on your hole?"

"You make it sound dirty like that, but, yes."

"Good luck."

She walks off, and Map hears her rummaging around in the kitchen, getting applesauce no doubt, and then he hears her slight footsteps going down the hall, and her door gently closes. A minute later, Map hears the soft grinding sound, as she slowly turns her pointed metal nail file into the thin wall.

He eventually wheels himself out of the room, down the hallway (where he pauses for a second to listen for a wheeze, which he doesn't hear), and into his room. He closes the door behind him, rolls across the room to his bed, and starts the painful process of dragging his limp lower body into his bed, and if that wasn't enough, the pain begins before he even starts moving, the thought alone tortures him.

In bed, he stares at the ceiling, rubbing sand out of his hair and onto his pillow. He hears Tonya's holing continue, a faint noise, especially over the wind and the waves, but he concentrates and focuses in on the steady sound, backed by the wind, the ever-blowing wind, and sometime just before dawn, when Tonya will be going to bed, he falls asleep.

The front door wakes him. The door, normally closed, is opened. Then it closes again. Sand skids across the warped floor.

He looks at the windows and sees that it is bright outside or as bright as it gets here in fall with all of the gunk particles suspended in the air. Gulls are fighting with each over just outside his window. He hears heavy footsteps in the hallway, moving slowly.

He tries to think back just five seconds ago: what was going on just before he woke? He was in bed dreaming about walking, but did he hear a knock on the door? No. No, so maybe it's just Ehab walking around, but that's just a sleepy thought, because Map knows that Ehab's never getting up and walking around, at least not without a hundred hacking wheezes and coughs. The footsteps are too heavy to be Tonya's.

It's Ms. Nevershe; oh, wait, he remembers, now awaking more from his sleep, she's doornail dead.

Then he hears a door open and close, gently, but not the front door to the unit, a bedroom door, or maybe a bathroom door, or the hall closet door.

He holds his breath; nothing, no hacking from Ehab, no whimpering from Pist (Map begins to worry that the reason the dog is quiet is that it is in the other room chewing away at the fat of the late Ms. Nevershe). The only sounds he can hear are the ones from outside: the surf breaking on the salty trash; an ambulance driving slowly, not in a hurry to save one of the residents of a seaside unit; he hears gulls fighting to the death, and then the eating of the loser's feathered and bloodied corpse. Good times at the shore, indeed.

After a couple minutes, maybe three, he hears another door open and softly close, and then footsteps walking away from him, down towards the kitchen, and then they get quiet as they enter the living room, where Ms. Nevershe is covered still, hopefully. He hears the footsteps coming back down the hall, but going past the front door, and walking down to his door. The footsteps stop in front of his door. Map turns his head and waits for a knock. But there is nothing. No sound at all; for a minute or two there is complete silence, even the barbaric cannibal gulls outside quiet down.

And then Map hears footsteps, heavy but muted, walking back down the dreary hallway and the front door opens, and then closes and he hears the deadbolt being locked from the outside. Ten seconds later a car door opens and then slams closed. It isn't until a minute or two later that he hears the engine turn on, and then the car sits there, right outside the door, before it pulls out into the empty beach road. Then the gulls start fighting in the air just outside of his room, and the wind picks up, and he licks his lips and they taste a little salty and also a little dirty, and he has sand in his teeth again, of course, and he yawns and he can almost taste those burning ships out in the ocean, still floating in place, burning slowly just like his nerve-ends are.

Map reaches over to his cheap bedside table, and opens the drawer and pulls out a pill container. He opens it and pours four pills into his left palm and then scoops one pill back up with the open mouth of the container. He tosses the three pills into his mouth and swallows them dry, sand and grit rubbing his throat as the pills go down. He's gotten used to it by now.

He puts his head back down onto his pillow. He thinks about the pillow, which is oddly the most comfortable pillow he's ever had. 'If I have to suffer here, convalescing by the sea, at least I have a nice pillow', he thinks.

It is light outside; the sun appears high, but it is not quite noon at the nasty beach. He could get out of bed, but there's nothing to do and nowhere to go, and he's tired from keeping Tonya's late night schedule recently. He thinks about his schedule for the day; he has no appointments with the nurses today: they all come by on the same day, two nurses, and four patients to a unit, those are the guidelines. So he decides to go back to sleep. He decides to sleep either all day or all day and all night, because if he gets out of bed, he'd have to get into his chair, and getting into his chair equals a lot of pain and a lot of nausea, so he is going to let the pills do their thing, and fall asleep.

And he does, as the gulls are eating each other's young and pecking out each other's eyes, and the wind is smuggling sand into his room, and the trashline collects more dying fish, and crabs rot on the beach: Map sleeps. He sleeps like the drugged patient that he is.

He awakes in near darkness and does not hear Ehab coughing, or the dog whining, or even the wind blowing. He strains to hear the waves. Silence.

Utter silence.

He wipes sand from the corners of his eyes.

He wonders if the pills are making him deaf. It's never been this quiet here.

He lies in bed until the pansy-purple over the ocean becomes navy blue and soon everything is black, eyes-shut-during-an-orgasm-black.

Then he hears a door open, not the front door, a thinner door, a bedroom door. But it does not close, and he hears footsteps coming towards his door, light footsteps. Tonya. There's a slight tap on his door.

"Map?"

"Tonya?"

"Yeah."

"Yeah?"

"Can I come in?"

"Yeah."

She opens the door, and then closes it behind her. She walks across the room and sits down in Map's parked wheelchair.

"How did you sleep last night?"

"Well, I was up almost all night, but I slept fine all day today."

"Good. You were looking pretty bad yesterday. No offense."

"Did you finish it last night, or this morning, whatever, your peephole?"

"Oh, yeah. That's why I came here."

"Hmm?"

"I finished it last night, my hole. And I woke up this morning when I heard someone coming into the unit."

"Yeah, you know, I did, too."

"Don't interrupt; this is important. So, do you know who it was?"

"What?"

"Who it was that came in last night?"

"This morning?"

"Whatev."

"Who?"

"Doctor de Gouge."

"Hmm."

"Yeah, because I didn't call him, did you call him again?"

"No."

"And the nurses weren't scheduled to look in on us today. So I got out of bed. To check it out. Curious, you know?"

"And?"

"I saw the doctor injecting something into Ehab. While he slept."

"Into, this time?"

"Yeah, into. I saw him prepare a syringe of something, but I didn't hear Ehab talk, but then I've never heard Ehab talk, but he wasn't coughing either. And the doctor was just so hush-hush, you know, like he was sneaking around."

"Hmm."

"But I definitely saw him sticking a needle into Ehab's chest."

"His chest?"

"Yeah."

"Effin' eff."

"Yeah."

"That would wake me up."

"You'd think so, huh?"

"Yeah."

"…"

"Well, did it?"

"What?"

"Wake him up? Ehab?"

"No, that's the weird thing too, because it wasn't a small needle or anything, I almost gasped when I saw it. I'm not even not sure that I didn't, if that makes any sense; I'm not even sure what makes sense anymore, you know?"

"Hmm. Maybe."

"I think maybe I did, and I'm not sure it's not just my meds messing with me again or just the fact that it was the middle of the night…"

"…the sun was up…"

"…but I got freaked out, like he knew I was watching, and I got back in bed and I pretended to be asleep and stayed there all day. See, I didn't say night that time."

"Did you hear Ehab cough?"

"No, it's been quiet."

"Yeah, weird, huh?"

"Yeah. Well, I need to go walk the dog. I'll be back in about ten minutes, if you want to wait here, I can help you to your chair when I get back, and we can watch the Med-t.v. or eat or whatev."

"Okay. I'll be right here."

"Bye."

She closes his door as she leaves, and then a minute later the front door opens and closes, and Map is in bed, listening for the sounds of the wretched and wrecked beach outside, on the Barrier Island, on the Burial Island. He's gotten used to it by now, gotten used to the rot race; see the rat rot by the sea, sickie: now it is his fate, but soon it will be me.

CHAPTER FIVE

the Burnt and the Blistered

This is half of a sandy hour later, and he's been transferred, painfully, a little roughly accidently, to his government-issued wheel chair. Tonya wheels him down the dim and gritty hallway, over scabs of old wall paint, fallen bits of ceiling plaster, passing Ehab's quiet room and the empty room that had most recently been assigned to the late Ms. Nevershe, never will she use it again. Tonya parks Map next to the sofa, facing the medical-television.

She walks over to the covered corpse and makes sure the corners of the bed sheets are secured. The pink dog sits next to the tub containing her deceased master; Pist stares at Tonya. "Give me a minute, dog," and after a minute of stretching her arms and checking her remaining teeth, Tonya picks up Pist and says nothing to Map as she leaves the room.

The front door slams closed.

Ehab, apparently awakened by the door, starts a loud coughing fit, which Map ignores. After a minute or two the hacking subsides and the medical-television channels change from one surgical show to another.

Map doesn't acknowledge Ehab through his wall; he's not sure that Ehab actually knows that he, Map, is awake and in here. The first channel is showing the interior of an ear; the next, the interior of the large intestines, and Map sits there, slightly hazy from the drugs, mesmerized in the trip he is taking via the dusty med-t.v. through the virgin-pink interior of someone, somewhere, maybe someone who is now convalescing by the sea, but most likely dead, Map thinks to himself, but that's just the pills talking.

These pills cause morbid thoughts, exhaustive and dreary suggestions; he hasn't gotten used to it by now.

The med-television switches channels to one showing a man in the early stages of becoming a woman, and then after a moment or two, up one channel to show a woman in the end stages of becoming a man. Ehab has either fallen asleep or likes to see this woman with the man's things dangling down. After a few minutes, Map hears a deep cough, and then the channel changes again.

The med-t.v. remains on the current channel: a man being operated on with skin grafts because of burns all over his body. After four minutes, five tops, Map wishes that the channel would change; but the volume of Ehab's television increases from the other side of his wall.

The front door slams again.

Map hears three paws trotting down the pissy hallway, stop at the water bowl for a quick sip, and then run through the living room. Pist pauses for a second to lick Map's hand and then the dog goes back to sitting next to the giant tub, with her back turned towards her late master, as if she's guarding an entombed queen.

The channel has not changed; Map lowers the volume on the medical-television, and the sound of those homicidal gulls outside fills the room, cawing at each other and flying over the house, the beach, and the trashline, dive bombing with their infectious silver-gray droppings.

Map begins to think of the trashline as alive, he knows it grows, and sometimes he's sat looking through the filthy sliding glass door and he can see the trashline ebb and flow slightly, and it looks like it is breathing.

Tonya enters the room, tosses a treat to Pist, and then sits on the sofa near Map and stares at the screen. After a minute of silence, she turns to Map and asks, "Why are you watching this?"

Map looks over at her, blankly, and doesn't respond, but nods his head to the wall.

Tonya says, "Oh, right. I forgot for a second."

"Was your walk okay?"

"Oh, sure, even though it was the second one in an hour."

"..."

"Didn't see anyone at all. Just an ambulance."

"Was it in a hurry?"

"Have you ever seen one in a hurry here?"

"No, no I haven't."

"And it still smells like hell out there."

"The ships."

"They stink. Stink but won't sink."

"Yet."

"And I've never understood why they're even out there, anyway, you know?"

"Oh. Yeah. Well, the first one, not one of these out here, but the one down south, two years ago? I remember hearing that one was an accident, and then it just drifted out into the international waters and no one wanted it anymore, and then it was ransacked by some pirates somewhere, and set on fire."

"Ahh."

"I swear I heard that one burnt for so long because of all the bodies of rats on there … breeding during the slow burn, eating the bodies of other dead rats, rat droppings burning, rat hair burns, and generation upon generation being born in a hurry in this sheltered, if not slightly smoky and crowed, rat haven, a rat heaven."

"Nice."

"And probably some dead high-sea pirates, too; you know that those ships are going to be fought over, just for the copper alone."

"Yeah."

"But then what happened, I hear, is that some of those captains just couldn't afford to operate them anymore: the fuel got to be too much, the crew all wanted more pay just to put up with pirates out there, and then the sky high insurance costs, and the final nail in the coffin was all the regs, those government regulations. I think that it was an owner of a big tanker down in Florida, maybe. I remember this one, the second one, was on the news a lot, too. His wife left him, he went broke, I think he killed his sister-in-law, whom he had been sleeping with and hence the wife moving out, but not divorcing him, and he just set out on the huge thing with some wine and weed and a little water and not much fuel."

"Yeah, yeah, I remember that now that you mention it; but I can't remember the guy's name."

"Neither can I; it doesn't matter. But anyway, it was kind of quiet when he left, because he was sneaking away before the body was found, the body of his wife's dead sister, and rumor was, on the news casts, was that he took a Russian hooker with him, a young one of course. She must not have known he was a broke murderer, and a week later, after a call on the radio for help from this woman, one of the hotshot news reporters took a helicopter out there with the intention of landing and getting an interview, maybe a rescue even. But they never landed the thing, they reported little fires being everywhere on the deck, smoke coming out of windows, things like that.

"I think they flew around for a bit, and no one came out, but they couldn't land. And a day or so later, the ship was on the news again looking like a giant smokestack out there. But then the real news happened."

"What was that?"

"The wife, the presumed widow. Insurance money. She was a co-owner of the company or the ship, and had life insurance on him."

"And he died on the ship?"

"He was declared a doornail, yeah. She made a pretty penny, a few million if I recall."

"Bet she's glad she didn't divorce him."

"Yeah, right? And then when word of the insurance money went around, a few other similar incidents happened, and I think two or three of those got insurance money, tons of it, but there was still all of these giant ships out there, burning, and not sinking, and when they do sink, it's not like they were emptied properly of whatever was in them."

"Hmm."

"And then more regs came into play and eventually insurance policies were changed, retroactively, and then that appeared to be the end of the burning ships."

"For a while, at least."

"Right, for a while. And then later there was this one," he points out towards the Atlantic, "then these two. Lucky us."

"Our two."

"Our two. You know why they're there?"

"No; why?"

"Pure convenience."

"Really?"

"Really."

"Just got to be too expensive?"

"And no one would buy them. Cheaper just to let them go adrift towards international waters and let come what may, you know?"

"Nice."

"Yeah."

"So, why are they just sitting out there, out here, in front of us?"

"Good question."

"…"

"My guess has something to do with currents, stagnant currents perhaps. Sand bar, maybe. I don't really know."

"Hmm."

"But that's just a guess. Maybe somehow the trashline keeps one closer in to shore and one further out."

"Hmm. I don't know much about science…"

"Neither do I."

"Hmm."

The dog, next to her deceased master, groans loudly; Tonya turns around quickly to check on the dog; Map turns his head a little slower, groaning in pain, and thinking about taking another pill. As they are watching, Pistachio groans again and burps once, then twice, smells the air, farts and looks confused, and then swells up to more absurdly grotesque proportions, and then proceeds to empty her decrepit canine bladder onto the floor, which flows towards the sliding glass doors.

The med-t.v. channel changes.

"I thought that you walked her? Pist."

"I did. Twice."

The med-t.v. channel changes again.

"Hmm."

"And she peed when she was out."

The channel changes again.

"Maybe it scares her when she swells up, and that's why she peed the floor."

The channel changes again.

"Yeah, or maybe it hurts like hell, and that's why. I think I peed myself when I pulled my first tooth out."

They both glance towards the sandy television set, expecting the channel to change; it doesn't.

"You mean, when a dentist pulled your first tooth?"

"No."

"…"

"No, I mean when I pulled my first tooth."

The channel does not change.

"…"

"Literally, I pulled it out and it hurt like hell."

"I imagine."

They both turn their eyes away from the poodle, as she is lapping up the pee off of the floor with her liver-spotted senior tongue. They both look back to the medical-television, it's a close up of a pap smear; Tonya picks up a spoon and chucks it against Ehab's wall.

The channel does not change.

Tonya looks in vain for another spoon, and when she cannot find one, she shouts towards the wall, "Ehab, you perv, c'mon!"

The channel does not change.

Map looks at the screen a second too long and Tonya gently reaches over and, with her fingers on his cheek, turns Map's head to the right, away from the med-t.v., away from the sordid ocean, and he's being forced, gently, to look towards the kitchen.

"Ehab!"

Map closes his eyes for a minute to appease Tonya; when he opens them again, he finds himself staring at a naked man in the kitchen, bald as a baby, and covered with scars.

Tonya is still looking at the medical-television, strangely attracted to the pap smear on the screen, and she's about to open her mouth to shout again, when a deep scratchy voice from the kitchen croaks: "What?"

Map stares at the nude man, confused. Tonya looks over, first at the whole scene, a scarred stranger in the kitchen, naked; she looks at his face, doesn't recognize it; she looks down at the scarred penis and wilted sack, and doesn't recognize either.

Map is silent, biting his lower lip and scratching his ear.

Tonya, after a moment of silence, asks: "Ehab?"

A gagging noise come from deep within the scarred torso, "Ggrwarrk!", followed by a violent coughing fit, during which Tonya and Map exchange glances and nod to each other, affirming that this mangled mess of a man is in fact the heretofore invisible Ehab.

Map speaks next, hesitantly, "I'm Map."

Ehab just looks at Map, and says nothing.

"I'm Tonya."

Ehab slowly turns his hairless head and face towards Tonya, stares at her for an uncomfortable while, and then turns back to Map for a second, before fixing his stare at a point somewhere in between the two of them.

He licks his thin lips and then raises a hairless eyebrow and says, "That her? That Nevershe?"

"Yeah."

Ehab: "Good God."

"No."

Ehab: "Hmm?"

"You should have seen her a couple days ago."

Ehab: "Good thing I can't smell anything. I bet that washed up whale is rank right about now. Ugh. I feel sorry for you two."

Map nods; Tonya tries to think of something to say. Ehab coughs, then spits onto the floor.

Ehab continues, "When's she going to be gone?"

Map shrugs, "Who knows; the doctor said it may take a few days and to just open the door when she smells."

Ehab: "Well, it won't bother me none."

Map: "Right."

Tonya: "Lucky."

Ehab: "Hmm."

Tonya: "Yeah."

Ehab: "No."

Tonya: "Hmm?"

Ehab: "No, not too lucky, not at all, not much at least. Look at me. Look."

Tonya stares, seeing him there naked and burnt, and she looks down at his parts maybe for three seconds too long, and Ehab says, "That's not what I'm talking about; talking about the burns, the pain, hairless like a fish ..."

"I guess that I was just thinking you were lucky that you didn't have to smell the ocean. Or smell Ms. Nevershe."

Map nods with Tonya's statement.

Ehab says, in a gruff, gnarly voice, "Sand," and then proceeds to spit onto the floor, "I swear my mouth got full of it just walking down the hallway." He spits again. Coughs. "I feel like I'm drowning in sand."

Tonya looks at him, naked and scarred from head to toe, and she's not sure what to say, but decides not to smile or stare, and then decides on: "That's why I wear pants. And underwear. Always."

Tonya looks away from Ehab; Ehab looks down at his nakedness; Map looks away from Tonya, now thinking about her underwear, and stares straight between Ehab and Tonya towards the medical-television.

Ehab, not caring about his nudeness, rubs his genitals, getting sand off, and glances from the med-t.v. to Tonya, and then over to the corpse in the tub, and the dyed pink dog, sleeping on the sandy floor.

Ehab asks, "Ya'll got any kava kava here?"

Map and Tonya look at him blankly. Tonya says, "I have some wax. Want a dab? Dab dabs?"

"No kava kava?" Ehab glares at Tonya. "Then fix me a Confederate Clot, huh?"

"I'm not sure…"

"I make mine USS Merrimack style; half a shot of sea water, a drop of motor oil, and then stir the rum with a chuck of burnt wood."

Map: "Is there a Monitor style?"

"Why would there be a Monitor version of the Confederate Clot? Don't you read any history, gimpy boy?"

"Sorry."

"Whatever. That would be a Slick Sided Steamship, and I ain't no vodka drinker. How about a Rusty Radiator on the Rag?"

"…"

"You know sure as fate's fucked that you want to know what a Rusty Radiator on the Rag is. I know you do. No salt water or oil in that one, sweetie, but of the three of us, only you can make it for us, and then only during your cycle. Stir it with your finger with some blood on it; I'll supply the radiator moonshine. A few hot pepper flakes are the rust. Mmm. A rarity but a favorite of mine."

"…"

"…"

"…"

Ehab nods his head towards the covered corpse, and hacks and coughs for a minute, then nods his head towards Ms. Nevershe again, and says, "That's how we get out of this ward, huh?"

The room is silent; the dog looks up at her doornail master and whines.

Ehab continues, "Not me, no way." He hacks again, spits a mucus-filled gray glob onto the floor, "Not me, man, I'm going to recover, recover just fine." He nods, smiles.

Map and Tonya nod affirmatively in unison.

After a moment of silence, Tonya asks, "Want some applesauce?"

Ehab, who had been looking out of the dirty window, hearing the nasty wind whipping around the corners of the house, says, "No. Do I look like I want some stupid bowl of cheap applesauce?" He coughs and coughs. He spits more sand from his mouth.

"Well," Tonya says, "You look like you could use some clothes. Or at least some boxers."

Ehab: "I think the nurses like me this way."

"They're not coming today."

"I'll make that tall one come hard next time I see her, now that I am feeling better."

"Ehab!"

Ehab: "Just saying. But you are right: why would I care if she comes or not as long as I do, right?"

Map, readjusting himself in his wheelchair, says, "So, uh, Ehab, what happened? What happened to you?"

Ehab, who has been standing in the same place this whole time, walks slowly over to where Tonya and Map are, and he stands right in front on them, with his burnt penis and shriveled sack at eye level and just a foot away from Tonya and Maps, says, "Well, I got burnt up like a mother. You know? Out there." He nods his head towards the grimy windows, it gets silent, and the trio can hear the waves crashing trash down onto the ruined beach outside. "Out there."

Map asks, "What do you mean, out there?"

Tonya says, "Sit down. Please."

She moves to her left, out from directly in front of his flame-fried genitals, and Ehab slowly turns and lowers his naked scars onto the old and gritty sofa cushions.

After he sits, he contemplates for a minute and no one says anything, and then he smiles through his thin lips and says, "Man, I'm so glad these cushions aren't covered in plastic. Used to be that all the sofas down here near the beach were covered in plastic, I hated that. But that was back when families used to come down here; no one cares about the shore these days." He spits.

It is silent again, except for the hot-pink dog farting, the ocean spewing filth onto the dark beach, and the waves dragging bottles and syringes back out to the sandy breakers. The wind whips around the house and somehow it gets into the house, as usual, and Tonya feels sand getting into her ears and hair; sand collects at the corner of her eyes. Ehab coughs and spits. The dunes outside are getting smaller and smaller every second.

Tonya, looking over at Ehab, but up high, to his flame-wrinkled face, asks, "Now, what were you saying? About out there?"

Ehab pauses, spits and coughs a few times each, and says, "Well, I guess I can tell you two." He looks back and forth from Tonya and Map a couple of times before continuing, "Well, I was working downstate for a man, a captain, on one of his big tankers. I was broke. I was in debt. Bad. I'm not going to lie, okay, and I'm not ashamed, no, but I liked to give my money to people. To women. To two women. Maybe more. For sure more, now that I think about it, yeah." Cough. Hack. Gag. Cough. Burnt lips smile.

"I'd have taken some."

"Oh," his scarred, thin lips curve into a smile, "Oh, child, I didn't give it away for free." He openly looks down at Tonya's breasts; she crosses her arms over her chest.

Map says, "Go on."

"Well, I had gone out one night, drinking at a bar, and I saw a couple of ladies, nice looking, nice and drunk; I didn't care that they had wedding rings on, why should I care?, I just cared that they had something different between their legs than I did."

Tonya crosses her legs, keeping her arms across her chest.

Ehab hacks some, spits towards the med-t.v., misses it, and continues with a huge smile on his face, "So, I took them out back, to one of their husband's cars, and I leaned them both over the hood, and pushed up their skirts, and just went from one hole to the other, back and forth. It was nice and dark back there, they seemed to be enjoying it, I was for sure. But one of them, the one I enjoyed most, forgot to tell me that her husband worked at the bar. Bartender. Whatever, no big deal. I was packing, of course; I always carried a gun when we went off shore, because of pirates out there; I didn't care if it was against some law or whatnot, neither did my captain, we all carried on the tanker. All of us, some legal, some, uh, doctored guns, too. They were the most fun, if you were on the right end of the gun, not facing the barrel of course. On and off, yep. But especially we all carried 'em when we were off of the tanker, yeah, yeah."

He goes into a hacking fit again; the dog behind them moans and barks along with Ehab's coughing.

The dog lets out a huge howl, like one never heard before from the bright pink poodle, and then the swollen dog shrinks back down to her normal size, appears to smile and wags her little tail. She leaves her dead master's side and walks over towards the sofa and sits in front of Ehab and Tonya.

Ehab takes a deep breath, his face's hue jumps from pale to cinnabar, and he clutches his chest. He closes his eyes.

Tonya touches his scabby shoulder, says: "Ehab, Ehab, are you alright?"

He holds up his pointer finger to say 'hold on', and he inhales slowly and deeply for a minute, his hands are on his chest.

Map asks, "Ehab, should I call for help? Tonya, hand me the phone."

"No, no. I don't know what that was, it hurt, it was excruciating. But I feel better now."

"Sure?"

"Yeah. Mostly better. A bit, at least, yeah. I'm used to it; I've been drowning in pain for some time now. Yeah, just drowning in it."

Map and Tonya: "…"

"Anyway, as I was saying: I was out back behind the bar, going from one to the other, I think I'd promised them decent money, which I had with me, and as I was inside the one whose husband worked there, I heard a door open and close. Not a car door. A building door."

"Yeah?"

"Go on."

"Well, it turns out that there were video cameras back there. I'm sure those women didn't know, I guess; no, sometimes I wonder if the one did it simply to mess with her husband, you know? I don't know. But I was in her, and then I was about to go, and then I heard a noise closer to me, and then I feel a whack at the back of my head, and the alley went from dark to light, and then the next thing I remember, is that I wake up, naked, with my hands and feet duct taped together."

He hacks, coughs, spits up more sand. Coughs again. Hits his chest with a scar-covered fist.

"And…"

"So I wake up, and I'm in some sort of boat, a small boat, and then I realize that I'm in a life boat, and I'm rolling and rocking like I'm in the water. But I'm a seaman, or was at least. I knew that the life boat was not in the water, just the larger ship it was attached to was out there. Floating.

"And I was there, duct tape over my mouth and around my hands and feet, and the ship's rocking, and I figure that sooner or later someone will find me … I figured that they wouldn't leave port without me, shorthanded, but it appears the captain did. So I lay there, naked as the day I came into this world, except for the duct tape, under the sun, my pecker burning, my eyes dry, and I listened for voices, but didn't hear any. None at all. I didn't hear any deck hands at all, or any deck noise for that matter. A little weird…

"But I wasn't worried, not then. I decided to sleep some, I was dehydrated from drinking the night before and being in the sun all day, exhausted, dizzy. I closed my eyes, figuring the sleep will do me some good, you know? And then when I wake up, I still don't hear any voices or noises."

He stops. He doesn't cough, he doesn't hack, he just stops and stares at the medical-television in front of him.

Map is quiet, just looking in Ehab's direction.

Tonya, looking at Ehab's upper part of his body, but not glancing down at his scarred member, says, gently, "Yes? Then what, Ehab?"

Ehab is quiet; Pist walks over and places her French-pink head on Ehab's wrinkly knees.

"That's when I smelled it. The smoke. That thick smoke. I'll never forget it. Never. I thought I was dreaming for a minute, or smelling something else, but I smelled smoke. And there was nothing I could do. I tried to scream, but couldn't, like in a dream. I hate those dreams, you know?

"And then those flocking gulls saw me. They were circling overhead, like salt-water vultures, all of them. All I could do was stare up, and by that time I could see the smoke in the air above me, with those gulls flying around, cawing like crazy, and fighting each other. Then, after a bit, the life boat I was in started to get hot.

"The life boat, old and wooden, had caught fire, and was starting to burn, and I couldn't see the flames, but I could feel the heat, and see the smoke, and then the first of those gulls landed on the edge of the boat, followed by another and another. I could tell they were hungry; they were sick of the polluted sea food just like I was."

Tonya shivers at the mention of gulls. She looks towards the windows, hears a bird shriek, and quickly turns away.

Ehab continues, "And then the wood beneath me started to crackle and pop. Pop and crackle. Like firewood. I was tired and dehydrated, and for a minute I fell asleep and I was back home, inland and safe, in front of a fire in the winter, back when it used to snow clean snow.

"I woke up to the smell of my flesh burning, and I tried to roll around, but couldn't get that far, the whole life boat was slowly starting to burn up, with me there, and no one to help. The gulls didn't seem to care; they'd stare at me when I moved and then fight each other, and if I got still, they'd get closer. When I opened my eyes, they were right above me. Dead zombie eyes just looking right back at me...

"And now, the good news: The boat caught on fire, and those nasty gulls flew away, and I started to burn, and I was hoping for death; I hadn't prayed in years, but I was praying for death, was sure I was going to die, and right then and there, I wanted to die, too. Quickly. Then and there."

He gets quiet, for a minute, then two. He coughs, scratches his left ear.

"Oh right, the good news: As I heard my skin popping, and smelled the hair on my head and my leg hair and my public hair and my arm hair burning, the ropes that held the life boat over the water snapped, and I, or the life boat rather, dropped into the water. Hard. Splash! Boom.

"I had the wind knocked out of me when it landed. It hurt. The impact. And I must've passed out for a while, from the impact, and from the burns. But I guess when it landed, since it landed so hard and had been on fire and all, it knocked some holes into the boat, and put the flames out, mostly, and some water came in, and I was laying there in about three, four, maybe five inches of water. But I was still naked and duct taped, and slept all night, thinking the boat would sink and finally drown me, but it didn't. I expected to drown that night, duct-taped and nude...

"All the next day I was out there, burned and shivering, under the unforgiving summer sun, and the sun just beat down on me, burning my already burnt cock, my cooked nose, and I was dehydrated as a whore in Hell. And then those gulls landed there again, and one got so close it started to bite my left nipple. Tearing at it. That's when I finally heard some voices, human voices, and, ha, just assumed that I was going crazy. Finally. But I heard a boat, and some men, and then the next thing I knew, it was three days later and I was in an ICU unit. I was there for a while, I'm not sure how long, but a month at least. More, I guess.

"And then I was brought here, to die by the beach, or as the doc says: to convalesce by the sea. Screw them, huh? You follow me?"

Map is silent.

Tonya says, "Say it again, brother."

Ehab looks over at her coldly. "Screw them."

Silence, but for the wind whipping the sand against the house taking away bits and flakes of the old paint; the unit has never been repainted since it was a vacation rental unit years ago, before the ocean became the gunk and junk that it is.

Silence.

Tonya says, "I wish you'd change the channel."

Ehab looks at her coldly again.

"Or I guess I could get up and do it; I want some applesauce anyway."

She gets up from the gritty sofa and walks towards the kitchen, followed by the oddly pink Pist, and she disappears down the hall and into Ehab's room; seconds later, the med-television in front on Ehab and Map changes channels from one health show to a surgery to another surgery.

Ehab and Map stare ahead at the screen.

Silence.

The channel changes again.

Map scratches his head, and looks over towards Ehab, who is watching a dental hygiene program now, "Ehab?"

"Yeah?"

"Hey, uh, Tonya said that maybe she saw Dr. de Gouge give you a shot of something today, or yesterday or whenever?"

"What do you mean that Tonya saw the doctor give me a shot? I've been in that room for freaking forever."

"You'll have to ask her; she'll be back in a minute. Anyway, did you get a shot? What did it do?"

Ehab stares ahead for a minute, and then looks over to Map, and says, "Well, you know, it's funny; you know how it is, always on pills, all the time, sleeping here and there dreaming while you're awake, thinking you're awake when you're asleep."

"Yeah, yeah."

"Speaking of which, you got anything?"

"Yeah, yeah."

Map reaches into his shirt pocket and takes out four pills, gives two to Ehab, and swallows the other two dry. Ehab tosses the pills down, also swallowing them dry.

Ehab asks, "What were those, anyway?"

"I'm not sure, just something the doctor gave me. They've made us all feel a little better."

"Let's hope. But, as I was saying, I wasn't sure whether it was a dream or what, I thought I had a dream that de Gouge came into my room last night, I thought it was just one of those vivid narcotic dreams. But then, a little while ago, I woke up, and where he stuck the needle in my dream hurt like hell, I tell you. But, the rest of me felt great. Feels great actually. Look at me!"

"Oh, yeah. We see you. We see all of you."

"Ha. Man, Map, this is the first time I've been able to get up and walk in, what, weeks? Months? And hell, I can talk without coughing up a gooey junky lung, and when I do cough, it doesn't feel like I'm going to die. And my skin, hell, it's been hurting like a mother since I woke up in ICU, whenever that was. What is today?"

"Do you know what he injected you with?"

"No. No, you know what? He didn't even say a word. He just came in quietly, did it, and left. As I said, I thought it was in my head. A dream."

"Yeah, that's what Tonya said he did. He just crept into your room like a thief."

"How did she know again?"

"I didn't tell you; I said you'd have to ask her."

"Yeah, yeah, I will. But, as I was saying, he didn't say anything; he just came in and left, like in a dream. And I woke up, and the first thing I felt was nothing … which is great … because all I'd been feeling for all of those months was just pain, pure soul-drowning pain. I wanted to peel my skin off, I'd thought about killing myself, but couldn't get out of bed to do it; and I would've taken a lot of pills, but I didn't have enough to do the job properly, and I didn't want to end up as a vegetable or anything.

"I don't feel bad at all! Everything feels great," he stands up, "I haven't felt this good in years," all nude and scar-covered, he makes a fist and pounds his chest, "Years, I tell you. I wish I knew what that was that he gave me, I'd inject more right now!"

Ehab pounds on his naked chest again, then his face turns crimson, his eyes roll up into his head, and he coughs a little, but the sound is muffled, and white foam comes out of his mouth, as if he were a rabid dog, and he falls down onto the floor, on his side, with his dead eyes facing the med-t.v. The channel does not change, of course.

Tonya walks in the room now, followed by Pist, and she looks down at Ehab on the ground and then looks over to Map in his chair, who shrugs his shoulders, and Tonya says, "Crud. He's dead."

Map nods.

Tonya, after a minute, looks over at Map, and says, "Hey, why is it that whenever I leave you alone in a room with someone, I come back and they are doornail dead?"

Map shrugs again. He's gotten used to it by now.

Outside, over the Burial Islands, the moon light is obscured by the pollution in the air, the ships keep on slowly simmering, the fish are dying and washing up on the shore with the plastic containers that should have been recycled; dead sea turtles and beached, rotting dolphins litter the shoreline. The rot race; see the rat rot by the sea, sickie; now it is his fate, but soon it will be me. The wind whips the nasty sand around, and the trashline grows, and it glows in the moonlight, and the dunes in front of the house are eroding away more. More and more. More and more and more.

Craps of fate, he's gotten used to it by now, gotten used to the burnt, the blistered, and the dead.

CHAPTER SIX

the Sinkers on the Burial Islands

This is when he feels he might be losing his mind:

"What did you say?"

"When?"

"Now. Just now. Did you say something to me? Were you talking to me?"

"No."

"Oh. Hmm."

"It's your pills, Map, that's what you're hearing."

"Oh."

"It has happened to me, too; I kept on hearing cats in the closet. I'd get up, open the door, and still hear them, but didn't see anything."

"Yeah."

"So then, it makes me wonder if the others things that I hear or see are there or not."

"Yeah, I know; me, too."

"Like, does it actually smell this bad around here? Like the Devil's bloody diarrhea, or is it just me? You know, you see, maybe, maybe we're just dreaming this stuff. Maybe, it's just me that smells bad."

"No, no. It's not just you..."

"But I can't be sure, you can't be sure..."

"No, I'm sure."

"You can't be sure that we don't smell the same fake smell. They're giving us the same thing. They don't care about us; you know that, they don't give a flying flock about us, what happens to us, how it all ends, when it all ends for us."

"..."

Tonya: "They think you're just as flocked-up as I am."

"..."

Tonya: "But I know they're right. I know it inside, deep inside."

"Yeah, we are all flocked-up."

"..."

Map: "You smell an ocean full of oil; it's not in your head; it's in the air. You're sucking up the smoke from those ghost ships out. It is nasty. It's rancid in your hair even now. The dog smells like it; urine and smoke. Like bars used to. The good ones, at least." A smile. "Now the sand is death black; it looks like little bugs all inside my bed. Sand bugs. Furious bugs. Trash bugs. Making my fingernails always smell nasty, you know? You know that smell. The one that wasn't always here, but now you doubt that it will ever go away: that one."

"..."

"It just smells like death all the time. Like death, of death. This rotting world. Rotting away. Wilting away."

"An ocean of rot."

"An ocean of oil, of rot, of trash. Take your pick."

"Well, what are we going to do about him?"

"Who?"

"Ehab."

"Ah."

"Yeah."

"Well? What are we going to do about him?"

"You should call him. Call de Gouge."

"Right now?"

"Right now."

"Where's a phone?"

"I think it's under him."

"What?"

"I think it's underneath Ehab."

"No, for real? Ugh."

"I think I saw it on the floor, near him, before, you know, he keeled over."

"Nice."

"…"

"Well, you're going to have to get it for me."

"Why?"

"Because look at me, I can't get it."

"Oh."

"Yeah."

"Gross. I don't want to do it. Can't you, well, never mind, I don't know."

"I can't; you'll need to get it."

"That's gross and I'm tired."

"Come on."

"I mean, isn't someone going to be here and get Ms. Nevershe at some time? Soon?"

"Well, yeah, it could be today, tomorrow, the next day, you know we don't know."

"But it could be soon?"

"Right."

"Well, I say we leave him there. They'll find him soon. Just go around him."

"What about the phone?"

"Really?"

"What?"

"Has it rung recently?"

"No."

"Are you expecting any calls?"

"No."

"Then I'm going to leave it; feel free to move him and get it."

"…"

"I think it's probably under his cock."

"Nice."

"Yeah, nice."

"Well, how about you at least go and change the channel."

"I can do that."

"Thanks."

"Just throw something against the wall when you see something you like."

"I know the drill; thanks."

"Yeah…"

Knock, knock.

She knocks on his door, pushes it halfway open.

"Hmm?"

"Hey."

"Hmm … What time is it?"

"Not quite dawn; almost my bedtime."

"…"

"…"

Map: "Well?"

"Oh. I was just thinking of something. Got me thinking. Something she once said to me."

"She?"

"Ms. Nevershe."

"Okay; go on."

"We were out there, in that room, watching the moon over the trashline, burning incense so we could open the doors a little and get a breeze in because she was always hot. She looked over at me, and smiled, and said that I should smile more."

"You should."

"Anyway, she told me I should smile more, but I told her I couldn't, that I was embarrassed about them, about my teeth, or how I talk. And she told me that I shouldn't be mad, because she said that she could feel me mad, angry, and told me it was just a waste, just a waste of time and of my energy."

"Go on."

"And I said to her, 'Aren't you pissed off, you know, at what's happened to you, at what you've become? The pain. Of just becoming pure pain? And becoming alienated from people, the ones who aren't thinking 'Why is this happening to me?' And she was silent for a while. And she just stared out over the dying dunes, and it was like she wasn't seeing the trashline anymore, or smelling the death out there, and she sat there, in that tepid tub, and just stared out."

"…"

"And she looked at me and she said, 'Do you believe in a god? In God? The God?' And I didn't answer, I was thinking about what to say, and I guess I took too long, so she went on and said, 'Well, I do. I do. I do believe in God. And when I get up there, to where He is, and it won't be long from now, I think, but when I get up there, I hope He asks me about this, about this sickness, this pain … and I think I'll look at Him, and say, 'It's no big deal, it was worth it, the rest of life's beauty, to go through some pain at the end.' And then we just sat there, and watched the moon through the smog. Then after a while she turned and said to me, 'Just never give up. That's what I did. And by the time I regretted it, it was too late. I was already on my way here.' And then I couldn't think of anything else to say; so I didn't say anything at all after that."

"…"

"Does it sometimes feel to you like the walls are breathing?"

"Sometimes? No."

"All of the time?"

"All of the time."

"…"

"But I've gotten used to it."

"Yeah, me too, for the most part, most of the time … except about right now."

"…"

"The walls are breathing."

"You'll get used to it. Again."

"Yeah."

"Yeah. It's gonna be alright."

"…"

"…"

"No. It's not."

"Yeah: No. It's not."

"Yeah."

"Hmm."

"Do you think you're ever going to stop hurting?"

"Sure; yes."

"…"

"Well, no. No. I just can't see it right now."

"Yeah, yeah, I know what you mean. I know what you mean."

"How about you? Do you think you'll always be hurting?"

"Hurting? Like, feeling pain?"

"Yeah."

"Oh, Map, I quit feeling a long time ago."

He awakes, hours later, to a gloomy noon, the sun obscured by the fine particles of destruction in the air. The first thing he feels is pain: that burning sensation from his thigh to his ankles, with a large grapefruit-sized area where he is sure that Ehab must have come in and hit him with a baseball bat on the ankle, knee, and hip while he slept; but Ehab is dead now, was dead then. Doornail dead. Dead on the floor. Out there. In the living room. On the sandy carpet. Dead, as dead as many of the dolphins in the sea, washed up on the beach. Doornails. The Barrier Islands have become the Burial Islands.

The first thing Map smells in bed is that nasty ocean. He hears the rabid crack-head gulls outside, pecking each other's eyes out, snapping at scabbed feet, ripping lice-infested feathers off of each other; defecating on the deck. He's gotten used to it by now.

He coughs.

Again and again, he coughs.

Then the gulls quiet down their yelling and bickering, and large rain pellets hit against Map's window. He reaches over, irritated by the pain, but ignoring it, ignoring the urge to vomit, ignoring the urge to take too many pills, and he opens the dusty, grimy plastic mini-blinds, probably contaminated with whatever killed the guy who lived in here before Map. He opens the mini-blinds and the rain drops are the size of small locusts and are swarming all over the window, drop by drop; thump, thack, tack, thack, it sounds to him as if the drops are almost solid. Hail? No, no. He looks closer and sees that the rain drops are rocket metallic gray and full of particles of smoke like a spiders sack is full of tiny spiders, waiting to run away in hundreds of directions.

Thump. Thack. Thump. Bump.

Thud. Boom.

He realizes he's woken up to sounds, footsteps; someone is in the house, in the unit.

He hears thumping, hacking, and an electrical sound, like a faraway drill. It starts and stops over and over for a few minutes, and then it is quiet.

Map grabs a few pills that are on the bedside table, swallows them down, and goes through the hell-on-earth feelings of getting from the sandy bed into his wheelchair. He rubs behind his ears and scratches his thinning hair and when he looks at his fingernails, there is brown-black sand beneath them.

He coughs again and feels like he is going to throw up. The ocean smell only makes him sicker. These old windows let the sea stench just flow in; as he sleeps at night, feet away from the leaky window, he dreams of drowning in sand, almost every night, drowning in black sand and bits of trash and oily sea gull feathers. He coughs up gray, gritty goo in the mornings. He ignores the pain as he transfers himself from the bed into his wheelchair; he thinks about drowning, drowning in sand, drowning in trash, drowning in pain, distracting himself for a moment from the pain if only just briefly.

Now the moment is over, and the pain returns.

He wheels himself to the door, awkwardly maneuvering through the door frame, and Dr. de Gouge is standing in the hallway, with that faded black bag in his left hand, and his right hand on the front door handle.

"Doctor?"

"Ah. Ah. Hello."

"Are you here to get them out of here?"

"Oh, no, Map, but I promise it will be today … for Ehab, at least. I hope."

"…"

"But, no later than tomorrow, by evening, perhaps late evening I'm sure."

"Are you here to see Tonya?"

"Ah, er, no. No."

"…"

"I'm just here to identify the victim, I mean, to make sure it is Mr. Ehab."

"Well, okay. Good to see you, I guess, doctor."

"Oh, er, right."

"Sir…"

"Yes?"

"Don't forget about them."

"Uh?"

"In the living room."

"Oh, right, right. Alright, then. Goodbye."

The door closes and Map sits in his chair for a few moments. Then he wheels himself down the hall towards the kitchen, past empty rooms, past Tonya's door. He rolls himself into the kitchen, and sits there, looking at the countertops.

He's lost his appetite recently, except for an insatiable craving for sugar. But there is none left. He's eaten it all. He sits staring at the empty countertops and picking sand out of his hair. The dog starts to whine and whimper.

"Pist?"

Whimper.

"The door is this way, don't make me wheel in there and get you."

Whimper, then the clicking of three paw's worth of toenails on the floor.

Map turns his chair around and starts wheeling down the hall. He opens the front door before the dog is there, and waits for the pink fossil to shuffle down the hallway.

The dog is unbloated now, as how Tonya would describe it if she weren't in her bed, hiding from the weak sunlight deep under her covers.

The dog stands next to Map, and looks up at him, confused.

"Go on, Pist. You're going out by yourself today."

Whimper.

"For real."

The dog finally turns and walks out slowly and stands there, like a fur covered statue; Map closes the door.

He wheels himself back down the gritty hallway, and turns the corner into the living room and he sees that Ehab is still there, dead and nude, on the floor. But, instead of being face-down, as he was, he is face-up, with his dead mouth slightly open, his doornail eyes open and staring at the ceiling, collecting sand.

Map sees that the doctor has turned the dead man over from being on his stomach to on his back, but neglected to cover him up. Map peers at the dead man who he only met hours ago. Map peels off his long sleeve shirt and wheels closer to cover Ehab, although he's not sure if the shirt can cover both the dead man's face and genitals, and he can't decide which is more appropriate to cover up.

As he gets closer to the pale, scarred corpse, Map sees that numerals have been written on the man's chin. He looks closer, and it doesn't look like a pen or a marker; the number has been tattooed onto Ehab's rubbery doornail dead chin.

Map stares and he forgets to cover the corpse. He's gotten used to it by now somehow, the burnt sac, dead eyes.

Map wheels himself over to the giant tub that still holds the sloshy remains of Ms. Nevershe; he gets close and he gags. It's time for her to go. It is past time for her to go.

Her head and face are uncovered now. He sees her chin is tattooed also. He wheels himself away from the large body; he's thinking about opening the sliding door to let the nasty breeze into the room, which, soot and all, is sure to smell better than these two doornail bodies.

"Map?"

He hears her muffled voice coming from Tonya's side of the wall; she must be looking out through her peep hole.

"The sun's up, Tonya; what are you doing up?"

"You need to cover him."

"I know."

"It's creepy to look out through my wall-hole and see him looking up, dead and all, and besides, I see his thingie when I look at the med-t.v."

"Which part should I cover?"

" ... "

"His face or his, uh, you know ... I only have this one shirt, unless you can bring me something else."

"Maybe they'll be gone by dark."

"No one seems too concerned."

"Who were you talking to?"

"Huh?"

"A little while ago?"

"Oh; de Gouge was here."

" ... "

"He tattooed them. On their faces."

"He tattooed their faces?"

"Yes, that what it looks like. He tattooed their faces."

"With what? I mean, their names?"

"No. Numbers."

"Is it their social security numbers?"

"Hmm, let me take a closer look." Map wheels closer towards Ehab and bends over in his chair, "No, no, too many numbers. And there's a letter or two in this one. D427B8764635. Unless that's two eights in a row."

"That's weird."

"Yeah."

"Have you ever seen anything like this before?"

"No; you?"

"No."

"…"

"Did he say when they'd be gone? The bodies?"

"Well, not really."

"Nice."

"Yeah."

"…"

"Well, so what should I do?"

"Cover some of him; I'm staying in here."

"Well, I don't just want to sit by myself … I'm going back to bed."

"That's the spirit. I'll see you at dark."

"Alright."

He wheels himself away from the rank-smelling living room, through the kitchen, past the empty rooms that once housed Ms. Nevershe and Ehab, and he pauses at Tonya's closed, quiet door, and then he slowly wheels himself into his room. He wheels himself over to the gritty, smeared window and looks out at the sand dunes and the blowing oats.

The oats are getting smaller every day. The razor bits of glass and metal in the rocky sand hit it and beat it down, beat it down every day, just like it does to the dune that the undernourished roots are holding onto, just as it's done to the unit that Map and Tonya are in, just like it's done to the spirits of Map, and of Tonya, to their hope, to their dreams.

He struggles, sweats, cusses, spits, yet he gets himself (through the burning spasms) back into the gritty bed. He closes his eyes, trying to imagine the living room corpse-free. He has to decide whether to try to throw up in the trashcan next to the bed, or to fight the feeling, fight the constant sickness, fight it back down the hole. So he does. He ignores the sickness and tries to concentrate on the pain in his legs, his thighs, his hips feel shattered. His toes feel broken, smashed. He's gotten used to it by now.

The wind blows; the trashline grows and acts as a black-out curtain over the dying reef; the corpses in the living room slowly decompose; the unclaimed corpses of the homeless in the medical region rot on the beach and are eaten by the hordes of flea-bitten sea gulls. Ships burn all day and night, stuck in some sort of stagnant current, or perhaps stuck on some sand bar, or maybe on another trashed reef; no one cares anymore; the smoke goes up like intergalactic distress signals. S.O.S. S.O.S.

The trashline floats, and begins to get its own gravity, pulling to it shark heads, turtle shells, shoes, toys, dolls, trash, and dropped heirlooms.

And in his bed, Map closes his eyes and lets his mind go to wherever the pills take him, away from here, away from the pain, away from where he's just a number, to where the wind is no longer just trash and putrid smells. And outside the waves get bigger, the wind blows harder, the trashline swells, the gulls peck out each other's eyes, and on the front steps to the unit, a pink poodle whimpers in the increasing north eastern winds, shivering on her three legs, and alternates between swelling up, and shrinking down, swelling up, and shrinking down, swelling up, and shrinking down.

The nasty wind continues to howl; the crazed gulls continue their rhypophagy. The dying keep dying; the healthy begin to die cell by cell; the dead begin to be forgotten, rotten. Craps of fate; they've gotten used to it by now. Can there be a winner in the rot race? Now it is his fate, but soon it will be me.

CHAPTER SEVEN

the Sooty, Flocking Gullers

This is her at his door: knock, knock.

"Hey."

"Hmm?"

"Map?"

"Huh?"

"Map? Wake up."

"Oh, Tonya, hey. What time is it?"

"Dark; time to get up."

"..."

"..."

Map: "What's going on?"

"Why is only one of them gone?"

"What?"

"Why is only one of them gone?"

"Who?"

"Ehab's gone. Ms. Nevershe is still in her tub. And it stinks like a cult a week after the cyanide party."

"I don't know..."

"Did you hear anything last night?"

"When? You mean today? No. Nothing. I was out cold."

"Me, too."

Map: "I guess the two nurses were sent by. You've seen them. It's probably all that they could manage just to get a dead Ehab out of here; there's no way that they could move the dead weight of Ms. Nevershe."

"…"

"So, what's up? What now?"

Tonya: "Well, I don't want to go out there into the living room; it'll make me sick."

"Yeah."

"I guess I could sit in here with you."

"Sure."

"…"

"I could even turn on the lights maybe. Are you hungry?"

"No. Are you?"

"Oh, no, I haven't had an appetite recently."

"Well, we could go walk Pist; I could push you this time, you could carry her in your lap, in the chair."

"Yeah, sure."

"Okay, you work on getting up and ready and I'll get Pist. Do you need any help getting into your chair?"

"I think I'll be okay."

"Alright; I'll be right back."

"Okay."

"Uh, Map?"

"Yeah, I'm getting ready."

"Uh, have you seen the dog?"

"Have I seen the dog? Oh, no. Oh, craps of fate…"

Map and Tonya are outside now, on the cracked, sandy sidewalk, bits of plastic wrappers and shreds of aluminum foil sparkle in the hazy moonlight. She's pushing him; he's holding her tennis racket. They alternate calling the dog's name.

"Pistachio, come here sweetie!"

"Come on, bitch, come here, I'm tired of the smell out here."

"Come on sweet girl, I have a treat for you, c'mon, Pistachio."

"Pist, come here!"

"Does it even matter?"

Her: "Well, I guess she's my dog now."

Him: "..."

"Unless you want her."

"..."

"I didn't think so."

"Alright, let's keep looking. It's just, where in the furious flock could she be? I mean, she is the oldest dog I have ever seen, it's not like she goes off and plays."

"I'm not sure. She could be anywhere, I guess."

"Okay. Let's keep looking."

"Thanks."

Map: "You know, the weird thing, and I'm getting used to being up at night with you and all, but the weird thing is just never seeing many other people, you know?"

"Yeah, well, I don't miss it as much as you do; I rather like not seeing a lot of people."

"And it's weird seeing so many houses with their carports all empty all of the time. A little creepy, you know?"

"Yeah. But people are there. In those houses, those units."

"Right."

"People like you. People who don't drive, who can't drive."

"..."

"Or just won't drive, like me."

"..."

Tonya: "People that are hurting like you; or like me, not feeling a thing at all."

"C'mon, Pist! Get out here. Come on!"

"It's okay to talk about it."

"What?"

"This. Being here."

"..."

"Feeling like this, like I know you do, all the time. Blurry. Hazy. Foggy. Down, all time down."

"..."

"..."

Map: "Yeah. I hate it."

"I know. I know that you do."

"..."

"I do, too."

"Yeah, yeah."

"..."

"So, how do you sleep at night?"

"Or during the day, eh? I guess you're asking if I sleep okay."

"Right."

Tonya: "I sleep for a few hours here and there, then wake up for a while, and eventually sleep a few hours more. How about you?"

"Once I get to sleep I'm alright, I guess, it's just right at first I just lie there and listen to the wind and the waves, or the occasional siren outside, always those flocking insane gulls … And, when I get into bed from the chair, this sandy one, it's a little bit of a workout. I feel like hell afterwards. But once I get past that, I sleep a little better. I just wish I could sleep without pills, I feel like I can't…"

"Yeah, yeah, I know. Well, I guess the dog isn't going to come to us if we don't call it."

"Come here, Pist!"

"Sweetie, Pistachio, come on over here, I have something for you!"

They are slowly making their way down the cracked sidewalk, littered with gull feces, pill bottle tops, prescription papers floating in the breeze. To their left, the east as they walk south, is a row of houses being used as convalescent units, and to the east of the units, the diminished sand dune (here mostly old car tires and both old Christmas trees, all brown, and also artificial trees, greener, but bleached by the sun and scraped by the sand.) The ocean, that sick sea, is just beyond the dying dune line.

The beach, the sandy once pristine shoreline, is now dark and empty. On almost every block there is a clearing in the houses from where a wave has come up and broken down a unit and pulled it out to sea, and all to no fanfare, hardly any witnesses, no commotion, and no emotion. Often at night it goes unnoticed; in the day it doesn't even get news coverage anymore, it's become old hat.

As they slowly pass by, on foot and in chair respectively, they turn their heads left towards those empty lots. Their heads tell them they should see a house there, they hope to at least to see a deformed hot-pink poodle, but there is often just a driveway, sometimes maybe a pole from an old basketball hoop, and then there is the mighty ocean, spewing forth a trashy roar.

On the roofs of the oceanfront units, flocks of sea gulls perch and are as still as statues even in the powerful beach wind, like feathered gargoyles. The birds stare at Map and Tonya as they slowly progress down the uneven sidewalk, occasionally calling out for the Persian-pink bitch. Map is nearly oblivious to the gulls; Tonya can't push Map's chair straight for looking at the brooding birds. Brooding birds by the burial beach.

"Hey, watch it."

"Sorry; I'm going to pee myself with all those nasty things up there staring at me. They creep me out, they really do."

"Pist!"

Tonya: "I wonder where she went?"

"..."

"You don't care, do you?"

"I'm just not a dog guy."

"Ah."

"And I'm not a cat guy either."

"..."

"Or a bird guy." He motions towards the gulls. "Filthy, feathered freaks..."

"Well, thanks for helping me look for her, even more so."

He looks up, to his left, towards one of the stilted residential units. A curtain in one window is peeled back; eyes are peering back, eyes from a pale face, eyes from a bald head, thick glasses, sunken eyes. Lonely, hopeless, sickly.

"Wait a second."

She stops pushing his chair; rubs her arms, stretches, looks across the street for the pink poodle. She sees no dogs, and she looks down the street towards a store.

Map, however, peers up into the window. The face stares back at him. In the night, with the poor light and all of the grime on the unit windows, he can't see much. Are the eyes watching them?, or are they staring, medicated and blurry, out into the night's darkness, not focusing on anything?

As Tonya is looking the other way, and as Map continues to peer up towards the dirty window, the face withdraws from the window, the curtain falls back into place, and moments later the room light turns off.

"What's up, Map? What's wrong?"

"Oh, nothing. We can go on."

"We should go ask Thom. Ask if he's seen her."

"Who's Thom?"

"Thom. From the store."

"No, sorry; I'm not sure what, or who, you are referring to."

"There's a store up here. Across the street."

"..."

"In about two blocks."

"What makes you think the place will be open now?"

"Well, how do you think I'd know Thom if the place wasn't open when I was up and about?"

"..."

"Duh."

"Yeah, duh. Okay, fine. Let's go to Thom's store."

"Cool. Maybe Pistachio hobbled down there for a treat or something."

"Yeah, maybe."

They stroll in silence for a minute, three minutes; she strolls actually, while he sits in his chair. Most of the windows in the units to their left are dark; some are boarded up with hurricane shutters.

He says: "I remember a time when there was no way these units would be shuttered this time of year unless there was an actual hurricane coming. They were always rented; rented for a lot of money, too, from March through October."

She says: "Yeah, and on this block, these three houses in a row have been boarded up since mid-summer."

He: "Why?"

She: "Really?'

"Yeah."

"I heard from Thom that these convalescent units were shuttered early as a rouse, pretending it was for the upcoming hurricane season."

"It wasn't?"

"No. Not at all."

"Well? What was it?"

"Now, I can't prove it, like don't ask to see a signed death certificate, because I just can't provide it…"

"Of course."

"But, from what I hear, it was pox."

"A pox, huh? Hmm."

"Yeah."

"No. What? Are you sure?"

"Yeah. A beach pox."

"I never heard about that; you'd think it would have been on the news, on the internet or somewhere. You've got to be messing with me. Are you?"

"I'm not."

"Craps of fate..."

"Yes, indeed ... I heard it was one case, just one, in the center unit. One guy died. A kid, sixteen or so. And then, of course, the rest of the people in the unit were, uh, relocated."

"Relocated?"

"Relocated, and never seen again."

"What about the other two units?"

"Oh, just as a precaution."

"What? What, just as a precaution?"

"They were also all, uh, relocated. Everyone in the units to each side of that one."

"Never to be seen again?"

"Yep. Never to be seen again; it looks like their end."

"Hmm."

"But don't ask Doctor de Gouge where they might be."

"Why?"

"He'll just tell you the state-issued line, which is the state-issued lie."

"What's that?"

"That they're all just convalescing by the sea: happily and healthily, of course."

"Weren't they all convalescing by the sea already? Here?"

"Sure. They're just doing it somewhere else. The houses had to be boarded for the hurricane season; or torn down because better units are going to be built."

"With what funds?"

"Exactly. There's nothing. No funds for something like that. You know it and I know it, but most people don't know, don't care, and don't care to know."

"But were there any hurricanes in the forecast prediction then? Even since then?"

"Nope. That doesn't appear to matter. Willful ignorance."

"..."

"Hey..."

"What?"

"What's going on there? At Thom's place?"

"I don't know."

"Let's go ahead and cross the street. Hold on, I'm going to bump you down over the curb."

"Ahh! Ow."

"Sorry."

"It's okay."

"Thom! Thom?"

She covers the distance of the next block faster than any other. They approach a small convenience store. A neon-orange Open sign flickers in the grimy window.

Peering against the glass into the store is a large figure that Map mistakes for Dr. de Gouge in the dark light until Tonya's "Thom!" gets the man's attention and he turns his substantially sizable frame towards them.

"Ah, Tonya, Tonya, Tonya. What a pleasant surprise. What's up, dear?"

"Thom, what's going on? Did you lock yourself out of the store?"

Thom looks Tonya in the eyes, smiles a toothy but brown smile from behind a bushy beard, and says, "No, no, ha, I have my keys right here." He pats his left pants pocket, which jingles.

"Well, what's going on then?"

"Well, an hour ago or so, the doctor, you know, de Gouge," Map and Tonya nod, "Well, the doc came by, a bit delirious if you ask me, and he came in and bought a bottle of water and as he was leaving he just stood in the front door, holding it open while drinking his water and he kept on talking about this and that and then a lone gull landed just outside, with feathers dropping out," he points to the sidewalk below them, they see a handful of feathers, "and it just stands there. Well, ha, de Gouge is fascinated all of a sudden, and he just stares at the bird, all stoned like, holding the door open as I'm behind the register. And, then the bird takes one step, and I blink my eyes and look away at something real quickly, a flash of something on the computer screen, and next thing I know, ha, the gull is inside the store."

"Oh. Gross."

"Yeah, but then as the doctor is holding the door open, so I can chase it back out," he points to a broom leaning against the building, "the bird takes flight and flies to the back of the store. I, of course, chase the sucker; I want it out before it poops on food or something. And, when I turn around, the doctor is still holding the door open, that frigging moron, and three more of those feathered freaks fly in, and then before he closes the door, four more swoop in, and then a couple more, and I decide that it's more than I can handle, so I run out here, followed by that twat-leak of a doctor, and I closed the door. I'm not going to try to get a whole furious flock out of the store; I don't want to get sick. I think that those feathered rats carry the beach pox."

Her: "Right. Maybe. Maybe, Thom."

"So, I did what they always tell us to do. I called the Animal Control. And I've been waiting out here since."

Map asks: "How long has that been?"

Thom spits on the sidewalk, and he rubs sand out of his thick beard, "Well, let's say, in this breeze out here with this grit in the air and all, let's just say that I feel like I'm drowning in sand here, like the whole trashed beach is getting in my beard … in my nose … in my mouth. Just drowning, you know."

Map: "I hear you, man."

"Oh, Thom, this is Map; Map, Thom."

Thom extends his right hand towards Map in his chair, "Schrittweischern."

"Uh, say again?"

"I know, it's a hard one, ha, Thomasson Schrittweischern. Ha. Call me Thom." He smiles.

"Thom. Nice to meet you."

Thom looks down, "You hurting?"

Tonya answers for Map: "I make sure he takes his pills. Plenty, too."

Map agrees: "I don't think I've missed any recently."

Thom: "Well, as I always say, more is better than less, especially in matters such as this."

Tonya: "So, where's the doctor now?"

Thom: "Oh, as I said, the doc was acting all weird, wired but stoned-like at the same time, and delirious. He just took off, dropped his water bottle and turned the corner." He points to a plastic bottle being blown against the building by the wind.

Tonya cups her hands and peers in, "How many did you say?"

"Ten, maybe eleven. Twelve tops, hopefully."

Tonya continues to peer into the grimy window and a battleship-gray gull swoops towards the window, defecating in midflight, and the infected crud lands on the window where her eyes are. "Ahh! Oh, I think I'm going to pee myself," she feels her remaining teeth with her sandy fingers, "I think another tooth just got loose. Flock those feathered freaks..."

She looks back to the glass door; the bird droppings are a combination of ghostly grays and radical reds, pretty pink in places. She asks, "Why isn't the bird poop white?"

Thom, without looking closer, answers, "Blood. Gull blood. They eat too many other gulls, too often. They're sick suckers, I tell you. Sick, sick, sick, ha."

"Gross. I don't feel so well all of a sudden." She places her hands onto her stomach; she gags. She spits.

"See what I mean, I hated to do it, I hate to call the authorities, as I hate them, ha, but I had to call them. Had to call the animal control..."

Tonya interrupts and looks down to Map, in his wheelchair, to explain, "The animal control here is just a couple of angry cops in an old mainland vehicle or whatev. Usually drunk asswipe cops, to boot."

Map nods.

"I couldn't try to go in there and take care of it myself; you know what I mean, Tonya?"

She looks down to Map and explains: "Bad ticker." She nods towards Thom's barrel-like chest.

Map nods. "Ah."

"It's gone out on me once already, twice actually, but once was almost the last time."

Tonya adds, "It was the end of him for a minute there."

"More than a minute actually, ha, yeah."

"Yeah, it was, wasn't it?"

Electric crimson and violent blue lights cut through the dirt particles in the night sky; the murderous cries of the ferocious flock inside the store is drowned out by the scream of sirens. A police truck pulls up to the curb. The truck pulls in facing the wrong direction and idles there with the windows up and the engine on for a few minutes as the driver taps into a laptop; Map notices a second person in the passenger side, seemingly sleeping through the shrieking siren.

Map notes, "You think they'd turn off those sirens. It's past midnight and they know where they are; there are ill and recovering people trying to rest."

Thom explains, "That's the point, Map. They know, they just don't care, no. That's why the sirens are on now, in the middle of the night. Blaring, ha. They know exactly where they are and they don't care, no. To them, it's just a barrier island full of sick patients, a burial island of dying people. Sickies and deadies, sickies and deadies. Or rather: deadies and soon-to-be-deadies, to them at least. They hope we all get washed away soon so they don't have to deal with us anymore. I'd say so they don't have to worry about us anymore, but they don't worry about us now, na, ha."

Tonya adds, "Those gull-bite-fever bullies."

With the engine still on, the truck's door opens and an officer slides out, scratches his crotch, feels instinctively to make sure his hand cuffs are with him, and spits on the ground, not once making eye contact with Map, Tonya, or Thom.

Thom is the first to speak: "Thanks for coming, sir. Those nasty things got all in, and I'd have had another heart attack for sure if I stayed in there any longer."

The officer stares into the glass doors: gulls glide inside. One flies against the door, breaks its neck, and falls to the floor, dead. Within a minute, a handful of gulls have descended on the corpse to pluck its eyes out and eat them, fighting with each other the whole time.

Another gull, walking on the store floor, stares up through the glass doors towards the people watching him. The gull opens its mouth, looking angry, and is about to shriek, when instead, it drops over on its side, twitches, and then stops moving. A handful of gulls swoop down on the bird's body; the corpse-pecking begins.

"That is nasty," Tonya says to no one. "Nasty." She turns away, gags, and covers her mouth with her left hand.

The officer stares into the store. He reaches into his pocket and pulls out a stick of gum, unwraps it, dropping the wrapper on the sidewalk below to be blown away by the putrid wind, then sticks the gum in his mouth, and begins to chomp away, noisily, as he watches the dirty gulls cannibalize their fallen feathered brethren.

Without turning from the window, the officer says, loud enough to be heard over the wind: "You people need to learn to respect wildlife."

Thom nods, "Yes, sir, sir, we were, it's just…"

"No. You people need to learn to keep away. Wildlife. That's why it's called wildlife. Wild. Life."

They nod.

"There's a fine for this. It's a steep fine, too, a hefty one for each of you involved."

Thom starts again, "Sir, no, sir. I don't think you understand…"

"Understand what? Are you the one that called us to come here?"

"Yes, sir."

"Did you hurt those animals? Did you hurt any of them? Because it sure as hell doesn't look like they hurt any of ya'll."

"Well, no, sir, they …"

"Because did you know there's a fine for that, too? A fat fine indeed. You're racking up a lot of fees here, sickie."

"Well, officer, it's just…"

Tonya interrupts, "Hey, you don't understand. Listen, will you? Thom didn't hurt any of them. He didn't put them in there. No."

"Then who did? Was it you?"

"No, it wasn't me. I don't work here; I wasn't even here."

"I didn't ask if you work here, or live here, or sleep with this sickie here; I'm just asking if you were involved in putting these poor birds in here, or harming any of them at all." He points through the front windows. "I'm sure that those two weren't dead when they flew in there."

"What? No. I wasn't even here."

"How am I to know that?"

"Well, I've been pushing my unit-mate down the sidewalk, ask him."

"I'm not asking him; I'm asking you."

"What?"

"How did all these birds get in there? Trapping wildlife is a crime, sickies. A serious one."

Thom: "They just flew in. One got in first, and the rest followed."

Officer: "I've never heard of that happening down here."

Thom: "Well, it happened."

Officer: "Doubtful."

Thom: "…"

Map clears his throat, looks up towards the officer, "I just don't get it … they're just nasty gulls. They're sick."

"They're sick because of us, because of people. People like you. Sickies."

Map: "Maybe so or maybe not, but they're not in this store because of us. I mean," he motions to his legs, to Thom who's holding his chest and breathing heavily, and then to Tonya, as she wiggles one of her teeth looser and looser, "we're patients down here, convalescing by the sea."

The officer grunts. "I can't be sure of anything."

Thom: "I called you here because I needed help. I still do."

Officer: "..."

Thom: "I thought it was the right thing to do, the thing we are supposed to do if this ever happened."

Officer: "Did you? Is that what you thought?" He spits again.

Thom: "So no one gets sick or something. Sicker."

Officer: "I'm just so sick of people messing with the wildlife down here."

Tonya, smiling to hide her erupting anger, points down to the ground, says, "See. See. See those feathers? Thom said that flocker was dropping feathers before it even went into the store. See?"

Thom: "Right, officer. Doctor de Gouge was down here, talking and gabbing, ha, and he held the door open and one got in and then the others followed in after it."

Tonya: "Call the doctor. Call de Gouge."

"I'm not going to call any doctor; it's the middle of the night." Without looking at the truck or changing where his eyes are focused, the officer raises his right hand and makes a brief, swift movement in the salty night air. A moment later the second officer is lurking in the shadows behind them, silently.

"Well, officer, what can you do about those birds, those nasty things in my shop?"

"That's a secondary concern right now; at least now, in there, those birds are safe and out of harm's way."

"Harm's way?"

"Right, away from you people. I'm convinced you hurt those birds … I think you were trying to trap them. Then poison them. Try to fix this fictitious 'beach pox' you sickies are always bitching about. We are tired of people trying to take care of things themselves down here."

"But I called you here. Why in the world would I trap a furious flock, illegally as you say, and then call you here? Call the cops here, to the scene of a crime, of a crime I committed, ha, huh?"

"I don't know why people do the things they do. Maybe something is off in your sickie brain. I don't know what's wrong with you, pal. You could have the pox or you could be a pervert. Both, maybe."

Tonya is irritated, fidgets with a tooth, licks her dry lips, and says, "Thom didn't do anything. We didn't do anything. No one did. Map and

I just got here. Thom runs this place, why would anyone want to put these diseased flockers into their own store? Gross, nasty."

"For the insurance money."

"Insurance money, what? No way. Thom didn't do this, it was an accident."

"Officer, I have a security camera behind the counter." He is pointing at the door. "You can see for yourself; the things just came on in when Dr. de Gouge held the door open."

"Sure," the officer says, emotionlessly, "Go on in and get this security video for me, would you, huh?"

"..."

"We'll wait."

"Well, I can't go back in there, that's why I called you here, ha."

Tonya bends over and picks up a feather. "Gross. Just look, look. On the ground. One of those birds was sick before it even went into Thom's place. See? See?" She holds the feather in the air with one hand and points to other feathers on the sidewalk with her other hand. "One of them was dropping feathers before it went in. It's sick. They're all sick. Do you even live out here? See these nasty things? Smell it, smell this feather, it is oil and bacteria and germs and crud ..."

She shoves the feather towards the officer's face.

"Get that thing away from me now, sickie!"

"Smell it! They're all sick, rotting, and nasty!" She pushes the feather closer and it rubs against the officer's nose.

"Hey!" He smacks her hand and the feather away from him.

Brisk footsteps come from behind her as the partner rushes up and grabs Tonya's frail, pale wrists and cuffs them together, roughly.

"Hey! What's going on? What do you think I am, some kind of bird whisperer, huh? I'm scared of them, yeah I am. There's no animal abuse or gull sodomy or anything at all going on here!"

"Quiet, now," says the first officer, who has extracted some kind of anti-bacterial gel from his breast pocket and is rubbing his hands together and rubbing it on his face. "I can't believe you touched me with that sick thing."

The second officer, the one who cuffed her, says, "Assault and battery. That's what this is. Assault on a peace officer."

Map: "Oh, come on? This is a little uncalled for..."

"Hush, sickie."

Thom: "Officer, officers, sirs, I think we've lost track of what's going on here. What about my store? The infected, flying rodents in there? Tonya meant nothing. Tell him, Tonya."

"No."

"Tonya."

"No. He was blaming us, almost all of us, wrongly."

"Tonya, you're in no position to make a point now."

"No."

First officer: "Say, uh, what are the two of you doing out here, anyway?"

"We're looking for a dog. A poodle. My poodle, kinda sorta, whatev."

"A pet poodle?"

"Yeah, a pink one, have you seen it?"

"You have a dog down here?"

"Well, yes. I mean, I recently kind of inherited it."

"Do you have a license for it?"

"A license?"

"Yeah, do you have a dog license for it?"

"No, but, uh, I'll get one."

"I can't believe that they let you people have an animal down here."

"You people?"

"Yeah. You know what I mean. Sickies."

"..."

"Let me see some identification. You got any on you, sickie?"

"Well, my hands are cuffed."

"Just tell me where."

"Let him get it." She's referring to Thom; the officer nods. "Back pocket."

Thom pulls out a medical identification card with her photo, name, unit address, and other data and hands it to the officer. He stares at it and holds it up next to Tonya, comparing the photo to the woman handcuffed in front of him.

"Is this you?"

"Yes."

"You look different."

"Well, it's my teeth."

"What? What about them?"

"I don't have as many as I used to. And I've lost weight from the meds."

"Hmm. Okay." He hands the card back to Thom, looks behind Tonya to the other officer, "Write her up for assault and battery then put her in the back."

Map: "Wait, officer. Sir?"

Thom: "What about my store, sir? What about the gulls in there … this is, uh, well, someone could get sick, or something. Don't you think?"

Officer: "Frankly," looking into the store, "I don't give a flying flock about your sickie store."

" … "

"Alright, let's get her out of here."

Map: "Tonya, hold on, sit tight; we'll straighten this mess out."

Tonya: "Ahh, come on, you catamites!"

" … "

The doors slam; the truck peels off down the darkened, sand-covered asphalt.

Thom and Map watch the police truck speed off into the dirty-misty night.

"Well," Thom finally says, "I'm not going back in there tonight."

"Good decision."

"Here, I'll push you back to your unit."

"That would be great. Now tell me about this pox, this beach pox?"

"Ah. You heard me mention the pox, I see, ha."

Thom, with his considerable frame behind the chair, begins pushing Map north on the sidewalk, towards his unit. The waves get higher and higher up on the thinning beach, bringing in some discarded plastic toys with one lurch, and then taking dozens of mismatched flip flops from summers-gone back out into the sea to be part of the trashline; the fish die, the diseased gulls fight, entire pods of whales beach themselves to die in the polluted air away from the trashline and the ocean of oil.

All around them, the wind howls and spits and throws millions of tiny particles of dirt, sand, and dead skin into Thom's beard. Thom coughs, spits up sand and dirt and skin particles, his tongue is dry, and he says to Map, "I'm drowning in sand out here, Map; I'm drowning in sand." Drown, baby, drown; drown in the rot race, the rot riot. Drown, sickie, drown.

He's gotten used to it by now.

CHAPTER EIGHT

the Helpless and the Hapless

This is now, a few sandy meters from the rising tide:

"Well, there's nothing we can do for Tonya right now, not tonight, at least. They'll take her over the bridge to the mainland station. I don't have a car. Do you?"

"No. No car. In fact, I haven't driven in months, maybe a year even…"

"And I think it is Friday night, Saturday morning whatnot, ha, do you know for sure? Friday or not?"

"Do I know the day? No."

"It's been all the same to me, since I got here. I've been able to run the store, but with no one else to help me out at all. I just work every day; it doesn't matter the day of the week. But, I'm fairly sure it was Friday when I got here; Saturday morning now, of course."

"…"

"So, they've arrested her and she won't go before a judge until Monday morning at the earliest."

"…"

"At least she'll have a cell all to herself, probably; they try to keep us sickies separated from the healthy herd. The cops who get assigned to this area hate it, you know?"

"Hmm, no, why?"

"Because down here all the calls are all for deaths, or for contagious people; but over there, all the calls are for drunk driving or for a d.v."?

"D.V.? Sounds contagious."

"No, no. Plate-smashers! Bong-breakers! Phone-throwers! Only in some parts of the country is domestic violence contagious."

Smiles appear on both men's faces.

Thom pushes Map in silence; after a few minutes, a group of gulls lands and lingers like gangbangers on the sidewalk ahead of them.

"Crud, ha."

"Nasty."

"I'm going to push us to the other side of the street; hold on." Thom looks both ways before crossing the street and then laughs to himself, "I don't even know why I look both ways, especially this time of night."

"..."

"Besides medical staff, ambulances, and that one trash disposal truck, run by a guy named Linc, there's nothing else driving around down here. Nice guy, Linc, ha, he always has a lady-friend along for the ride. And not the same one every week, see? Oh, to be younger... No, no one else is driving down here but cops, and then only occasionally. They're not driving here tonight; the one patrol that covers the sick beach beat is taking Tonya to jail."

Map: "Those mother-gullflockers."

"I remember when these roads were crowded, day and night."

"I remember when a pile of dog droppings smelled worse than the ocean breeze."

"Ha, yes, yes."

Thom stops pushing Map's chair. They are in front of the unit that Map saw a pair of eyes watching him earlier.

Thom: "That's the doctor's car, isn't it? De Gouge's?"

Map looks over, nods his head, "It is." The car shifts side to side on stressed shocks. "There's someone inside. Must be him."

"Hold still." Thom lets go of the wheelchair, rubs his sore hands, and starts walking towards the car in the driveway.

"I'll just sit here, no worries."

"Ha!"

As Thom walks up the sandy driveway the driver's door opens and the oafish doctor begins to get his massiveness out of the car; he hasn't noticed Thom or Map.

"Doctor!"

"Ah!" The doctor falls back into the car, shocked. The car rocks side to side.

"Ah, er, Bob, from the store, eh, right?"

"Well, actually Thom, ha: Thom from the store, yes."

"Yes, eh, I wasn't expecting you here at this time of night; it's the middle of the night, don't you know?"

"Oh, I know the time, doc, I was just leaving the store full of gulls; it'll probably be shut down now, for contamination. At least for a while."

"Well, craps of fate."

"Fate has nothing to do with it, more like craps of gulls, ha. You held the door open and let those flockers in, doctor."

"Well, er, okay then, indeed. But, good to see you, Thomas."

"Just Thom." Thom frowns.

"Eh, right, Thom. Good to see you, Thom, but I must go on and get inside the unit and see about something, someone rather."

Map says: "Dr. de Gouge! Doctor, what about the last body?"

The doctor turns his neck towards Map, and asks, "Who's that? Matt?"

"Map. Not Matt, still Map. What about her body?"

"Er, which body is that, Map?"

"Ms. Nevershe. The one still in my unit. The big one in the tub." The doctor is silent; so Map continues: "You know, sir, you've seen her. Ms. Nevershe."

The doctor rubs his dreadlocked beard, sand falls to his shoes: "Oh, yes, yes: is she still there?"

"That's why I'm asking about her being taken out, doctor."

"I'll make that a top priority … tomorrow morning, by lunch, or dinner at least."

"Good. Because it is stinking bad in there, like a pod of whales is rotting in there."

"The big one?"

"Yes: Ms. Nevershe."

"Oh, yes, er, the whale. Right, right. I'll make a mental note of that, eh, yes…"

"And Tonya's been arrested. Wrongly, I believe. I thought you should know…"

"Okay then, great to see you gentlemen, and I hope you both feel better and enjoy your time in your units down here, convalescing by the sea."

Thom and Map are silent and stare at the shaggy doctor.

De Gouge continues: "You know, plenty of people would like to live here, in these exact units."

Map: "Who?"

Doctor: "Eh… er."

Thom: "Doc, just because we're sick doesn't mean that we're stupid."

The doctor ignores Thom, reaches into his car for his bag, and then turns and walks up the wooden stairs of the unit.

Map speaks up: "Oh, and doctor?"

"Yes?"

"Have you seen that dog from my unit, the pink one? The three-legged pinked-up bitch?"

"Ah, yes, Pistachio."

Thom and Map exchange glances in the smoggy night; Thom says, under his breath, "Flock it, he forgets everyone's names but some mangy dog's…"

Map continues: "Right, Pistachio. Pist. The bitch. She's sick, and old, and she's disappeared. Gone. Ka-pooey. Bye-bye-doggy."

Dr. de Gouge says, "Well, good luck to you, I hope you find her. She could be important for research, expanding and contracting her mass so much as she has been doing lately. Very important. Best of luck, and let me know."

Then the doctor turns and slowly walks up the wooden stairs before he unlocks the door and steps inside, quickly closing the door after him.

Thom: "What a gull."

Thom walks back over to Map, and instead of wheeling the chair away, they both stare at the unit the doctor entered.

"It's like he never remembers any of us."

"Oh, he should remember me."

"From the store?"

"No. Well, yeah, but not only. Not only from the store, no, ha."

"…"

"Long story. Ready?"

"For the long story?"

"No; to head on."

"Sure, whatever."

"Let's go." He pushes Map, and he huffs and puffs and sweats in the nasty night's polluted breeze, and between hacking fits he states, "He's a hellrake, a fop, ha."

"Sorry?"

"A fribble, you know?"

"No, who?"

"That flockin' doctor! De Gouge, that dink."

"Ah."

"A medical slut. A short-thinking selfist, in fact."

"Hmm."

"Ah, what the hell, but we need him, don't we? Hmm. Bit of a predicament, I'd say, huh?"

"Maybe."

"He's one of the last ones that'll take the measly monthly pay to haul his fat butt over here, to where we sickies all live."

"Ah, yes, I guess since you put it that way, yes."

"I need to stop again, sorry; the crud in the air goes right to my bad valves."

"Take your time; I'm in no hurry."

"Hmm, me either."

"Why don't you sit down and catch your breath."

"Then I might not be able to get back up, and I don't think you'll be able to help me."

"No, no I won't."

"Are you contagious?"

"No. No, just a burden on the system I guess; I can't walk, so I can't work. Or, rather, I can hardly walk, so I can hardly work."

"Yeah, I can work, you see, but they're, or he rather, is expecting me to keel over and die any second now."

"…"

"But I won't give them the satisfaction, ha. No. No, screw 'em."

"Amen."

"You know, but of course you don't, that when I first got down here, three years ago maybe, that cockrot de Gouge drove all the way back inland to see my wife, my late wife, God bless her soul, to give her what he called a demonstration in 'healthy masturbation techniques'. Ha, he's a flockin' unsuc-sex-ful libertine, a pus-dripping wannabe bed-swerver. A rakeshame fopdoodle!" He spits on the sandy sidewalk, coughs, and spits again. "Ugh … such a clodpate."

"Healthy masturbation techniques? For real?"

"Yep."

"Well, I'm sorry about your wife."

"Unless you were the guy drinking and driving headfirst into her car, then you needn't be sorry; and I know it wasn't you, because he's dead, too."

"Still, sorry."

"Water under the bridge, Map, under the falling bridge, ha."

"Have you asked him about that?"

"No, no; I'm sure he doesn't know that I know. I won't say anything about it or I'm afraid that the next thing I know, he'll be messing with my meds, and not in a fun way. I know they want me dead, they were hoping I'd be dead long ago; I know he wants to kill me personally … but he can't just murder me, now, can he? What's left of the system is still working for me, a little, just a little. He's seen me almost die once, and I think he danced for joy, shook his fat rear end in joy."

"Huh."

"Yeah. He's flockin' insane."

"Hmm."

"Sometimes I'd like to drown him in that nasty ocean out there, but I don't want to go near it myself, you know?"

"I hear you."

"Hmm. Or him; I don't want to get too close to him, either, now that I think about it. I believe he's gone and gotten himself all frenchified."

"What's that you said?"

"Oh, nothing, don't sleep with him, and you'll be fine, insofar as that goes."

"Say, I just can't tell; how old is he, the dreadlocked doctor?"

"Oh, ha, he's like the Kensington stone, you know?"

"What's that? Sorry?"

"The runestone. He's like the Kensington Runestone, out west; he's like the Newport Tower, up north; that vagina-pimple could be any age. No one seems to know, and no one can agree. Ask four people and you'll get eight answers. Sometimes I think he's mid-fifties, sometimes I think he's much, much older than I am."

"And how old are you, Thom?"

"Older than you, Map, much, much older than you are," he coughs, then clears his sandy throat, then says, "Older than I should be, ha, that's for sure."

"Looking good, then."

"You don't know me well enough to lie to me yet, ha."

"Sorry."

"Whatever, no worries, okay?"

"Alright; cool."

"And there's another thing that I know about him, that dirty doc."

"Oh, what's that?"

"Something my wife, my late wife, found out, and she wrote it to me, in passing, in one of the last letters she sent over here to me."

Map: "..."

"Tonya obviously, you must've noticed by now, also suffers from a serious case of ornithophobia, among other things."

"..."

"..."

Map turns his head, and looks up towards Thom; both men smile and then simultaneously begin to dislodge sand stuck between their teeth. Spitting sand, more sand than saliva.

Thom says, "You know what I hate about all of this, Map?"

"I can guess a lot."

"True, true, yes. But I always told my wife to make sure that I wasn't buried in a suit ... I hate suits ... I haven't worn one since my father's funeral. I always told her to bury me as I was, just however I dropped dead to leave me like that, not to dress me up. I always assumed that my heart would give out before she died; we both did."

"Well, I can try to make sure that happens, I guess."

"No, no, you don't understand. Down here, we sickies don't get buried ... regardless if we have kin that want our remains or not. Not that I do, mind you, we had no kids and I have no siblings. No. They cremate us. And then they toss our ashes out into the ocean."

"Crud."

"Right ... we get to become part of the trashline, or we wash up with the crud on the beach."

"And worse ..."

"What's that?"

"The sand that's always in my teeth, my hair, my nose..."

"Oh, right ... it's sand, pollution, oil, and cremated people ... nice huh? But it's better than being embalmed and buried."

"Why's that?"

"All those chemicals ... methanol, toluene, formaldehyde, ethylene oxide, and, of course, ethyl benzene ... they're horrible for us."

"But we'd be dead."

"I mean for the rest of us ... for the ones of us still living here, or anywhere for that matter, and the ones of us yet to be born. Burying xylene, having toluene in the soil, benzyl phythlate in water, it's horrible. Horrid. Simply horrid. Look around us ... you can smell we've flocked up the air, when it's light tomorrow, or hell, you know what the oceans look like now. And what we can't see, imagine all of the stuff that we can't see. We're messing the place up, Map."

Map: "Flocking-a."

Thom: "Yeah, yes, yes. You said it. But, personally, for me, well, I don't mind being cremated. Although I'd rather just be stripped of my clothes, give them to the poor, and then bury me naked in a hole, let the worms and centipedes and ants eat me. Of course, ha, it would have to be a mighty large hole, maybe they'll have to use the Oak Island money pit to bury my fat arse in."

"How are you feeling?"

"Well, I guess it depends on how much further it is to your unit."

"Not that much ... a few blocks I guess."

"Well, I'll need a rest and maybe a pill or two when we get there."

Map: "No problem."

Thom: "..."

"Oh, and Thom, and please don't take this as an insult, but I don't understand half of what you're talking about."

"That's okay; you're not the first," and he lets out a hearty laugh, only silenced by the nasty wind blowing bits of sand and grit from oil and bodies into their ears, and just over the dunes to their right, the contaminated waves scream, and overhead the infected gulls scream and fight in midair, and the wheels on Map's wheelchair begin to squeal as the oil picks up more of the dark, dingy sand and of the cremated ashes of former patients of the seaside convalescent units.

Now they are inside of Map's unit: Thom opens the door and gags, "Wait here, sit tight, ha," he says to Map, who is in his chair just outside of the door, "let me go and open windows to let in some of that nasty ocean breeze to clean up the rank air in here, good god man, this is horrid."

He disappears down the hallway; Map sits in his chair, legs burning as if napalmed, his hip feeling as if a gang of punks has beaten him with skateboards for a week. The stars twinkle gray in the polluted sky. As he stares across the street at another unit with dark windows, a gull lands on the railing near him. In the dim light exuding from the unit's grimy windows, Map sees the once white bird is no longer white, but is an ashen gray, except for some wine-red stains around its cracked beak.

Thom exits the house, gagging, saying "Whoa, does it smell in there," and then the nasty bird caws and catches Thom's eye. After a heart-cough and one more nauseated gag, Thom takes in a lungful of the sordid atmosphere, and then lets out a huge bellow, directed at the bloody-beaked gull, which squawks back at Thom, and then, slowly and reluctantly, spreads its filthy wings, stares at the men, and then casually takes flight.

"I can't believe I used to feed those pox-ridden feathered rats when I vacationed here as a child."

"…"

"Let's get you on inside before that sucker and its friends get back here and poop all over the place."

"Okay."

"Just point me towards your room; I don't think you want to go into the main room. Nasty, nasty."

"To the left, at the end of the hall."

"Okay; let's go."

Thom has trouble getting Map's wheelchair up the few inches into the door frame, and after a few minutes of sweating and cussing, he wipes his brow, coughs and gags, and says, "Hey, I tell you what … if it's okay with you, and let me know, let me just pick you up and carry you on in there; I'll lower you onto your bed. Nicely, of course, ha, yes, yes!"

"Um…"

"Nothing weird; I'm old enough to be your grandfather, well your father at least, and I swear I have no interest in hugging you … I'd rather put my fingers into the nurses, if they ever come back to my unit," a breeze of the interior air comes out of the front door and he gags again, "or to this one, for that matter, crud."

"I guess I could hobble down the hall. I've taken enough extra pills to numb the pain a little."

"Nonsense."

Thom bends over, surprisingly agile based on his age and the gray in his hair and the sweat on his forehead; Map leans forward and Thom lifts Map's thin frame into a bear hug and stands up as if he is just carrying a canvas bag of produce, and walks into the piss and vinegar hallway, heads left, pushes open the door with his foot, and lowers, as gently as a giant can, Map down onto the sandy mattress.

Thom stands, huffs and puffs, wipes sweat from his brow one last time, and says to Map, "You find me some spare pills; I'll go close up the unit and make sure no birds have gotten in here to eat that body out there ... not that that would be a bad thing, granted."

Map is silent as a response and watches the giant man turn and disappear down the hall; a moment later he hears a gag from the front room, and a moment after that, the door to the unit is slammed shut, the latch is engaged, and Thom comes back and stands in the doorframe of Map's room, almost taking up the entire space with his muscular girth.

"If it is okay with you, I'm exhausted, I'm just going to stay here tonight; the place is almost empty with Tonya gone and all. It is just you and that decayer in the front room."

"Sure. I mean, I just live here, it is not like I own this place, you know."

"All too well, Map, I know all too well how it is."

Thom turns to go, momentarily forgetting the pills he asked for; Map says, "Hey, Thom, earlier tonight, you said that they wanted you dead? Who? Who is that? The government? Is that what you meant?"

Thom nods, silently and slowly.

"Why? Why is that?"

"Because I kept on warning them. I warned them. I did. I did and they know it." His face turns burgundy.

"..."

"I warned them about it, about all of this," he nods his head towards the dark windows, indicating the outdoors, "I warned them all, and they mocked me to make me look crazy. They tried to ticket me, to arrest me, for doing the call of nature in my own private yard, instead of in the toilet. I mean, I have full title to the place."

Map: "..."

"No liens, either; not anymore."

"Hmm."

"Yes, you see? You follow me? My yard was fertilized, and I wasn't polluting any streams or water. Oh, I still let my wife use the inside john, and once in a while, back when it used to snow, I'd go inside, but mostly I went outside, and used leaves. They tried to make me look poor; I'm not. They tried to make me out as a fool, an uneducated peasant. I'm not. Ha!

I wasn't always a shopkeeper, for Christ's sake, I have an undergrad degree in biology, a master's in chemistry, and a PhD in physics."

"Oh, I had no idea."

"Well, how would you? We just met; unless of course you saw me on the news, or read one of my articles..."

Map: "No, sorry. I don't think so."

"Why apologize? Most people didn't read any of them. Most people didn't listen to what I was trying to tell them. They just dismissed me as some sort of crazy fringe green anarchist nutcase, and I was a green anarchist, I just don't think I was crazy. No, not a nutcase. Not exactly. Sometimes, to try to discredit me, I was called a green terrorist. Which I wasn't, not totally. I knew it was going to happen; I know all of it was just going to get worse. Much worse, actually. And I'm not mad about it; I'm sad for us, as a species. I'm sad for the seas, sad for the shores. I'm sad about all of this, about what happened."

"All of what, exactly?"

"About all of our blinders being on, being blind about sustainability. Most of what the government tells us is incorrect at best, but probably just lies ... it is not real sustainability. It is bull-manure ... manure is, however, sustainable. As long as we can keep on eating we might live, but I'm not sure how much longer that will be."

"..."

"I tried to tell everyone, to warn everyone, years ago. About waste. Recycling. The flockin' trashline."

"..."

Thom: "Cancers. Not for us ... there are too many of us, or were, there are less of us now, but still too many people. Cancers for the oceans: we are the bad cells killing the ocean. We are the ocean's cancer cells."

"..."

"And those gulls? Something is really very wrong with them. Yeah. I mean, that's as obvious as the trashline is our own fault; but what is wrong with them? Exactly what? I mean, besides just being carriers for that wretched beach pox. Is it a breakdown in their natural society, or is it a collective cancer? Maybe too many cigarette butts for dinner ... and that is part of what was killing the sky, too, at first little by little, but now, once the sun comes up and peers through the smog, you'll see the biggest ashtray you've ever seen, with those tankers out there just simmering, smoldering."

Map: "..."

"And here we are down here, choking on this nasty, trashy sand. The ashes of the dead. The smog from the living. And where are they?"

"…"

"No, no. Where are they? Where in hell are they as we are in hell? I mean you see them on the television, news stories on the internet, but trust me: it is all orchestrated. Highly orchestrated. Puppets. Where are they? The big ones?, the important ones?, the powerful ones?"

Map: "The mountains."

"On the mountains? Some people. But the ones in control? Where are they?"

Map: "…"

"See, not on the mountains, ha. Under, in. In. In the mountains."

"In the mountains?"

"In. They're at Cheyenne Central. In Cheyenne Mountain. Some are a mile deep under the Mile High tarmac, ha, you know? Or, across that wretched sea, someone's got to be squatting in Yamantau up there. Knowing it's going to get worse, ha, and it is, it is. And who knows where most of the Bilderberg Group has ended up, some dead in the sea, the others still working hard, at what?, who the flock knows … maybe the New World Order they've been whacking off to, or maybe just capitalist domination, whatever gets them off, you know? It won't last. This is nice, now, comparatively; compared to how it will be, to what this all will become, yeah." He pauses and scratches his chin through his beard. "There is no way to hide from this, but people are trying. The ones who are well; not those sickies, we sickies, me sickie. But they're out there hiding in the middle of nowhere, in the mid-west, in missile silos. Silo condos, they have become all the rage."

Map: "Yeah, I never had that option…"

"Believe you me, if I had the money, and the well heart, I'd have one. Away from down here. But it doesn't even matter. Well, it does now. But it won't soon."

"No?"

"Trust me."

"Craps of fate…"

"Craps of pollution is more like it. We've been pooping the kitchen sink, all of us, everywhere. Can't do that. And can't hide from a sick world by hiding inside of her, no, no." He sucks in air, rubs his beard. A gull crashes into the dark bedroom window, attracted by the bedside lamp; a smear of *rosso corsa* red and beach-grim gray has appeared and is slowly dripping down the sandy window. Thom dislodges some sand from his ear. "I'm going to get myself too worked up … do you have some extra pills? My heart needs to slow down. Flock…"

"Sure."

"Thanks."

"Hey, Thom, did you say that the doctor once almost saw you dead?"

"Well, either he didn't look too closely, or my will to live was too strong."

"…"

"And I didn't always have this beard." He walks closer and bends down towards Map, who is sitting on his bed. "Look here."

Thom parts his thick beard with his stodgy fingers; Map looks up, squints in the dim light from the small lamp next to his sandy bed, and says "…craps of fate…". From the left side of Thom's chin to the center of it are blue numbers, about half the amount of numbers that Map recently saw tattooed on the late Ehab's scarred chin. "What in hell is that about?"

"I died for a minute, just one, one and a half at most, but not enough to hurt my brain, well not much at least, and not long enough to crash my hard drive, if you follow. The doctor was there the whole time. It was before my wife died in that car. He didn't even try to revive me."

"Really?"

"Oh, yes, yes. He heard my heart slowly fade, and immediately reached into his bag and pulled out the tattoo gun."

"Craps of fate."

Thom: "Indeed; but he's an idiot in a way. The best doctors have moved to the mountains, following the money. If he had waited a couple more minutes then I'd at least be brain injured, probably dead."

"But? What happened?"

"The tattoo gun surprised my brain into shocking my heart back. I woke up as he was bending over me, tattooing away."

"What did he do next?"

"Apologized and left. Real quickly, ha."

"What did you do?"

"Nothing."

"Nothing?"

"I had just been dead; I was in no position to kick his balls up into his throat, which is what I should have done."

"For sure."

"Oh, I still plan on it … I still think about it every day. That's why I wear these gull gutters every flockin' day." He stomps his right booted foot on the floor; the sounds echoes throughout the unit.

Thom looks down at his boots, and then Map looks down at them. "Nice."

"Steel toed gull-gutters. Top of the line."

"Nicer."

"Flock yeah."

"So, why are you so, er, civil to him? Why don't you just crack his balls open like a walnut with your boots? You're big enough to take him down with one kick."

"It's not about that."

Map: "…"

"Well," Thom licks his lips, rubs his eyes, "It's like this. There are a couple of reasons, from timing to the element of surprise, to honestly I believe they'll just kill me. Poison me with the fake manmade nutrients they put in my food. Our food, actually. Yours, too. Overdose me with squalene, perhaps. Or just throw me in some sandy jail without any of my heart pills, which would have the same ending. Me, dead and cremated and being scattered in our nasty ocean out there. And I know they would. I'm no nut. No. No, I'm worse than a nut. I'm a menace. Well, not anymore, I haven't thought seriously about bombing a power plant to take down parts of the grid in a few years. Well, at least a couple of years. Okay, a year…"

"Maybe people will listen to you?"

Thom: "Maybe, but they never did before, not many at least. And as I said, I know the government wants me dead. One way or another, ha. The ends justify the means. They've been waiting for it. Waiting to bury my fat arse under the Georgia Guidestones, where no one can hear me fart… government, ha! Maybe more of the Bilderberg Group; they're not crazy, they're not fake; they're killers and this, all of this junk in the water and the smog in the air, it's just what they want."

"But maybe you can help."

"If I help, even a little, ha, it just shows that they were wrong all along."

"But it shows you were right all along, too."

"That's of little consequence now. Besides the planet being sick, have you happened to notice that we're all sick down here, but what the hell is wrong with us? What the hell is wrong with Tonya, with that lady roommate of yours? Even her crazy pink poodle is sicker than sick. Plastics. Fertilizers. Genetically engineered foods. Mining. It's killing me; it'll kill you too."

Map: "Hmm."

"Oil tankers, oil spills... Anyway, I'm getting tired ... I don't keep the kind of all-night hours that Tonya got you into."

Map smiles. Thom continues, "Besides, those pills have kicked in; I'm getting a little tired."

Map: "We'll talk in the morning. I have some questions for you."

"Yes, we can talk in the morning. I'll tell you about the time I threatened a handful of members of InfraGard; I was ready for those flockers to pull a pistol on me. Those rancid you-know-whats. Hmm. I guess I'll have to check on the store at some point tomorrow, but it's probably going to be condemned soon anyway, if not by the time I get there, damned birds."

"Maybe."

Thom turns to leave, and then turns back and says, "Oh, Map, your chair is just outside. I'd bring it in so it doesn't get all rusty ... but I'm literally about to fall asleep ... I'll move it back to your room in the morning. Yell if you need it, or me."

"Okay, thanks, Thom."

"No problem, Map. See you in the morning, or whenever you wake up, being on Tonya's crazy schedule now. Thanks for the chit chat."

Thom turns and heads down the hall. As Thom walks down the mildewed hallway, Map hears Thom talking to himself in a whisper: "The caps, the ice caps are going to flood us. And the formaldehyde seeping ... the formaldehyde raping, the fucking formaldehyde!" He spits sand onto the nasty wall. He groans and scratches his tattooed chin. "The fucking, fucking formaldehyde!" His face turns beet crimson. His neck swells like an angry cartoon. His palms are slick with sweat. His heartbeat-beat-beat accelerates. His ears are snare drums. The nasty hall smells like piss and vinegar; Thom is as mad a man on a piss and vinegar diet.

Map hears a door open and then close, and then he hears the springs on Tonya's bed scream under Thom's considerable weight. Map smiles and reaches into his shirt pocket for an extra pill to help him sleep, pulls one out, ponders it for a minute, and then decides on taking two. As he swallows them down, he feels more sand in his mouth than he's noticed in days. Ash. Dust. Skin cells. Feather bits.

As he falls asleep, he feels bits of grit being forced through the window by the increasing wind, the screaming wind, or is that those sick gulls? He thinks it must be a mixture of the two, banshee gulls in the screaming wind. And the waves continue to crash, washing up bits of hundred-year-old plastic, discarded tires, bleached dolphin bones. The waves are louder every night, just by a bit, as they inch themselves closer to the dunes, as the screaming wind takes down the dune line in front of the unit, grain by grain, and blows the sand with the ashes of the dead into Map's mouth, and ears, and nose, and hair, and he's exhausted and falls asleep as gulls fight on the deck, next to front door, drips of blood staining the rotting wood. He's gotten used to it by now.

Rotting away, just like Map and Thom feel, like they are slowing but surely rotting and no one cares enough to help. They are the helpless and the hapless. The sickies. The ones who sweat when they've gone too long without their pills.

The sick, the dying, the forgotten, the rotten.

CHAPTER NINE

the Damn, Damned Deadies

This is silence, and then this is muffled voices.

That's what wakes him: Muffled voices. Whispered words. Curses. Grunts. Movement. Map wakes up and stares at the ceiling, confused. Sand dunes are in the corners of his eyes; his throat is raw and scratchy. Hushed tones. Syllables, but no syntax. Shushed sounds. Sshhh.

He sits up, reaches for his wheelchair, and then remembers that Thom did not bring it inside when they got back to the unit.

He turns his head towards his door, which is half open. A dragging sound; muffled voices.

He looks over, wipes the sand from his eyes, coughs, and then he sees Thom's boots. He recognizes the boots from their conversation last night, Thom's steel-toed gull-gutters, being dragged across the floor towards the unit's door, toes pointing upwards and dragging along lifelessly.

The boots stop momentarily and then continue being dragged out the door.

Map sits up, howls from the stabs of pain, and collapses back onto his bed again, with beads of sweat dripping from his forehead. He reaches into the drawer on the bedside table, blindly grabs a pill container. He opens the canister, swallows two pills, closes it and places it back onto the bedside table.

Bumps, bangs, and thumps. He stays on his sandy bed and listens.

Finally: "I thought they said there was only one left?"

Map turns his head, it's the shorter nurse. Map: "Sorry?"

Nurse: "One deadie. Not two deadies."

Map stares at her, wordlessly. The nurse turns her attention from Map to an unseen person still outside of the unit. "Princess? It said one, right?"

Map: "What do you mean?"

"There are two. Two deadies were in here this morning. Three if you include the burnt one yesterday."

"Who?"

"Oh, I don't know: a big deadie and a bigger deadie."

"What?"

"That's the best I can do. I don't know their names, I don't even know yours."

"..."

"Well, we were sent for one, and we can only take one, so we're gonna have to come back for the big one, the bigger one that is, another time."

"When?"

"When we're told to, that's when."

"Oh."

"And, hey, she," she nods her head outside, "has another shot for you."

"..."

"So, don't leave." Laughter; mocking looks.

"Would you bring me my chair?"

"No."

"Please?"

"Perhaps later."

"..."

Map closes his eyes and the pills take over and he's sleeping again, with his mouth open and collecting sand blowing in from gales outside through the old windows.

"Barons?"

He doesn't move.

"Barons?"

"..."

"Barons?"

"Hmm?"

"It's me, Princess."

"Sorry?"

"Princess, the nurse."

"Oh, right. Okay."

"I have something to make you feel better."

"The same as last time?"

"I'm not sure," she looks onto her screen of her clipboard computer, "I think so, something close to it at least, a little different. I don't know, you need to ask a doctor."

"Oh … okay."

"Can you roll over onto your stomach?"

"Sure."

He slowly rolls over, painfully; she pulls down his pants a few inches and then rubs a dark liquid in a circle where she will make her injection.

Map: "You didn't do that last time."

"Are you sure?"

"Yeah."

Her: "Hmm. I should have. Oh well, whatever. Hold on, this is going to hurt."

"Well, if it's going to hurt a lot can I take a couple extra pills to take the edge off, for now and later?"

"Go ahead. Take as many as you want. Take too many and I don't need to worry about you anymore."

He reaches over and grabs two pills from the table next to his sandy bed; he swallows then down dry.

Princess: "We call that sand, those pills."

"Sorry?"

"We call them sand. Those pills ya'll are always taking: they are sand."

"Oh, yeah?"

"Yeah, and when ya'll take too many, we write D.I.S., for 'drowning in sand', as the cause of death. The cause of some patient's death. Your death."

Him: "Yeah?"

"Yeah, and the sand, your pills, they have some slight amnesiac in them."

"Oh, yeah? I didn't know that."

"I've told you all of this before; I'm surprised you remember how to piss sometimes."

Him: "You've told me this before?"

"Yep. Oh, and pretty soon Wrecks is going to move into this unit."

"Wrecks?"

"Northern Wrecks."

"Who is that?"

"Oh. Hmm. Never mind, just make sure he takes his sand. Okay, got it? Plenty of sand, plenty. And don't call him, uh, hmm, nevermind; I need to get this done and get out of here. If I tell you you'll just forget anyway; it's a waste of time. Besides, no one has a history here, didn't you know? Only a future. Future deadies."

Him: "Hmm."

She readies the syringe. "Hold on, I hear this is going to hurt."

"I hurt all the time. Always."

"Don't worry, this will hurt more."

And it does hurt more.

But he falls asleep quickly on his stomach, with his pants still pulled down. And he sleeps hard, and long. The nurses left shortly after he drifted off to sleep; neither of them moved his wheelchair closer to him, but instead just brought it into the hallway, in sight but out of reach.

He sleeps all day with the wind howling a constant, sandy lullaby; trash flies by the window, and he's counting trash on the crests of waves in his dreams…

He wakes up; pulls his pants up; the old windows let in too much of the dirty Atlantic stench; it adheres to flesh, grips onto hair, creeps into lungs.

It's not dark, but it's not sunny.

He's not sure if it is a particularly bad air quality day, with soot so thick in the air that the sun gets grayed out, or if it is dusk. The sunsets aren't as brilliant as he remembers them being when he was a child. Hazy.

He reaches onto the table next to his sandy bed for some pills.

"Sand; hmm."

He sits up, prepares himself to be sick, he prepares for the lurch of pain and the surge of stomach acid up his sandy throat. But it doesn't happen.

He feels pretty much okay.

He sits up, and just rubs his upper legs, to get circulation going, he blinks his eyes a lot, and they are sore, dry; he spits some grit onto the floor. He no longer looks to see what color it is. He no longer worries about spitting on the stained floors.

He sees his chair, halfway down the hall; at least it's inside.

He thinks about standing up; he stretches his legs off the side of the bed. A sharp pain in the ear, into his neck; then that sharp chest spasm;

his heart stops for a millisecond, and then pumps blood full of sand around his body once again.

The wind howls; a stench comes through the old windows and he can taste it. It tastes gritty; it feels like old musty coffee grinds are always stuck in his teeth, in his throat. Drowning in sand. Coughing out sand. Spitting out sand. Shitting out sand. Sitting in sand. Sucking in sand. Sleeping in sand. Suffering in sand.

A sickie in sand. Sand sick.

Sandy sickie. Sickiecide.

He does it: he stands up.

He stands slowly and painfully.

And then his chest hurts; but then it doesn't. He coughs out more sand. He feels his toes in his sandy socks. A sour taste is his mouth, always lingering, supplemented by the nasty after taste of the sea air. Convalescing by the sea, dying by the ocean, suffering next to the suffocating salty sea. Dying. Ocean. Salt. Dying dunes. Decimated dunes, decimated sickies. Drowning in sand, drowning in trash.

He's taking steps, towards his wheelchair, instinctively. He walks through the doorframe that Thom's bulky mass filled up completely just last night; Map rubs his three week old whiskers, sand falls to the worn, havisham carpet.

He walks past his chair, next to the front door of the unit, facing away from the ocean. He can hear the sick ocean even here at the front door. He feels wind from between the cracks in the doorway and it smells like the dirty brown and gross gray foam that floats on the crests of the filthy waves. He washes his hands five times an hour with industrial soap but the ocean's rotting skunk smell never disappears.

He can hear gulls outside on the front steps, eating one another, killing cousins, passing on viruses. A bird plague. A gull flu. A beach pox. A sea shore virus bug no person has had before. Yet.

He looks, just to reassure himself, or convince himself, that the big man is gone; Map looks into Tonya's room as he passes, hoping to see her or the giant Thom asleep in her bed. It is empty. Not even a corpse.

He passes the other empty bedrooms in the unit, pauses at each one to double check, takes a step in, and as he's nearing the kitchen, the wretched smell hits him, and he has to turn around and cover his face. It is the smell that was known as Ms. Nevershe not too long ago, but long enough ago that she shouldn't still be here.

Map stops in his tracks and vomits onto the floor.

He straightens up and turns around. To no one, or rather maybe to his decomposing late unit-mate dead in her tub, he says, "I have to get the flock out of here for a while."

He walks back down the dreary hallway, and when he reaches the back door, he swings it open, and steps out and finds himself near a couple of one-eyed bloody-beaked gulls.

He kicks at the birds, (one growls back, more like a feral cat than a shore bird) and takes a step forward, and the gulls back up, and then all turn and quickly take flight as a gang into the filthy sea breeze. Map gags again.

He walks down the steps onto his sandy driveway, which is always empty, except for when the doctor or nurses show up for the brief assessments. He sees tires tracks leaving the driveway, and heading north.

Map walks, slowly, to the end of the driveway and turns to follow the tire tracks.

A couple of blocks up, the tire tracks pull into a space where a unit once was, before a wave or a fire destroyed it.

Foot prints and drag marks show in the feathers and sand, leading from where the tire tracks end and on towards the desecrated sea shore.

Map walks forward and follows the prints.

He slowly walks over the crest of a sand dune, covering his eyes from the blasting sand, the screaming winds, the screeching gulls, the bits of trash flying towards him, the brown foam blowing in the air, empty crab shells blowing near his feet.

He squints, looking in the direction of the ocean. He has to squint to looks towards the sea. Gusts of death in the air. Bits of plastic, hair, clothing. Sickie ashes, no, deadie ashes.

He scans the beach, the landfill next to the sea. Trash blowing, birds swelling and rotting, the sea getting closer and closer and picking up items and blowing the trash closer to Map's unit, and the wind blows trash from the sea to the land, and from the land to the sea, where it joins the trashline, outlining the continent like a ring of dirt in a tub. The floating trashline, the now eternal trashline.

To his left on the shoreline, he notices a huge heap of feeding gulls. He takes a few steps that direction and notices not one heap, but two, one significantly smaller than the other. The birds are crawling over each other like maggots on old meat. "Must be something that washed ashore."

For no reason, he walks closer, having to almost cover his ears at the sonic assault of the screaming gulls. Three more steps, rather painlessly too, and three more and he's closer. Closer to a heap, the two heaps. Closer to the throngs of infected birds, those poxed and feathered flying rats.

His nose has stopped working from the stench; or maybe his mind has chosen to protect itself by shutting off his sense of smell: order the olfactory off-duty.

He picks up a glass bottle, and throws it towards the heaps. It lands closer to the smaller heap, and the gulls are startled enough to fly up away from a second, and Map sees what the heap is.

He can't make much out from just a glimpse, but it appears to be a body, a dead body, a naked, partially bird-eaten human body. Ehab. Ehab's naked, burnt, and pecked pecker.

Map reaches down and picks up a bucket, dumps out the trash that's accumulated inside of it, and tosses the bucket, underhand, high and far, into the air, and it lands on top of a gull on the larger heap. The birds scatter into the air.

Map sees this is another body, although most of the face is eaten away.

He recognizes the clothing and the bushy, sandy beard.

He recognizes Thom's gull-gutter boots, doing him no good now.

He suppresses vomit, and looks on long enough to see the riot of gulls swoop back down to eat the rest of Thom, and Map turns and walks away, feeling sicker, muttering, and kicking dead birds on the beach.

The waves react by getting larger; the wind reacts by getting stronger; the gulls react by eating Thom more; Map's leg reacts by starting to hurt again; his brain reacts by wanting sand, lots and lots of sand, enough to drown himself in. S.O.S. D.I.S.

Map is limping a little now. He is in pain, but not as much as he normally is, as he recently has been in. He stops and throws up on the sidewalk, getting some vomit on his shirt and pants, wiping his mouth with his hands and then wiping his hands on his pants. He's not sick from pain this time, or from lack of sand, but rather from seeing Ehab and Thom's faces being devoured by the diseased gulls.

He's staring down at the sidewalk, watching his feet, when a dog starts barking.

He is one block from his unit. He looks around, says "Pist?", but doesn't see a dog or hear a bark again. He looks up into the polluted sky and sees a pair of gulls trailing him like vultures. He looks up at them, screams, "Flockers!" and looks around for something to throw at them, but finds nothing.

He walks past seemingly empty unit after empty unit, hears crying in one, muted screams of pain in another, probably someone screaming into a pillow. The single paned windows of the unit do not muffle the sounds from inside the unit and they don't keep the dirty sand from being blown inside by the trashy wind. He stops to listen for the dog bark again, and he turns in a circle, looking down the empty street, seeing no people and no vehicles.

Behind him, in the direction of his seafront unit, he hears a car ignition turn over. He turns, getting hit in the face by a blast of putrid air and stinging sand. He wipes the sand out of his eyes, and looks towards his unit's usually empty driveway. He watches a car back out of the driveway and then drive down the road away from him, gray sand mixing into the charcoal-black exhaust. The exhaust hovers in the air.

When he is a few steps closer he hears his unit's door slam shut.

He walks more confidently than he has in many months, years even.

He spits out some junky gunk.

These are what he sees and smells: salty plastic winds; feathers and gull-feces-speckled sands; bits of trash burrow in his hair; a feather attached to his three week old stubble, and he pulls it, sees the bloody gull feather, and dry heaves unexpectedly, bending at his stiff waist, leaning over the sandy sidewalk. The bending hurts more than he expected that is would.

He spits out taupe gray bile onto the vacant sidewalk.

His eyes water; his nose drips. Sand gets into his open mouth; he spits a little and gags again, but then he straightens up, and continues walking towards his unit.

His legs don't betray him and he finally gets to the rotting wooden stairs of his stilted unit with its trashline view.

He pauses, inhales some of the wretched sea air, and lifts his stronger right leg first, and slowly walks up the rickety steps.

He swings open the unit door, steps in, and closes it behind him.

He glances towards his assigned room, then turns and sees that directly behind him is a tall man wearing safety goggles and a white fabric air mask covering his nose and mouth.

Map: "Ah!"

The man stays silent.

Map: "Oh, you scared me."

"..."

"I'm Map. Welcome. I assume you're going to be living here for a little while?" Map nods towards a suitcase on the floor next to the man's boots. "Convalescing here?"

"..."

"Well, why don't you go and ahead and take that room." He nods to the room furthest from his own.

"..."

"There's another one of us living here, too. She's not here now. Tonya."

From behind the mask: "Shh. I don't care. What in a bird's buttocks is going on in the other room?"

"What? Which?"

From behind the mask: "Out there. There appears to be someone large, colossal. And dead; very dead indeed."

"That's Nevershe."

"Shh. I don't care. Just get her out of here."

"Well, um, I can't haul her; I guess with your help maybe..."

"I'm not going anywhere near her."

"Good choice..."

"Shh. When's that woman going to get back here?"

Map: "Who, the nurse?"

"No, fool, the woman who lives in this unit, in that room, you just mentioned her?"

Map: "Tonya."

"I couldn't care less about her name; when's she getting back here? I haven't been around a ... shh, never you care."

"Well, as I said, I'm Map. What's your name? Northern Wrecks? Is that what the nurses said?"

The goggled man takes two quick steps towards Map and he's right up in his face, and he growls, from behind the dirty mouth filter, "Don't you ever flockin' call me that again, you understand?"

He reaches up and has both of his hands on Map's throat before Map can respond or react, slowed as he is from all of the months in the bed and chair. His airway is being blocked and the blood is slowing to his head and he gags some and the man in the mouth filter and goggles says nothing and just keeps applying pressure. Then the goggled man rears back his head and throws it forward into Map's forehead.

Map collapses onto the hallway floor into a heap of clothes, skin, sand, and blood, smelling like piss and vinegar, craps of fate, he's gotten used to it by now.

The first thing that Map smells is the sea breeze, the rank, sick ocean odor. Gag.

Then he tastes the salt and the grit; the salt in his blood, and grit of a shattered tooth mixed with the salt in the smog and the sand in his mouth. There is a loud ringing in his ears.

Next, he hears the steady moaning of the ocean, like the moans of a dying patient. With his eyes still closed, he hears the other noises nearby: the quiet talk of a medical diagnosis coming from the too-loud med-t.v. through the too-thin walls; and deep, labored almost-mechanical breathing of a heavy ex-smoker sucking for oxygen from behind a mouth filter. That is when Map opens his eyes, expecting to be in his sandy bed, forgetting that he is slumped over on the dim, gritty hallway floor; and he looks up just in time to see a boot coming towards his soccer ball forehead. Boot from hell; beat down like hell; hell smelling like piss and vinegar.

Now, all Map smells is the sea breeze, with all of the tear-inducing, throat-swelling junk that floats in the air.

Next he tastes salt, a little from the sea air, but mostly salt from his blood, which is swimming freely between his teeth now.

He swallows a piece of a tooth. He swallows it before he realizes that it is part of him, not some wayward morsel of an old veggie from the food bank on the mainland.

Then he doesn't hear the ocean as well as he did a little while ago; the thumping of blood in his swollen ear is deafening; he can feel and hear his pulse in his broken tooth, in his busted ear drum.

He opens his eyes to a sticky darkness.

He licks his dry, cracked lips; his tongue feels chalky. Ashen. Swollen. Dry.

He sticks his tongue out and tastes stale plastic. Between bursts of the rancid sea breeze, he smells the familiar odor of damp duct tape. Salty duct tape.

His wrists feel agitated from rubbing together, taped together along with the trashy sand that's always blowing around. He strains to open his eyes; he can feel hair on the back of his head being pulled and then he realizes that a loop of duct tape is encircling his head.

The tape yanks on his hair even as he tries to remain still. It grinds particles of sand into his wind burned cheeks. It smells worse than a thousand sweaty and bloody Band-Aids from sickies, no, from deadies, from doomed, deceased deadies.

The taste on his lips begins to make him sick, but he can't stop himself from licking his lips, licking the fiber on the thick tape: dirt, plastic, sweat, spit, blood.

He tastes bile in his throat; it burns as it goes up; he briefly wonders about gravity. He gags, begins to throw up, and, he has to swallow it back down. He chokes some, feels pressure in his throbbing head, in his pounding ears; his bruised and trampled temple feels like it will explode. His eyes are swollen and bloodshot. His left ear is deaf; in his right ear he can't hear much, but can feel the waves move in the junky ocean as each wave makes the dune line smaller and smaller; the trashline gathers and grows, and expands and spreads.

"There once was an ocean…"
Map awakens.
"…clear and peaceful…"
He tenses up.
"…with blue sky…"
He imagines it.
"…and clean sand for the people."
Smack!
He's hit on the left side of his face.
He grinds his gritty teeth.
"But the waves' motions…"
The grit tastes bloody.
"…constant and thrashful…"
He wonders if his eyes can bleed internally.
"…carried chemicals and trash…"
He can smell the chemicals.
"…'twas crassful!"
He can taste the crass crap.
Slam!
He's kicked in the ribs.

He can taste pain in his mouth like thick, bleeding smog.

"Soon the State set in motion…"

He hears a gull's cannibalistic shriek.

"…a healthy chore…"

His tongue is swollen; it is hard to swallow.

"…have sickies…"

He's kicked in the left shin.

"…convalesce at the ailing shore."

Slap!

He's backhanded across the face; another tooth is loose.

His tongue is drawn to the newly bleeding tooth.

"With almost no commotion…"

The wind howls.

"…the sick and crazy…"

The tooth throbs with each accelerated heartbeat.

"…the thick and hazy…"

A hand reaches down and hovers just above his sandy, trashy hair.

"…went to live by the sea."

Grab!

His hair is grabbed by a fist and then yanked upwards.

He feels himself lifted up off the floor; he feels some hair rip out of his sandy scalp.

"She's sick, the ocean…"

His eyes are closed tight. He is shoved back onto the floor.

"…and so are we all…"

The voice gets louder; the waves crash closer.

"…but that polluted tide…"

His heartbeat in his bleeding tooth is a marching band on speed.

"…shall be my pall!"

Heave!

Map is yanked up again by his hair; his legs are weak and shaking.

As he starts to topple, the masked and goggled man kicks Map's feet out from underneath him, and he falls duct-taped face first. When he hits the floor he's knocked out cold, and he's dreaming of a time when the filthy waves weren't so close, the wasted beach wasn't so trashed, and his aching mouth wasn't so bloody-bloody.

Bloodied body, battered brain, best wish now is to sleep, to sleep in the sea, the sick, sick sea.

In his head-full of day-dreams and day-mares, under the matted hair, sand, and blood; in his bruised brain dreams, the beach still smells like a landfill of rotting whales; even in this concussion sleepy-sleep, the gulls continue to cackle, claw, and carry-on like cracked-up crazies.

But here he can run. Fast. Painlessly, painlessly, painlessly. Instead of burning, burning, burning.

And he's here in trauma dreamland, daydreaming, and he looks down and there he is, some other him, another Map, slumped down on the cheap sandy carpet in the convalescent unit. Even in this dream, the trash makes the ocean swell like a bloated whale carcass, and it reaches and stretches constantly, flowing and ebbing, tidal pools full of fish eyes, running shoes, and fishing line wrapped around discarded and forgotten children's toys.

He leaves himself; he leaves the version of him that's down for the count and bleeding out, legs tucked up awkwardly, itchy raspberry-colored fresh spots and older maroon scabs on his spine where needles were jabbed and stabbed.

He throws open the door; the normal wind is there, blowing the foul stench and plastic bags around, trying to jerk the door out of his hands, but he's stronger now. He holds his own against the gale; steps out and closes the unit door behind him, effortlessly. He goes down the steps, nails poking up, wood rot every third step, gull droppings on each step.

He goes to the sidewalk, turns south, and walks. He calls the old canine's name, he listens for her weak bark, and he smells for her stinky, sandy pink fur. He hears nothing over the mad rants of the anguished Atlantic to his left.

He calls and calls; he sees no one; he hears no one; a piece of paper blows by; a single rain boot is sticking up out of the sand; bits of plastic, shards of glass, splinters of bone cover the sandy ground.

A lone gull drunkenly swoops down ten yards ahead of Map; it eyes him momentarily and then turns away and starts pecking at the ground. Map proceeds forward. After a few steps, the bird turns and starts flapping its dirty wings and charges at Map. No problem; Map kicks it away. He doesn't even hurt while doing it. The bird drops onto a cactus next to a crushed soda can and an empty mustard squeeze bottle.

Map walks on. He stops where the bird had been and looks.

He sees a three-legged small skeleton all curled up, restful in its rot. The jaw is open, as if trying to get out one last peep. Dead. And there's no more flesh or fur left. The sun still bleaches bones on the beach, just not as quickly as before all the pollution particles pervaded. The beach bugs and gulls have eaten everything. Picked it all clean. Bones bleached; cartilage replaced with packed, dirty sand.

Map looks down; he feels sick to his stomach.

The bones stay dead. He moves back.

He steps forward one more time, to look for a collar, and his knees burn, and then his toes throb, and his hip and back feel stabbed. He bends over, dizzy, passes out, and the dream beach goes dark, like a coffin closed on a vacationer.

And outside, gulls eat the rotten remains of their mates, and fight with their brothers over who will eat their dead parents.

The tides carry the deadly craps of fate, the trashline spreads like a virus and moves closer and closer to the pitiful dune line, waiting to storm the beach and sack the sick sea shore.

The wind howls, it never lets up, it doesn't care about the sickies, the near deadies, doesn't worry about the needy, doesn't nurse the bloody, the bleeding, or the suffering… doesn't pity the sickies, the bleedies, doesn't give a gull damn about the convalescents by the sick, sooty sea, or the rot race, or to see the rats rot by the sea.

And Map bleeds, he doesn't get up.

Bleeding onto the hallway floor, he doesn't get up.

He doesn't get up.

He bleeds.

CHAPTER TEN

the Sadistic Statistics

This is at the salt-air sandy Hell:

"This deadie just snotted a massive bloody."

His face stops being dragged over the sandy, cheap carpet. The two nurses are back, hung-over, and with tummies full of pills, as normal.

The other one: "What? Snotted blood? The deadie?"

"Snotted blood. A big fat blob of it. How dead is he? Maybe it's got a little broken off brain in it."

"Hmm, I don't think so. You sure that blood wasn't already there?" She points at a stain on the floor. "I know that blood was. And that puddle, too."

"Yes, yeah, I saw it. It came out of his nose, like a baseball-bat-to-the-face bloody nose."

The other one: "No. What? But this is a damned deadie. A damn, damned deadie. Gull fodder."

"No, yes."

"Well, it must have been residual, from us dragging him and all."

"I don't know. Maybe it's a really, really sick sickie."

"I mean, wasn't this just another drowning in sand?"

"I thought; but I don't know. Look at him. Looks worse than usual, which is never saying much down here. Looks like a flock of gulls went after him. I mean, I don't know: this unit's been dropping dead like great-grandmothers recently."

"Yeah, I've noticed. Frigging deadies. Frigging sickies." She fakes a gagging sound followed by a real gag.

They each involuntarily wipe their mouths with the back of their salty sleeves. They both let go of Map; he continues to bleed onto the floor.

He moans. Moans again.

"See." Princess says this.

"See what?"

"It moaned; it's alive."

"How was I supposed to see that, huh, you gull-sucker?"

"Shut up. Can't we just go ahead and leave?"

"We've got to get rid of this deadie first."

"Just this one?"

"That's what the order was: to get rid of the deadie in the hallway."

"But this one isn't a deadie; it's just moaned. It's a bleedie."

"Hmm."

"So, then it isn't our problem. Send the doctor a message; tell him this one is his now."

"Hmm; okay."

"We take care of them after the bleeding stops, whether they die or suffer. Or both."

"And then we get out of this place."

"Finally."

"Should we look in the other rooms?"

"..."

"..."

"Do you want to?"

"I don't care."

"Yeah."

"Put some pills in his pocket and leave a glass of water by his hand."

"Okay."

"I'll meet you in the car."

"Flockin' deadies everywhere…"

He vaguely hears them talking, thinks he hears them kiss but that's all in his head. Princess bends down and loosens the gritty duct tape, and leaves him passed out and bloody in the hallway near the front door. The door slams behind them; and he dreams about gull battles and dog bones, duct tape and face masks, and sandy, gritty blood.

It's the doctor, in the narrow hallway, bending over Map, his dreadlocks dangling down like blood-stained snow drifts in his burly beard.

Map: "..."

"Hmm? Matt?"

"..."

"He got you good, didn't he, eh?"

"What? Who?"

"Handsome Kelly. Northern Wrecks."

"..."

"That one balled lunatic."

"Sorry?"

"He was running around naked one day, naked save for his eternal face mask, and a sea gull swooped down, fast as lightning, and oh man did it grab one. And it got a good bite of it, too. Didn't get it all, but we can't spend all the time and money trying to save one sickie's left ball, right?"

"I guess not."

"I mean, we don't want that son of a loon reproducing, no, no. That hungry gull just did us a favor, that's all."

"What?"

"Nothing. Eh, nothing at all."

"That's crazy. A gull?"

"Craps of fate, yes."

"Ouch." He shivers.

"And I'm the one who had to take it out and sew it up."

"Ugh."

"Balls of fate, indeed."

Map: "Oh, Sure."

"Alright, here we go."

Map: "Where is he, anyway?"

"Who?"

"Handsome Kelly, Northern Wrecks, whatever you call him."

"Oh, I don't know; I was hoping that you knew."

"No, last time I saw him he was trying to kill me, I think."

"That sounds about right, yep. You wouldn't be the first, uh, no, no."

"Is he dangerous?"

"Let's just say it's better if we knew where he is. Craps of fate, he's one sickie I like to stay far away from."

"Ah."

"He poisoned his wife."

"Did it kill her?"

"Yeah, yeah, but not right away, no."

"Hmm."

"But it couldn't be proved."

"What?"

"Intent. Poison. He claimed she liked it. Wanted it. Begged for it."

"What did she say?"

"Oh, uh, she never spoke a word again in her life."

"Ouch."

"What a way to go; I suppose she could have been as sick as he was, or he could be sicker than we know; which is what I expect."

"What exactly happened?"

"Well," he pauses and scratches his dreads, sand falls onto the floor, "she was found gagged and hog tied in his bed, with rotten vegetables stuffed inside of her, in various ways."

"Damn."

"..."

"I still feel like hell almost all of the time, doctor. I mean, I felt okay for one day, but that was it, after that last shot. So, what do you think? About the pain; will it get better?"

"I don't think it'll get much better, no."

"I figured. Can I get another one of those injections?"

"Oh, um, you've probably had more than you should, certainly, actually, but I don't see what it will hurt. Maybe we'll have to do this one off the records; wouldn't want to be giving you too much."

"Now? I could use some relief."

"No. Oh, no, not now."

"..."

"Soon. Maybe."

"Hey, so, uh, what about the poison? I must've missed that part?"

"Er, what poison, now?"

"The wife."

"Oh, yes, yes: he had marinated the veggies in cyanide."

"..."

He wakes up in his bed, but doesn't remember getting there. His face and head throb and burn. His hair seems to be trying to pull itself out of his head. His spit is glue. His eyes feel chlorinated. His balls burn. His sack is shriveled; he feels there to make sure there are still two testes. They are there; but he thinks that they have shrunken some. His shaft is shrunken also; he rubs it, feels a rough spot on the skin; ignores it. He gets a little discharge from the tip onto his fingers; he wipes it on his sheet. One of his nostrils is clogged, and he has a taste of bile, blood, and salty, dirty sand in his throat. His left ear hurts; his right ear feels like it has water in it.

It looks like morning outside, but a hazy, dirty one. A loveless one; a sexless one. A scented one, but that scent is soggy, salty trash.

The gulls are oddly quiet, so is the sea. He realizes his ears are throbbing so loudly with his accelerated heartbeat that he can't hear anything.

He pries open both eyes, which were glued closed by sleep and blood, and some other muck and junk he can't identify and he doesn't want to even consider.

His tongue is the size of a camel's tongue. His teeth feel fuzzy and furry, and one or two feel a little loose. Maybe three.

It hurts his arms to move, and his left hand goes to rest on his throbbing left leg, and his right hand goes to console his cock and balls, and that's when he realizes that he's naked. That fact escaped him as he made sure his body was present, if not broken. Present, yes; presentable, probably not. Naked. Nude.

He tries to lift his head to look, but drops his head back in pain.

He feels like he might vomit, bile is coming up his throat, so he turns his head towards the side of the bed, towards the window.

And that's when he sees her: the nurse Princess.

She's leaning against the window; he sees that she has his pants, folded, between her uniform, acting as a pillow and a barrier between the windowsill and her derriere. She's smoking a joint. He can barely smell it through the crud in his nose and the blood in his mouth and throat.

She's looking at him, her patient, but paying more attention to her joint. She nods towards it and says, "My Great Burial Reefer, my smoky noonday demon."

"Mmm."

"When sickies die, they become slime in the trashline. But I'm a nurse, and as I'm a health-giver, when I die, I'll float high on the Ganga River."

"..."

"You seem doubtful, sickie." She holds the joint up between their faces, so the red tip is aimed up, and she lets it burn for a second, she then blows hard on the joint of her great burial reefer, so bits of the red cherry land in Map's eyes, eye lashes, nose, and mouth.

He clears his throat; it's rough and gooey. He wants to spit but doesn't know where to spit, and doesn't think he can get up, or even move much. He turns his head the other way, thinking he'd spit on the floor. He notices that the room door is closed; he doesn't mind; he doubts there's anyone else here, alive, that is. Then he remembers Northern Wrecks. The pain is coming back with the memory. He shivers; it hurts. Then he recalls the doctor coming over, but he still doesn't remember getting in bed.

He looks back at the tall nurse. She's looked away by now. Her joint has disappeared but there's still smoke slowly seeping out of her nostrils. She's playing with the buttons on her uniform pants.

He says to her: "Have you looked around for him?"

"Northern Wrecks? He's not here."

"You sure?"

"I think. The doc said I could shoot him in the ball if I saw him in here. And I'm a good shot." She doesn't smile; she doesn't even look down at him.

"..."

"The doctor sent me here to give you a shot."

"Good."

"I have it here. How are you doing? Are you feeling okay, considering the beating you got and all?"

"No, I feel like bloody hell actually."

"Ahh. You were out of it when I came in; we call that 'floating on sand'."

"Yeah?"

"Yeah. But sooner or later, everything sinks. Everyone sinks. Not to come back up again. D.I.S., sickie, D.I.S."

"..."

"Wouldn't that be bad, not to come again. Screw the not coming back up again, think about never going down again. Think about that."

She's unbuttoned her pants while she was talking; he hadn't noticed until they dropped to the floor, and he still didn't hear them, but notices her panties in his line of vision.

She has her thumbs hooked into the waistband of her underwear. She lowers them down, and Map sees that under that pair of underwear is another pair.

She notices him looking at her and explains, casually, "...keeps more sand out of my holes..."

Then she lowers the second pair. His sac doesn't feel so shrunken. He shaft grows some.

She looks over, shakes her head slowly. "Oh, no no no; I don't want to give you the wrong impression. I'm not touching that sickie shaft; your bushrod might have bushrot."

"..."

"You want your shot, right? Earn it then."

She climbs onto the bed, straddles him, and lowers her loins towards his mouth: "Lick the sand out and then lick me out, sickie."

He pauses a second and she turns ever so slightly and slaps his scrotum, hard. He winces and moans; she lowers herself even more.

"Do it. Do it now."

"..."

"Lickie my slickie, sickie, or I'll rippie your dickie. And I don't have bushrot ... at least that's what I tell fools."

"..."

She wipes herself off with his sandy blanket, gets off of him silently, gets her pants and her two pairs of underwear, and she walks towards the door.

"Your shot is in the bag on the floor, deadie." A few more steps. "Don't inject too much."

A couple more steps.

"I'm not going to inject it because my wrist is cramped from typing reports on you sickies who drown in sand."

She is at the front door. She pauses at the front door, puts on her layers of underwear, then her pants; she opens the front door and walks out of the unit, wordlessly and shoeless.

The door slams behind her, and it echoes throughout the unit.

Map hears it; ignores it; concentrates on the pelting sound that has started to hit the unit's windows facing east over the trashline and into the sooty clouds and the pillars of smoke from the derelict and burning ships.

He hurts. His leg is a whale that has been harpooned in the spine. His lungs sting, his ribs hurt, he feels a shortness of breath and some numbness in his left arm. His sees the nurse's bag across the room, but his legs can't get him there now. His eyes water, his tongue is dry.

The water pelts against the window across the room, but not against the smaller window next to the bed, the one that the nurse was just leaning against as she was getting high. Map wishes now, though it didn't occur to him then, that she had shared her joint with him; but he was too out of it from the pills the doctor gave to him to ask her for a hit.

He realizes that the window on the east, at the foot of his bed, is being hit by ocean water.

The bag across the room is too far for him to get to right now.

His mouth tastes like her you-know-what and smells like her you-know-where, plus the bitter pills, polluted sand, salty blood, and some sour duct tape residue.

He realizes that he's the only person alive in the unit right now. Or, he hopes he is, at least.

He knows that there are people who wish no one was alive in this unit right now.

He's tired; he closes his eyes; and soon he's floating on sand.

Peck.

Peck!

He was asleep when it started, so it seems to have happened quickly. He wakes up still aching mentally and physically, feeling hung over although he hasn't been able to find a drop to drink since he was first entered into the system, back over the bridge, on the other side of the smelly sound, back on the mainland.

Peck, peck!

It gets his attention now; as he turns his head he hurts from his stomach to his toes, with a bolt of pain going into his left testicle, too, which makes him think of Northern Wrecks.

Outside is one of those dead-eyed sickly gulls, cawing like crazy, fighting its own reflection in the grimy window. It bites at itself in the reflection, lice infested feathers falling off in the process. It kicks. It stares. It caws. It stabs its reflection in the face; once, twice, thrice.

Map is watching intently now.

The bird goes in for the kill; and this is the power hit, this is the sick gull's final fight, and it jabs its battered beak into the beak of its opponent, and as Map watches, the gull makes a crack in the unit's cheap window pane, and the gull attacks again and again, until finally it kills its opponent by cracking through the glass in its reflection's throat.

The gull's beak pokes a small hole in the window, and keeps on lashing. The hole gets bigger, and the gull, which only a moment ago was all worked up in hatred, is now worked up in fear and confusion. The hole in the glass gets bigger, small shards of glass are now falling down onto where the nurse leaned her butt as she smoked and waited for Map to awaken.

The hole is bigger and the beak comes through farther, until the bird's whole beak and face finally appear through the hole, and pauses only a moment until it spies Map on the skinny bed, and then the gull lets out a shriek, its sickly black tongue sticking out between its wide open jaw, and it shrieks with a ferocity that Map has never heard before. Then it tries to back out of the hole, to go and fly in the polluted air over the nasty beach, but it is stuck. It shakes its neck from side to side, forcefully, and each time it stabs itself from the points in the glass that it had created by attacking its reflection.

The edges around the glass change from whitish silver to rosewood red. Feathers begin to fall off, and then bits of bird flesh begin to be left around the edge of the glass. The gull bleeds more and screams less, and more feathers fall out and more flesh is torn out. Blood drips down the window and begins to form a pseudo lava puddle.

The bird stops shrieking but still struggles.

Then the struggling stops too, and the gull is alive, but dying, and Map reaches over to touch it, not sure if he should comfort it or break its neck and put it out of its misery, and at first he doesn't hear the footsteps behind him. When the footsteps echoing on the floors finally get his attention, it is too late.

He doesn't even have time to turn his head, but he hears the hollow thunk sound when he's hit on the back of the head. He doesn't even have time to feel pain before the room goes dark and he's floating on sand.

Floating on sand.

Floating on sand…

There is salty blood slowly dripping down his throat; there's bloody sand mixed into his salty tears; there's sandy, salty blood in his snot; there's a muted echo in his left ear; there's a throbbing scream in his right ear; there's a broken finger on his left hand; there's a gash on his right hand.

His left eye is swollen; his right eye is sunken.

His visions in his dark head are of a busty topless beauty, on top of him, riding him, and this is a memory, and he recognizes this memory, this bump from the past, he's about to explode deep within her, behind his shut eyes, but then he realizes what he feels down there, and he awakens.

He wakes feeling a warm pain in his midsection.

He can't open his eyes right away. His swollen left eye and his sunken right eye are both working against each other, and both are working against him, too, ignoring him.

But then the warm pain intensifies.

He can't hear out of his left ear, but the screaming in his right ear dies down finally, and he hears waves. He looks over, sees the bloody, broken window, where the nurse's butt had been leaning, and he forgets for a minute that the window had been unbroken and bloodless not too long ago. Both eyes are a little open now; his right ear listens. He turns his head towards the window and the pain shoots down his left leg.

He looks down at his body, towards his left foot, to see where the pain is going, and that's when he sees his crotch.

His bloody crotch.

He doesn't move; he freezes, feels for pain, inventories for his privates mentally, to make sure it's all there. Bloody. Bloody crotch.

Bloody feathered crotch.

He's feeling sick. Stomach bile in places that is shouldn't be. Testicles tighten.

He's feeling lightheaded; his right ear starts to scream again, the muted echo in his left ear gets quieter. His swollen eye shuts again. His sunken eye sinks in more. He blacks out for a second, and he's back to having a topless dream-woman on top of him, with him inside of her, and his crotch is happy, and maybe so is hers, but then the room spins a little and she disappears off of him and his world goes brick-to-the-head-black.

"Bollocks!"

"Ugh."

"Map? What is going on?"

"Tonya?"

"I wasn't even sure you were alive when I got here a minute ago."

"..."

"Didn't you hear me calling your name?"

"What?" He looks towards the window; it's dark outside, he can barely make out the bloody break in the window where the screaming beak shot through. "What time is it?"

"I'm not even sure what day it is."

"…"

"Do you know?"

"Huh? No. No."

"No matter. Are you ready?"

"For what? Do I look ready?"

"Doesn't matter, I guess."

"I'm not sure I even have balls anymore."

"Why is there a ripped up gull between your legs?"

"I don't know. I'm not sure."

"Your crotch is bloody; your face is bloody; there's half of a ripped up dead gull corpse looking like it's going to fellate you. Think harder."

"…"

"And faster. We have to go."

"Go? Where have you been, Tonya?"

"Can we talk about that later?"

"Later? You disappear for days and then wander back in the middle of the night like it's nothing? I'm just a little curious here."

"Well, of course it's night, when did you expect I'd come home, in the light?"

"Hmm. Well. Okay. Good point."

"And, as for you being a little curious, well, you should be standing here looking down at you…"

"…"

"…it's a sight for suicidal eyes, maybe, if that. I mean, what the flock happened to you, Map? Was a dirty, flockin' gull trying to peck your what-wheres?"

"…"

"Hmm? Well?"

"I'm not sure."

"Not sure? How could you not be sure that there either was or wasn't a gull pecking at your what-wheres?"

"But, what about you?"

"What? What about me?"

"Are you okay?"

"Er..."

"Well, sure, I see. I mean: are you as okay as you were last time I saw you? At the store, the other day..."

"The other night."

"Right, the other night; what happened to you?"

"..."

"Will you not tell me?"

"They didn't beat me; they fed me; and they let me go, without a charge."

"That's good, right?"

"No criminal charge; they'll fine me some cash of course. Cash I don't have."

"Right."

"How'd you get off?"

"They let me off; they gave me a choice."

"What was that? The choice?"

"Well, there wasn't much of a choice. There were two of them; nice looking flockheads, but flockheads nonetheless. They said that they'd let me out after their shift if I did what they wanted; they were all messed up, drugged up. They said that I had to either let them film me while I got naked and wrote 'Sickie' in magic market next to my, uh, you know, my what-where, or they wanted to both face-flock me, but not on camera, I think they'd get fired for that. I couldn't tell which one they wanted. I really couldn't. They seemed to have been happy to let that one go in either direction."

"..."

"Most cops just want to prick-stuff tonsils, you know? Their piggy-pig locker buddies' tonsils included, for real."

"Well, I mean, you've told me this much..."

She turns away; she turns a lust red. Her: "Well, I wasn't about to put some cop in my mouth. No way."

"Good point."

"Besides, no one's going to see that anyway. No one that I know. And I'd rather have some stranger see it and think I'm some sick pervert than to look in a mirror every day and see a cop-doll."

"Hmm. Yeah."

"Because I might be a sick pervert, but I'm not a cop's sex-doll. For sure."

"Well, I guess you made the right choice..."

"There were no winners in that game."

"Well, I had my own weird situation, just tonight, or yesterday, or whenever, I'm never sure anymore."

"What happened?"

"What happened? Oh, I guess all the pills and the stress and the pain and just age."

"No, you flockhead, you can't remember things because of all the pills; what was your weird situation?"

"Oh, we can talk about that later?"

"Really?"

Him: "Yeah."

"No, no way, I just told you I have the word 'Sickie' next to my, uh, you know, and you won't tell me your story? Argh!"

"Nah. I will later. I feel like hell. Anyway, didn't you say you want to go somewhere?"

Her: "Yeah, yeah. Pack your things. We're going to stay somewhere else, in another unit."

"Help me up."

"On second thought, you sit there and I'll pack your stuff."

Him: "Thanks."

"It shouldn't take too long for me to pack your stuff; where's your duffel?"

Him: "There, in the closet. Yeah, you notice how they don't let you bring a lot here? I thought I'd be able to get more clothes here, somehow, but I don't know who would know how to do that."

"Yeah, it's part of it."

"What's that?"

"It's part of the plan, not on paper, just barroom theory."

"I'm sorry, what?"

Her: "Three bras, seven panties, six socks."

"I think my situation was slightly different..."

"You know what I mean; ideally, they'd send me down here without any tampons, hoping that I'd die before I got a period here. Die quickly, quickly and quietly."

"Painfully, too, perhaps."

"Yeah, perhaps, but they don't give a flock; pain's not a statistic. Ha, their sadistic statistics. In fact, to them, pain and suffering are part of a cure. Flocking sadistic statistics…"

"A cure?"

"From their point of view. A cure, a conclusion, whatev: the ends justify the means, eh?"

"…"

"And who knows…"

"What's that?"

"What'd get me first? Or you first? Maybe my sickness. Maybe the pollutants in the air, or the bacteria in the water, or some gulls in a frenzy. Whatev. It all ends the same."

Him: "Curtains."

Her: "Curtains."

"Craps of fate."

"Craps of fate indeed … or, even, my end could come at the hands of that damned deranged dreadlocked doctor."

"Indeed."

"…"

Him: "Did you know that those nurses call all of our meds 'sand'?"

"Hmm; no, I didn't."

"Yeah, and when someone dies from them, from taking too much, they call it 'drowning in sand'."

Her: "Hmm; this is the first I've heard of that. Where did you hear this?"

"From one of the nurses; they both came by a couple days ago, and then one of them came the next day."

Her: "Hmm."

"Yeah, it was kind of a weird situation."

Her: "No, they come here all the time."

Him: "It was different this time."

"Hmm. How so?"

Him: "Nevermind."

"Okay."

"…"

Her: "That's how I want to go."

"What's that?"

"Drowning in sand. That's how I want to go."

"Yeah. Yeah, me, too."

"Drowning has always been appealing."

"Yeah. Yeah."

"But we couldn't do it at the same time, I mean, you are what is left of my friends, and I don't trust any government registered nurse…"

"Me neither."

"And if we were to both die here, well, who knows how long we'd just lie on the floor. I don't want to die and nastify in this place; I'd rather sink to the bottom of the ocean than rot on the unit floor, and you know sooner or later those flying feathered rats will get in here and eat us."

"…"

"Dead or alive, sooner or later, look at those suckers. I hope they all kill each other."

"Better them than us."

Her: "Yeah, but probably sooner us than them."

"Hmm."

"Right?"

"Probably, probably."

Her: "You know, I don't feel like I'm dying, not like they say I am, well, not all the time I don't at least, but I sure feel like I'm under-living."

"Yeah, yeah, me, too."

"And it sucks."

"Well, I guess that it's better to be a sickie than a deadie."

"Maybe."

"Yeah, maybe."

Outside, gulls scream death-cries while pecking at each other for food, rape, entertainment; the birds cackle loudly like diseased feathered hypergelasts. The trashline spreads; fish die a little faster; the human corpses in the sand are eaten by trash crabs; the waves get taller, reach further in, drop off more trash, drag sand back out away from the dunes, making the trashy beach smaller. And inside the sandy, damp unit, the blood of the decapitated gull congeals in Map's room, on the wall, on the broken window pane, on the gritty floor, on the cheap sheets and the used covers, the gull's mouth, across the floor from other parts of the bird, is open in a silent cackle, in a silent mocking pose.

The surviving sickies at the sea are just sadistic statistics.

CHAPTER ELEVEN

the Going, the Going, the Goners

This is where they are: In another seaside derelict unit.

This is her: "I was always bored back then. Imagine that, not being a sickie and being bored. But I was."

"Yeah?"

"Yeah. And I always wished to be somewhere else."

"..."

"Guess what?"

"You got it?"

"I got it."

"Wished the wrong thing, huh?"

"Yep."

"Hmm."

"Should have just wished not to be bored."

"Yeah."

"Sucks."

"Yeah."

Her: "But it's better now."

"Oh?"

"Yeah; I used to not care."

"About?"

"You."

"Me?"

"Well, no."

"People like me?"

Her: "Sort of."

"People?"

"That's it."

"Hmm."

"Yeah."

"How about now?"

"Like now-now, or just now-about?"

"Either. Both. Whatever."

"Well, they're the same."

"And? What is that?"

"Now I think about other people more than I think about myself."

"Yeah?"

"I finally felt close to people here."

"…"

"I finally felt close to people here, feel close, convalescing by the sea. It felt nice while it all hurts. Sometimes you just need to feel a little niceness while you hurt, you know?"

"I do; yeah."

"I thought you did."

"…"

Her: "And then they're gone. It doesn't even matter to anyone much. Their deaths just open up unit beds."

"…"

"Poof."

The breeze is a tepid stink: dead bird feathers float in it; bird bodies float on the brown foam on the nasty, nasty waves; the heavier trash sinks to live as an artificial barrier reef, seeping oil beneath the trashline just out from the Barrier Islands, the Burial Islands. He's gotten used to it by now.

He says: "I had one of those lonely dreams last night."

"What's that?"

"One of those dreams that make me lonelier after I wake up than I was when I went to sleep."

"That's why I don't sleep at night; at least that's one reason I don't sleep at night. What did you dream about? Parents? A pet, or at least a pet that isn't Pist?"

"Does it matter?"

"You tell me."

"Well, it was just a dream about someone who used to be close to me. Emotionally. Intimately."

"..."

Him: "It was just so real; I thought when I woke up I'd be back there. Or at least she'd be in the sandy bed next to me."

Her: "..."

"I hate this feeling. This emptiness. This sinkhole."

"I hear you. I know what you mean."

"..."

"So I try not to dream."

Him: "Can you teach me that?"

She smiles; he coughs.

"When was that?"

"Last night."

"No, no; I mean: how long ago was she in your life?"

"..."

"How about in your bed?"

"Oh, who knows; five thousand pills ago, three thousand pills ago, nine thousand pills ago. It all blurs together since I first went under the knife."

"Yeah. I know what you mean."

"She's like one of those sinkers out there; like right now, I know that she's out there, she's just below the waves so I can't see her, but that doesn't mean she's not on the bottom."

"Maybe she's floating and we're the sinkers."

"Yeah. Yeah, that's more like it. I've sunk, and I can't look up and see her through the funky sea water."

"Tell me how it all ended. What ended it? I love to hear about other people's misery, don't you?"

"I just upped and disappeared into the system. Then I got sent to these units eventually."

"What?"

"I went under the knife too many times. Or one too many times I guess."

"How so?"

"Well, the first surgery went alright, I guess; I was in a bit of a funk, pain, pills, depression, stuff like that; it happens, I've been told. And then after the next one, nothing got better; I just hurt more. Some of me thinks that was a bit of the plan."

"I've had similar thoughts. Their sadistic statistics."

"I just sank further and further into myself; and I was getting to be less and less like myself. I think I remember not being so angry; I think I remember not being so moody; I know I remember thinking I was a good lay, at some point, and I know I remember being not so pissed off and paranoid."

"…"

"…"

"Go on. Please."

"I disappeared after the third surgery because I knew I had already become a bad lay after the second surgery; and the third one would just make things worse."

"What was her input on this?"

"I told you; I just disappeared."

"You just bolted?"

"Yep."

"Does she know you're down here at the coast?"

"Doubt it."

"Does she know you are even alive?"

"Well, I image there's no obituary for me. Not yet, at least."

"That was kind of an asshole thing to do."

"It does seem that way, now, yeah. I'd blame it on youth, but it wasn't that long ago, and I was not a youth. Neither was she. Hmm."

"Hmm, is right. Jerk."

"Yep."

Her: "Tell me the medium-length story, not the two-second version."

Him: "You know the term 'bust a nut'?"

"I'm not a child, Map."

"It began to mean something completely different for me."

"How so?"

"It felt like my balls were exploding."

"I thought that's how it was supposed to feel."

"No, not in a good way, and not during orgasm. Before. An erection hurt everything, everywhere."

"Hmm. That's not good."

Him: "That's an understatement. But, the left one, especially the left one. Hurt like hell."

"Well, I guess I can't relate..."

He goes on: "So, if I got a hard on, my left nut hurt. When I entered her, my left leg felt like ice picks were stabbing into it. If she got on top, she had no fun because I was hurting so much and she could tell. And then she never came, because of me, because I was sweating from pain, a bit distracting I imagine."

"..."

"It sucks not to be able to enjoy sex; but it sucks even more to feel like I was the reason that she wasn't enjoying it either."

"Women are different than men; this maybe wasn't a deal breaker for her."

"As I said, it is clearer now, in retrospect, with distance. And how is it so much clearer now anyway, with more time, and more pills in between? You'd think my brain would be mush."

"It isn't?"

"Mushier, then."

"That's more like it."

Him: "But we kept on trying; trying different things; I just lost interest; I think she did, too."

"But you never asked her."

"Is that a question?"

"You tell me."

"No, I never asked her about it. I probably wasn't thinking straight. Well, heck, I know I wasn't thinking straight. Clarity left me long ago. I made up our minds for both of us. She was too hot to be with a broken man like me; she was too smart not to have a good and proper lay whenever she wanted it. Wants it. Needs it."

"..."

"For me, maybe for all men, I just got to feeling that she had no more interest in me. Like my needs were a bother. Like she no longer had needs; or, if she did, she was fulfilling them elsewhere. With something else. Or, rather, someone else. Or, other people, not just one."

"..."

"Anyone but me."

"Really?"

"Really, what? Is that how it happened? Or is that how I felt?"

"Both. Either. No, both."

"I don't think it matters, not now, not then. Especially not now. It doesn't matter which one it was, I felt like it was both, or either, whatever."

"Whatev?"

"Yeah. I just got to doubting. Doubting her. Assuming her needs were being fulfilled elsewhere."

"Maybe she just got to the age where she wasn't thinking about it all that much."

"She's just about my age; I'm not old enough to not be thinking about it all the time; it's always on my mind. Well, less now, thanks to all the sand. I don't know. I can't worry about it now. I just hope she's finally getting laid like she wanted to. I guess like she wanted to. With anyone else but me. I don't worry about it as much as I used to. I just assumed that whatever she wasn't doing with me, she was doing with someone else, behind my crapped-out back."

"Craps of fate."

"I don't worry about fate anymore either. That's something for someone in love. I'm just in pain."

"…"

"I don't have much to worry about now, not much to think about now. When is the pain going to be unbearable?, when is the next pill going to kick in?, how many pills can I take to feel less pain?, how many should I take to feel no pain?, when is the nurse going to put her clothes back on…?"

"What was that last one?"

"Nothing."

"I wish I had more pills in my mouth right now; this makes me shiver. This makes me sad."

"Don't be."

"Tell me about the dream."

"Now?"

"…"

"It was like it never happened, have you ever had one of those dreams? Where you are aware of the present, and the past, but you are in a future present which has a different past, like one where you make less mistakes, less screw ups?"

"The good dreams."

"I'm not sure if those are the good ones or not; I woke up feeling like hell. But, it seemed like a long dream in a short time. No, no it didn't, it was a short dream in a long time."

He stops. She waits, and then says, "Go on, Map."

"Oh, right. It was so simple, so simple and mundane, so common. But sublime. Ecstasy. Sublimely ecstatic. Like one of those dreams where I am making a peanut butter and jelly sandwich with my grandmother; where I can smell the peanut butter, and I can smell my grandmother, and taste the grape jelly, you know?"

She does, she nods her head, and she smiles. There are holes in her smile.

He goes on: "We were at a table, a round one, there was a checkered tablecloth, one of those tablecloths that feels like fabric on the top but has plastic on the bottom, or maybe vice versa; not a tablecloth that was ever in one of my places or in one of hers. It must have been from a restaurant that we both went to sometime. Or maybe it was from nowhere at all. And we had some friends over, I know who they were, good friends of mine, of ours; now maybe just good friends of hers. I know their names but that doesn't matter, you don't care about their names, do you?"

She doesn't: "…"

He goes on: "And we were all playing cards, which is funny because we might all hang out and play a game, but not cards, but it felt so natural. I could smell her. Actually smell her. I could smell the cards, too. They smelled like plastic; she smelled like heaven. I could smell her soap, and her lotion, the type I bought for her, and her cheap deodorant, her expensive shampoo, that one brand of hummus she ate, the tobacco on her hands. I miss smelling things like that; I miss smelling things that aren't rotten fish or salty air or disinfectant."

"Yeah. Yeah."

"And I heard her voice again, like she was right here, right here next to me, as close to me as you are now. That's how close and real it was, like you and me talking now. I could hear her, she was asking me how I was feeling, she was asking me if I needed help up off the floor, she asking me if …"

"…"

"…"

Her: "What? If what?"

"If it hurt too much to go on, and if we should stop, if she should get off. If she should get off of me."

"That's what she said? In the dream?"

"…"

"…"

"…"

"…"

"Oh, sorry; I just got lost there for a minute."

"No worries; go on."

"There wasn't much more to it."

"That's what made it so real to you, it is just like most of our days of most of our lives, there's nothing much to it. A mundane Monday. A typical Tuesday. A whatever Wednesday. A thousand Thursdays. A forgotten Friday. A so-so Saturday. A snoozing Sunday."

They both smile and exchange glances.

He goes on: "We were just hanging out, with our friends, and I could feel her hand brush against mine, I put my fingers in her hair and when I woke up, there was a piece of hair in my fingernail."

"Hair."

"Shorter then hers, and a different color."

"Yours?"

"Mine. I guess. Where else would it come from?"

"…"

"I smelled my fingers, and I tried to smell her, but her smell wasn't there. It was gone, or rather, it never left my head. All I smelled was disinfectants. It was just so real, I expected to turn over and have her next to me. I looked one way, and then the other, twice, just to be sure, just to be sure that it was all a dream."

"You thought she would be there, and instead you woke up in a unit bed."

"Yeah, yeah. I mean, I remember following her into the kitchen to cut some celery, or wash some carrots, or get some more hummus. I kissed her. Next to the fridge, one of those stainless steel ones, with the freezer on the bottom. There was magnets holding photos of some dogs on it. There was a calendar there; September. I don't remember what year it said. She had a veggie peeler in her hand; I had an ace of diamonds in my pocket. I had car keys in the other pocket; I could feel them against my leg in my pocket."

"Tell me more. Please."

"I tasted the hummus in her mouth in that kiss, in that kitchen which smelled a little like garlic all the time. She loved it. The kiss, not the kitchen. She dropped the peeler onto the floor. I laughed and washed it and then got the veggies ready and she walked back into the other room towards that random card game."

"And?"

"And I watched her awesome ass as she walked away; it looked good, just like it always did. She sat down. I munched on a carrot. And then I woke up."

"And?"

"And now we are here."

"I think I'd rather be there."

"Me, too. Me, too."

"It's an ugly night here."

"Yes, but you should see the days. They are even uglier."

"No, thank you."

"I think I am beginning to understand your night thing now."

"So…"

"So what?"

"Have you thought about trying to contact her?"

"No."

"…"

"No. I think that bridge is burned now. We all make mistakes we have to live with, right?"

"I guess."

"I just want her to be happy, and I don't think she would be happy with me. I'm not sure anyone would be happy with me."

"Oh, I don't know about that."

"…"

"But there's more to it than that, isn't there?"

"What do you mean?"

"There's something more; you didn't just walk away because she wasn't, you know?"

"…"

"That's a bit of a cop out, don't you think?"

"…"

"…"

"Yeah. Yeah. It is."

"…"

"I mean, that was part of it; but I don't know. I think I just fell into some deep, dark place. Way down. Down in the damp darkness, the one I always wanted to avoid."

"..."

"I fell in and just couldn't get out. Never got out."

"..."

"I think I'm still there. Only now, in this place, it's like a manifestation, you know?"

"I got you."

"Do you? Yeah, yeah, I guess you might."

"Explain it. Explain it to me. Please"

"Falling backwards. Loosing grip. Slipping away. No. No. That sounds too slow, too controlled. This was fast; more like rapids in a high river than a riptide in a low tide, see?"

"Okay."

"And the peripheral vision just closes up, blackens all around, swallows you up, swallowed me up, and held on. It was like slow motion at night. All the time."

"Yeah."

"And the uselessness. The all-invasive botched-gull of a feeling. Can't help others; need others to help me. You. Just to help. For everything. Anything. And then their resentment; they try to hide it, you try to ignore it..."

"Right."

"I could never ignore it. Never. It just got to be louder and larger and wilder and brighter."

"Okay."

"And it stabbed. I felt like I was being stabbed, all the time. Wounds. A wounded animal. A rodent."

"..."

"A gull."

"Ugh." She shivers.

"A sooty, flockin' gull."

"..."

"That's how useful I felt. Or, useless. Just a smutty, unwanted parasite." She nods her head.

"A burden."

"No."

"I felt like a burden. A big, broken, depressed burden."

"Tell me. Tell me more."

"I just couldn't stand myself, can't stand it. That feeling of needing others so much. Of not being able to pay my way, not being able to pay my part of the bills. Living off the checks the government sent me; way too small to live on, just big enough to make me feel small."

"..."

"Bitterness. Both ways. Bitterness."

"..."

"And, ha, of course, the endless pain, and the constant blurriness. From the meds."

"The sand."

"The sand. Yes, yes, the sand. All the time. Damn it."

"Yeah."

"Damn it to hell."

"Yep."

"It just feels like there's no way to stop, and no way to continue."

"I know."

"All the time, it felt like that, feels like that, like's there's nothing else but this big painful now. No past, no future."

"Just ouch."

"Just ouch. Right."

"I see."

"It's like always living in Antarctica. Alone. Alienated. Freezing. Frozen."

"Like living in Narcotica."

"Yes. Right, like living in the United Sweats of Narcotica, the United Suffering of Narcotica."

"The citizens of Narcotica are the Narcotized."

"Yes. But there are no neighbors; just empty neighborhoods, save one lonely tenant."

"That's how it feels?"

"That's how it feels."

"..."

"And I'd be lying, or course, a big flockin' liar, if I told you I didn't think about ending it, more than once."

"Drowning in sand?"

"Drowning in sand."

"…"

"But I feel even too weak to do that."

"…"

"So, I gave up."

"…"

"I gave up. I gave in. I quit. I quit pretending, I quit hoping, I quit seeing the glass as half full or half empty; I saw the glass as shattered."

"Shattered."

"Yeah, shattered. Just like I felt. Felt and feel. Still feel."

"Okay."

"It seemed the easiest thing to do."

"Easiest?"

"Yeah, maybe even the best. The best thing to do."

"…"

"So, I did it. I just did it."

"And never looked back?"

"Well, uh, not quite like that."

"No?"

"I always look back."

"…"

"But there's no going back, just always looking back."

"…"

"Just like the beach."

"The filth?"

"The trash."

"There's no going back, is there?"

"There's no going back."

"There's just always looking back."

"Yep."

"…"

"Just always looking back."

"…"

"Always."

Her: "And where in piss is Pist?"

Him: "I had a dream about her the other night."

"Do you want to tell me about that one, too?"

"That one didn't have a happy ending. Not that I've had a happy ending in mine…"

"I'm not sure, at this point, if the real Pist had a happy ending either."

"Must be better than her master's ending."

"Maybe. Maybe we'll never know."

"Sure is an ugly night out tonight."

"Always is."

"I've got some questions about Thom."

"I'm sure you do."

"Tell me about you and him."

"I loved him. But not like you and whatever her name is. Was. Whatever. I loved him like a father figure, like a mentor. He taught me a lot. I just never acted on it. He does, did. Did."

"…"

"And… and… I don't know. I'm kind of spent right now."

"…"

"I'm done."

"Yeah; well, the sun is going to be up sooner than later anyway, I guess."

"Alright. See you tonight."

Smack!

He opens his eyes, slowly. The dream images are wandering into the corners of his brain. The room is not too light and not too dark, and he tries to decide if it is morning or evening.

Smack!

Again. And this time it gets his attention.

He closes one eye; keeps the other just partially open. His lids have trapped sand; each grain of sand with its own tiny stench.

He sees her now.

"What are you doing here? Both of you, huh? Why are you in this bed, sickie?"

He looks around; it looks a lot like the view in the last unit; this one may smell better, but he is a little worried that his nose just hasn't woken up yet. Maybe there have just been less corpses in this unit. There is pain in his legs, his knees, his toes retain that crushed feeling.

"We left the other place."

"Don't make me slap you again. Or whatever: make me. I like slapping men; especially you for some reason. Slapping a sickie might seem mean to people on the outside; but I don't tell anyone, I don't even whisper it to my vibrator, and I love that thing. And if you complain, well, you might be dead before the complaint gets too far. And they'll just think you're some perv sickie. You smell bad, by the way, you smell bad like you usually do."

"Are you going to make me go down on you again?"

"Don't get your pissed boxers all wet, sickie, you weren't that good."

"Ah, good to know."

"Pretty piss poor, even for a sickie actually."

"Ah, thanks again."

"I had some twins yesterday."

"Twins?"

"Yeah."

"Brothers?"

"No; one of each."

" … "

"But don't worry; once they are, uh, done convalescing, I might be coming back to you. Maybe. I guess one of us might have something contagious though…"

" … "

"A little sunshine for you to make you feel good." She smiles, pleased with herself.

"Good to know."

"Is it? I'd only have you do something to me if you're still here, alive, and not looking too bad. Not that you look too good right now." She rubs her nose. "But you know that, of course."

"Of course."

"You got that sickie chic with you, huh? The skinny toothless vampire wannabe, I guess, right?"

Map: "She's here, yes."

Smack. She smiles, says, "That's funny, a toothless vamp; I have a good sense of irony."

"Better than your bedside manners, yes."

Smack!

Map: "I prefer that smack to being near your inbred loins."

Smack, this time with her fingernails pointed towards his cheek. Claws. Scrapes. Cuts.

"I didn't know you liked me at all."

"Professional courtesy and all of that crap."

"That's the worst courtesy I've ever heard of."

"Alright; no more of that; shut it or I'll pee on you."

"..."

Her: "Why did you two sickies come here?"

"The door was unlocked."

"Did you bring your stuff?"

Him: "A little; I don't have much as it is."

"Didn't."

"What?"

"Didn't. None of your stuff is back at that old wreck."

"Why do you say that?"

Her: "Because it is just a pile of debris. And one dead beached whale sickie, er, deadie now, ha."

"I don't understand."

She laughs a little, smiles. "The whole lot is a mess of four-by-fours, cheap insulation, a ruined roof, and probably at least one dead woman. Who flockin' cares about one less deadie, though, right? If those crabs haven't finished her decomposing fat off by now, then a flock of gulls will take care of it. In five minutes flat. Less than that, actually. And they'd kill their own brother just for the fun of it after they are done with the deadie."

"Nice. What happened?"

"Oh, and the one next to it is gone, too, the one to the left, the nicer one. Going, going, gone. Goners."

"Gone how?"

"A wave. Big one. I thought you were a goner; I thought it was going to be less work for me to do. Damn you. You damn, damned sickies. I was sure you were a water-logged deadie."

"You weren't looking for me here?"

"Why would I be going house to house looking for a sickie who was swept out to sea with the rest of, or most of, the unit he was staying in? You're a deadie now according to my records."

"..."

"I wasn't looking for you; now that I found you, it means one more person to check up on. Bad, bad luck. That's what it is."

"And Tonya."

"I'm sure she can take care of herself. But if she can't, I don't care."

Him: "Why then?"

"Why what?"

"Why are you here? And in my room?"

"This is not your room. Your room is in pieces floating around, in, and under the trashline."

"What am I supposed to do?"

"Do I look like an admin of any sort? No. Need a pill and I'll give you one; need a new unit assignment? Not my problem, sickie."

"That why are you here?"

"I thought the place was empty; I was going to come on in and smoke some stuff and entertain my crotch. Mmm. I was excited about that part. I'd have you do something to me but I think you're going to die soon anyway, and that kinda creeps me out. So, you're out of luck, goner."

"I'm sad to inform you, but I'm not about to die anytime now."

"I have literally heard that one hundred times, more actually, by people who said that, and died within twenty four hours. It gets to be funny after a while."

"You're sick."

"I think you're confused there, sickie." She starts fidgeting with the button on her pants.

"I thought you had those twins to take care of you?"

"Do you see them here, stupid?"

"No."

"Right. Come on. I'm in my prime, maybe not even there yet. Not like you. I can't stop; I'm always wet down there. But I bet none of your girlfriends were ever like that, not about you. Now that I think about it, I might have spoken too soon in ruling you out a minute ago. Your tongue wasn't that bad; I've had a lot better though, for sure, but some worse, too. A couple maybe."

"I'm not sure I was trying that hard."

"You were getting hard, I know; and I think you tried your best. It worked at least. But I'm not hard to get off, so it is not a real big accomplishment, so don't start to think too highly of yourself, okay? Any other woman would be dreadfully disappointed, unless they like deadies with small woodies and scars."

"When was it?"

Her: "What? When was what?"

"The wave."

"Dawn."

"Oh."

"When did you leave?"

"I don't know. Sometime before dawn."

Her: "Duh, dummy, I figured that one out. How did you get here?"

"With her. With Tonya."

"What, did she know about the wave?"

"How would she know about the wave?"

"I don't know; she's all flocked up in the head, I thought maybe she had some telepathic powers." She laughs at herself, smiles.

"..."

"Screw it; I'm going to smoke some."

Map hears foot steps down the hall, but pays little attention. She hears nothing. She opens her nurse satchel and rummages around and pulls out a joint. She sits on the edge of the bed Map is on, and messes with a sandy, oily lighter and lights her joint, and begins to smoke it, quietly and quickly, not talking to Map and not looking at Map.

She gets up and walks towards a grimy window and tries to look out at the landfill of an ocean. She takes a few more puffs and when she turns around towards Map he looks over and sees her eyes have become bloodshot. Her mouth is caught in a half smile, half frown. She still holds the joint in her hand and walks over towards Map. He thinks that she is going to hand it to him, but instead she turns the burning end down and proceeds to twist it into his exposed thigh flesh to extinguish it.

"Ouch! What the hell?"

"I thought you couldn't feel anything; I thought that those things were worthless."

"Ah, that hurt! They are not like they used to be; but my legs aren't worthless."

Her: "That's not what de Gouge says."

Him: "That doctor is flocked in the head. He's crazy as a gull."

She says nothing, but starts to gently rub one of her breasts, stoned. She stops when she sees Map looking up at her.

Him: "Hey, where is the doctor anyway?"

"I don't know. But last time I saw him, he said you were hopeless."

"What?"

"Hopeless, maybe even helpless and hapless, but I think hopeless is what he said, I don't pay attention to him anymore. Maybe he said he had little hope for you to progress much more; what's the difference? A sickie is a deadie sooner than later. A going, a going, a goner."

"Some nurse you are."

"I didn't get into this career because of my empathetic tendencies."

"Yeah, I can see that."

"Besides, if de Gouge says that you're a soon-to-be-deadie, I believe him, always have, always will. Don't always do what he says I should, but I believe what he says."

"Good for you, I guess."

"I mean, my old man wouldn't lead me astray, would he?"

"..."

"That's what I thought."

Map hears a few more footsteps and looks around the room, then towards the door; he says, "Is your nurse friend with you?"

"No; why?"

"No reason."

"No, I told you I came here alone; she's off with her boyfriend while her husband is at work. I told her not to worry about working and I swiped her time card for her."

"You're a princess."

"Of course I am. That's why they call me Princess, sickie. I'm also thinking that you're going to treat me like a princess."

"What?"

"I changed my mind about you; you're not contagious are you?"

"Yes."

"Liar; I just told you de Gouge was telling me about you. A hopeless gimp; but not a contagious prick."

"..."

In an instant her pants and her two pairs of underwear are on the floor and Princess is straddling Map with her exposed labia pushing into his face.

Her: "You want some meds and pills, you get me off. And better than last time, you sick gull-flocker, use your tongue more, pretend that you've made a woman enjoy it before, I know that might be hard. The fiction might be hard, wanker, not your little stub ... too much sand for that thing to stand, I bet."

She grinds herself in towards his mouth; pushing his forehead back with one hand and rubbing herself with the other. He grudgingly obliges her. After a minute, she starts to smile and he is hoping that she's about to go so she'll get up and go; but instead, she smiles down at him and says, "Oh, yeah, I've got the type-2 on my jelly roll, so if you get it, don't give it to anyone else; that would be irresponsible."

He pauses; she punches him in the side of his jaw. Bam!

He continues and closes his eyes for a moment. When he hears some more footsteps, he opens his eyes. He sees her eyes are shut and her sandy hair is swaying.

Then her eyes open and she's jerked backwards off of him. She falls back onto his legs; he shouts in pain.

She's pulled off the bed and hits the floor. Thump.

Then, Tonya stands up at the end of the bed, briefly looks over at Map, says "You okay?", to which he nods, and Tonya looks back down at the floor. Map assumes she is looking at the nurse on the floor. She has one end of a belt in her hands.

She starts walking backwards and Map hears some gagging. She takes a few more steps; Map tries to sit up to see what is happening. She comes closer, walking backwards. Map sees that Tonya is pulling the nurse with a belt that is looped around Princess's neck; the nurse is pants-less and gagging with her eyes open wide.

Tonya, looking down at the gagging nurse: "Where are your med-car keys?"

A finger points towards a bag.

Tonya raises a boot and kicks it into the back of the nurse's head. When Princess continues to moan and gag, Tonya kicks her again. When the nurse is quiet, Tonya still holds the belt around her neck.

Map: "You're going to kill her if you don't let up on that belt."

"And?"

"And? Well, you don't want to kill her."

"…"

"Do you?"

"I don't care. So, might as well."

"Don't."

Her: "…"

"Please. No one needs to kill anyone. Not right now."

"For Thom."

"For Thom? That's not going to bring Thom back; she's not even the one that killed him, I'm sure, if someone did in fact kill him. I mean, look at her; what would she be able to do to a big man like that."

"I saw her beating the heck out of you."

"Yeah, well, I'm not Thom. Look at me. Look at her, her face is like *Mardi Gras* it is so purple. This isn't the right thing to do."

"Okay, okay, fine, Map, fine." She releases the belt; the nurse is unconscious on the floor. "I'm going to piss on her though."

Him: "Whatever. Just don't kill her."

"Well, she's lucky; I haven't peed in the daytime in years. Too bad she's not awake to remember it, to enjoy it."

"Ah, she'd enjoy it for sure."

"I don't see how you like being awake in the day.... Whatev, where are those car keys?"

She walks over to the bag and fumbles around until she finds the set of keys.

"Here, let me get you into your chair."

"Won't they be looking for her? For us, even?"

"I know you heard her; these unit walls are so thin that I could hear your tongue on her what-where. I heard her through the walls myself: they think we are both deadies now, deadies who were washed out into the sea with our old unit. Cross us off the list and take a long lunch. Leave early for the day. Or, maybe sexually assault a handicapped patient, whatev."

"Yeah, okay, I guess."

She helps him out of bed and into his chair, turns it towards the door, grabs the nurse's satchel, and says, "This has got all types of meds in it; it must have yours. The wench better have some sunglasses in here, too." He nods and she pushes him out of the bedroom.

Her: "Hold up; don't go anywhere, I'll be right back."

"Alright."

She turns and walks back into the room; a minute later, she's back in the claustrophobic hallway buttoning her pants, smiling, a twinkle in her sandy eye.

"I'm hungry, I wonder if there is any applesauce around this place..."

Him: "What did you do?"

Her: "Don't worry about."

So he doesn't.

She has found some sunglasses in the nurse's bag, and she has them covering her eyes. "Let's go outside, onto the deck."

"Now?"

"Now. Why not? That's something I haven't done in years."

"Okay."

She pushes him in his chair through this empty unit. She slides open the glass doors leading out onto the warped, slightly rotting deck.

She scans the ocean; he stares straight ahead; neither says anything for a moment.

A gull lands nearby; she shouts at it until it flies away.

"Hey, Map, look. There are more."

"Huh? More of what?"

"Ships. Freighters. See?" She points.

"Yeah, I see them. I hadn't noticed them before now. There must be some change in the currents that are bringing them here."

They watch out over the horizon, silently for a little while.

"Hey, Map?"

"Yeah?"

"What's different about those two?"

"Well, they're a bit close together I guess."

"Good. What else?"

"Uh, what?"

"What aren't they doing, Map?"

"Oh. Huh. I see now."

"Yeah. There's no smoke. They're not on fire."

"Huh."

"Yeah, huh."

"I wonder what's going on. They must have smoldered out or something."

"Well, don't worry about it, I guess, don't worry about them."

So he doesn't worry. He doesn't worry about any of the drifting freighters, smoking or not. He doesn't worry about the shrill caws of the starving flock of gulls flying overhead; and he can't see the crab under the house, half grown into a piece of litter that traps and engulfs it, while it eats a human thumb. He can't tell that the waves are getting closer and closer, but if he could, he wouldn't worry about it, not right now, no, not right now.

Because what does it matter now?

Because ... because ... because nothing. Nothing. Nothing at all.

187

It doesn't. It doesn't matter now. Not at all. No, not down at the shore, with the sickies, and the dying and the dead, convalescing by the sea, the sick, sick sea. See the rat rot by the sea, sickie; now it is his fate, but soon it will be me. A going, a going, a goner.

The sea, the sorrowful, swollen sea is drowning in sickies, and drowning in sickly, salty sorrow.

He's gotten used to it by now.

Chapter Twelve

the Gull Fodder and the Sickiecide

This is now and this is what she's doing: She had taken the keys to Princess's med-car; it is theft of course, but she doesn't care. What do the forgotten care about consequences?; what do the once-abused fear of the ones they hate, who are now weaker?; what does Tonya fear of the flocking piggy-pigs at the police station who enjoy sexually abusing the ill, the pained, the dying?

Nothing. Nothing at all.

Nil. Zip. Zero.

She's beyond that now; far beyond all of that. They've taught her not to fear, not to respect, but to hate. The term 'forgive and forget' is not in her head now, and hasn't been for a while and won't ever return. Craps of fate.

The keys jingle in her pocket as she pushes Map in his chair down the rotting ramp outside their temporary adopted unit. She's hoping he won't fall through the old ramp and land in the gray sand, in the cactuses which trap trash and gull feathers. She pushes him slowly down and they struggle together to get him into the low, small car. He screams in pain here and there but tells her to ignore him, not to worry about it, that it is the norm now. She knows that now, it is so obvious, it has been so obvious ever since she met him in the unit, the old unit, the one that was washed away, torn apart, floating with the trashline now.

"Hey, wait here, okay? I'll be back in a jiffy-jif, don't go anywhere."

"Where am I going to go? I can't get my chair out by myself."

"No one wants your pissy pity party, Map."

"That's not how I meant it..."

"Whatev; I'll be back."

"..."

She slams his door; apologizes with her eyebrows and eyes, which tell Map that she hadn't meant to slam the door so hard. He nods his head, and then he leans his head back onto the headrest, closes his eyes and quickly nods off. Constant medication makes nodding off easy, but dreaming hard.

Slam!

The car shakes from the trunk closing; his eyes pop open. Sand is in his eye lashes; he's gotten used to it by now. He looks out the grimy windshield momentarily forgetting where he is until the driver's door opens and Tonya lowers her slender frame into the front seat.

She turns the ignition on, lets it idle for a moment, stares straight ahead, and then turns on the windshield wipers and the blue fluid to clear off the gunk that's landed there like a sandy smog tattoo.

After a minute, he asks, "You okay?"

"Yeah; why?"

"Well, we're just sitting here with the car on."

"Christ, Map, give me a minute will ya? You want to drive? I mean, come on, I haven't driven in so long, flockin' forever, give me a minute to settle my nerves and remember what to do."

"..."

"Sorry. I didn't mean to talk to you like that; you're my only friend down here now, I should treat you like it. I'm just a little nervous about driving."

"I'm your friend?"

"Well, aren't I yours?"

"Yeah, yeah, I just haven't thought about friendship in so long."

"Seat belt?"

"What?"

"Are you going to put your seat belt on?"

"Who are you going to have an accident with?"

They both look out the side windows at the deserted street; the sand in the road shows no tire tracks.

"Hmm. Good point, Map, good point. Screw the seat belts."

"..."

She grips the wheel; her knuckles are white. Map glances over at her, smiles, says: "Relax." She does; her knuckles turn pressure-pink again.

"Okay. Ready? Here we go."

She turns around to reverse, takes her foot off the brake, and the car lurches forward towards the house. She screams; he covers his face with his hands; she slams on the brakes; he reaches for his seat belt.

"I think you need to be in reverse…"

"Yeah, thanks. I figured that one out, Map."

She put the med-car into reverse, turns around, and backs out a little too fast, swings the car to face forward, put it back into forward, and starts to move on down the street.

"Where are we going?"

"Thom's place."

"What about the flock?"

"I have a key to the back office; it is separated from the store portion of the building. Stupid layout normally, but to our advantage now, as I'm sure those nasty, nasty gulls are still in there. You know no one's gone in there to clear them out, no one flockin' cares."

They drive in silence; looking into the passenger door mirror, Map watches the sand and trash fly out behind them as the car drives down the street, the only car in sight.

They reach the store and pass by it; Tonya takes a right onto a sand covered street, driving over soda cans and empty prescription bottles, and then takes a quick right into a sand alley. "If we get stuck, you're going to need to push us out, Map."

"…?"

"I'm joking, man."

"Ah."

"Here we are anyway."

The stops the car in the middle of the alley, she says, "I doubt any one is using this alley and if we get a ticket, it's not our car anyway. Heck, I don't even have a license for them to suspend or take away."

"They can fine you."

"They think I'm dead. They think you're dead, too, Map."

"True."

She turns off the car, leaving the key in the ignition, opens the driver's side door and gets out. She walks around the front of the car, opens the rear door, struggles to get the collapsed wheelchair out of the back seat, struggles even more to get it set up, but does, and then opens Map's door.

"Ready?"

"Ready."

"Grab onto me; let's do this."

After she gets him into his chair, she slowly pushes him to a rear door with the word 'Private' spray painted on it. "Thom was too cheap to buy a sign, so I spray painted one onto the door for him."

"That was nice of you. Hey, why do you have a key anyway?"

"In case I needed it, he gave me one. And, hey, look, we need it now. Convenient, huh?"

"Yeah, I guess."

She takes a key out of her pocket and reaches her hand out to the rusty door handle, and to her surprise, it is already unlocked. "Huh, will you look at that, I didn't need it after all..." She swings the door open on its rusty hinges, moves a brick from nearby and props it open, and then says to Map, "After you...", smiles, and pushes him through the door way.

"I'm Damn. Johnny Damn."

"What?"

"Um, you just asked me, 'Who the flock are you?', and I answered you. I'm Johnny. Call me Johnny, Damn, JD, whatever."

"Whatev..."

Tonya and Map are quiet for a moment and just stare at the bald man sitting at the desk, staring at two laptop computers. He looks too young to be bald from old age, so Map and Tonya silently deduce his sickness. He has on thick glasses, but is only looking through one lens, as the other eye is covered by an eye patch.

Johnny Damn notices them staring and says, "I know, funny, huh?"

Map: "Sorry?"

"This eye patch. All the nurses think it is a stitch: send the guy with an eye patch down to the shore, ha. You know, 'Argh matey!', and all that."

Map: "Ah."

Tonya: "Uh, Johnny, JD, what are you doing back here?"

"Oh, the front of the store is basically full of those poxed flockers. Some dead, some dying."

"Yeah, yeah, I know. But I mean, what are you doing back here, right now, at this moment?"

"I guess I could ask the same of you; I mean, I was here first."

"I asked first."

"Fair enough. I went out for an early morning, pre-dawn walk, to try to get some fresh air, which of course I didn't find any of. When I got back, I guess I have good luck, I mean my name is Damn not Damned."

Map and Tonya exchange glances; Map says, "I'm not quite understanding."

"I got back and my smelly seafront unit was gone. So was the one next to it. I guess I was walking west enough of it to be out of the way."

"Oh, the same thing happened to Map and me, too: our unit is gone."

"Do you ever feel that they like it when that happens? So, who are you guys, I don't think you introduced yourself."

"I'm Tonya. This is Map. We are unit mates, or were, when we had a unit."

"Ah, homeless, nay, unit-less sickies unite, eh?"

"I guess. So what are you going back here?"

"In general or specifically?"

"In general."

"Thom gave me a key. You know Thom?, the big guy who runs this store?"

Tonya: "I know Thom. Or, knew Thom rather."

Damn: "What?"

"Thom's gone. Dead."

Damn: "…"

"How about, what specifically are you doing back here?"

"Ah, I thought you'd never ask: I'm reading up on the Forever Floaters."

Map: "The Forever Floaters?"

"Yeah. Ya'll come on over here and look at this." He quickly closes a window on one of his laptops, and points towards the other laptop. "Ya'll are going to dig this."

Tonya: "Is that real news? All we've seen is the med-t.v. programs for the last forever it seems. Where'd you even get computers down here anyway?"

"I know, I know, they are contraband, but what are they going to do to me? Kill me? Put me away for life?" He rubs his bald head. "I probably only have a couple months left anyway. But don't worry about that; I sure don't worry none. Come here, come here and look at this stuff."

Tonya pushes Map closer to the desk, parks him next to Johnny, and then stands behind Map's chair, leaning over, looking at the screen.

Johnny points at some news footage. "This is from a helicopter, but I guess that's obvious. See these, these two freighters? They are literally right out there, just east of us." He points through the wall separating the office from the gull engulfed store and out over the diminishing dune line, over the expansive trashline, towards the horizon. "Have you noticed them yet?"

"Yeah, Map and I noticed them just a little while ago. What's the deal with them?"

"Those are them. Those are the Forever Floaters."

"What are they doing out there?"

Johnny turns his bald head, and looks out of his right eye, his only visible eye, through his thick lenses and says, "Why, they are floating, forever. Hence their name. They are the Forever Floaters."

Map and Tonya both say, "Ah."

"Makes sense now, huh?"

"Tell me, us, more. Please."

"Why do you look familiar?" He's looking at Tonya through his one good eye.

"From the store, maybe? Thom and I are friends. We were friends, rather."

"No. No, I don't think that's it. Hmm." He stares at her for a minute, rubs his bald head, then removes his glasses, cleans them on his long sleeved t-shirt, puts them back on, and continues, "Oh, well, no worries. I'll figure it out sooner or later. Maybe later. Oh, well. Now, the Forever Floaters. Hmm, where to start? Perhaps with a beer. Excuse me a minute, ya'll watch the news footage. I find the sand goes down better with beer."

Tonya: "Your pills? The sand?"

"Yeah, that's what it's called by the staff down here. Those rude flockers."

Map: "So we've heard."

"Ya'll care for one? A cold one? There's a lot in the fridge back here. They don't belong to me; so help yourselves to as many as you like. Thom won't be needing or selling them now, based on what you've told me. Cold one?"

Map and Tonya both shake their heads no.

Johnny Damn slowly stands from the seat he's been in; it appears to be a labor for him to rise. He grips the arms of the chair he's been in; his arms shake; his head appears heavy, sweaty. When he stands all the way up, Tonya notices that his fly is unzipped and his pants are unbuttoned.

"Uh, Johnny, your damn pants are undone; they might fall or whatev."

His face reddens; his glasses fog up in his one exposed eye. Slowly, oh so slowly, he reaches down and buttons the button at the top of his pants, and then zips his fly, then he wipes some beads of perspiration from his forehead, and then removes his thick eyeglasses, wiping them clean on his shirt, watching Tonya all the while with his one good eye. He places the glasses back on his face, and wordlessly he turns and slowly crosses the room. When he gets to a fridge against the back wall, he opens the door and removes one can of beer, pauses for a moment, and reaches in and grabs another one and lets the heavy door swing shut.

Tonya looks over and says to Johnny, "Neither of us wants a beer."

Johnny: "...?"

"You have two beers with you, but there's only one of you."

"Ha! Oh, you're a funny lady, ha!"

Tonya: "...?"

"Tonya, I think he's saying that those are both for him."

"Ha, yes, yes, Map, you told her right, ha!"

Tonya remains silent and turns back to the laptop on the desk. She's about to reach down to read the article on the screen when Johnny shouts, for the first time raising his voice since Map and Tonya found him in the storeroom: "Wait! Don't touch that! I mean, just wait, you never know who is contagious down here; could be me, could be you, could be him, could be all of us."

"Map's clearly not contagious."

"Just let me handle that; I'll show you everything you want to see."

"Okay, buddy, sorry, Johnny."

He lowers himself down into this chair. He pops open a can of beer, leans back his head and proceeds to drain all of the contents into his mouth, chug chug. Tonya notices the lights reflecting on Johnny Damn's bald head from the ceiling; Map pays no attention and is watching the live news feed on the monitor in front of him. Tonya is standing; Map is in his wheelchair; Johnny Damn is in a swivel chair seated in front of his computer. The first can is now empty and he crushes it in his hands and tosses it back over his shoulder; he pops the top on the second can, but does not take a sip, instead, he lifts it to his nose and inhales deeply. "Ah! Damn that smells like heaven, huh? Hey, sorry, sorry I snapped; I get a little possessive with my laptops. They are now my sole possessions."

Map: "Why didn't they get washed away with your unit?"

"I carried them around in my backpack when I walk; I never trust any of the staff down here. You can't trust those wretched, lazy nurses. If they found it, I might never see it again."

"Probably."

"So, where were we? Besides wishing I had brought a third beer over here a moment ago... The Forever Floaters. Right? You've really never heard of them, huh?"

Tonya says, "No. This is the first. I mean, we did notice the other ship out there, but didn't know much about it."

"Well, they would like us to remain ignorant of the news; ignorant and illiterate if they could get away with it. The same reason slaves were never taught to read hundreds of years ago. Knowledge is power." He turns and looks at Tonya with his good eye. "You sure we never met?"

"I think I'd remember you, Johnny. I'd remember a man named Johnny Damn."

"Oh; I thought it was because of my good looks..."

"No; sorry...."

"I'm just joking, honey..."

"My name is Tonya; don't call me honey."

"Sorry, Tonya. Tonya. Tonya. Tonya. I should be able to remember it now. Until I get to the end of the beer that is, ha! You just look familiar. This is going to kill me until I figure this out." He stares at her for a little bit longer, long enough to make her turn away; then he turns his one-eyed gaze to Map, and after the same amount of time says, "But you, Map, you are not familiar. Hmm. I hate it when this happens." He once again removes his eyeglasses and this time only cleans one lens, the one over his good eye and does not touch the lens that covers his eye patch. "As far as I can tell, from what is being reported, is that from a convalescent colony south of here, I don't know how far south, but still in one of the Carolina's, maybe this one, maybe the other one, well, it is what I would call a Sickie Rebellion."

Here he stops and just points to the images on the screen with one hand as he takes the remaining beer can in his right hand and brings it to his mouth, turns it up, and drains the contents into his mouth. He finishes the beer, and then once again crushes it in his hand and tosses it back over his shoulder. It hits the floor and skids to the wall, where it stops. No one has looked away from the screen.

From his chair, Map repeats: "A Sickie Rebellion."

"Well, that's what I'm terming it, at least; I coined that phrase. The national media, the few outlets reporting on it, aren't calling it that. They aren't calling it anything special. But it is, it is."

Tonya's turn to ask a question now: "How many people are we talking about?"

"That I'm not sure about; but it appears to be a few dozen at least, and those are the ones I'm able to count while they are being filmed on the deck of the one freighter. And it is unclear how many ships are out there floating. But, I'd assume that no one is being told, or shown, the whole truth, you know?"

"Sounds reasonable."

"And, since I think it is a safe bet to say that for every sickie that can come out onto the deck, there's at least one somewhere in a bed below deck, either unable to move, or perhaps unwilling to come out onto the deck of the ship. Fear, you know?"

"Fear of what?"

"You trust much these days?"

"No, I don't; I don't think Map does either. Do you, Map?"

"Nope."

"But, Johnny, what's their long term plan?"

"Long term plan? What's your long term plan? Or mine? Realistically my long term plan is to go out in a pyre on the beach after those flockin' nurses yell and insult me in my last days. Long term plans? No, no. I think it's much more immediate than that. Just short term plans, day by day, weeks by week, not even month by month. To get away from the sand that they force down our gullets, to get away from the insurance policies, the gov regs, to get away from being a sadistic statistic, to get away from the ineptitude of the doctors and nurses that are the only ones willing to come down to the stinking shoreline full of sickies, to spend their last days not staring out at the trashline and smelling all the rank breeze, but to go beyond it, and have a clear view of the beautiful horizon..."

"..."

"..."

"...and to die in peace. Die, die, die in peace, peace, peace. Not die being washed away by a filthy rogue wave taking away these flimsy convalescent units. Not having those flockers peck on my pecker."

"Amen, Johnny Damn, amen."

Map: "I see what you mean; you make it sound almost alluring."

"Almost?"

"Good point."

Tonya, "Hey, let me check out some other news sites." And she quickly reaches down, before Johnny Damn can stop her, and she takes control of the laptop screen and minimizes the window they are looking at, the one with the helicopter images of people living on the ships, and she just opens a window that had been minimized by Johnny Damn, and they all just stare for a minute.

Another minute passes.

It is silent until Tonya says, "Are you flockin' kidding me, Damn? This is what you've been watching? Me? Those fucking piggy pigs suck."

Johnny: "Ah, now I see; I told you that you looked familiar, and I can hardly see..."

"And I see why your pants were unzipped, you flockin' pervert! Damn it Johnny! Come on, Map, let's get out of here and leave this sicko perv to drink himself to death alone back here..."

Map is silent. Tonya gets up, throws her chair across the room, where it lands in a pile of crushed beer cans, and she starts to say something, stops herself, starts to say something else, stops herself again, and then slaps Johnny on his bald and sweaty head, positions herself behind Map's wheelchair, backs him away from the table (his mouth is open but he's not saying anything, looking back from the screen to Tonya to the screen and then to Johnny [who is staring at the screen] and back to the screen), turns his chair, and then she pushes him to the rear entrance of the storeroom, the one that they entered in less than half an hour ago, and they silently leave Johnny Damn sitting in his chair.

Tonya struggles to get Map's wheelchair out of the door and across the sand to the med-car that they've stolen from the nurse, and she turns back towards the building, when Map asks: "Tonya? What are you doing?"

"I'm going to shut the door? What did you think?"

"Well, I wasn't sure what you might do to him. But, hey, screw him, leave the door open; he's too drunk to notice and concentrating too hard on the screen; leave the door open: maybe some gulls will go in after him."

"Hmm. I guess Thom's done with the store. You, Map, you are a smart man. I didn't think you had it in you."

"Well, you're my only friend, Tonya. I'm just watching out for you. I'm on your side. About this. About anything."

"Shut up, Map."

"What?"

"Oh, don't make me say it. Just shut up."

"...?"

"You should know by now that's my way of saying you're my only friend too. Now shut up."

She helps him into the front passenger seat of the stolen car; folds up his chair and puts it in the back; a gull lands near the open door to the storeroom; she gets in the front seat and slams the door; two more gulls land near the storeroom door; Tonya turns the engine on, lets it idle a moment, turns on the wiper blades and washes the gray sand off the front window; more gulls land and start hopping to the open storeroom door; she drives away.

Inside, unaware that the storeroom door is open, unaware that gulls are coming inside to look for food, Johnny Damn is staring at the screen of this laptop, watching a video loop, the same one that Map and Tonya just realized that he had been watching before they came into the storeroom: the video loop of a naked Tonya at the police station writing the work 'Sickie' on herself with a marker...

He's masturbating to Tonya's image, unaware of the beach-poxed flock of gulls ganging up behind him, unaware that he's moments away from being gull fodder.

"What now?" They say that to each other, in unison.

Neither answers the other; neither looks at the other; there's a thumping from the rear of the med-car.

"What's that?"

"Don't worry about it, Map."

"So..."

"Yeah, okay."

"..."

"I guess let's drive to the causeway and leave this wretched sandy hell of an island."

"Is it that easy?"

"It is that easy. Bridge to mainland, bridge away from this sandy hell."

"Ah."

"..."

Thump. Thump.

"..."

"Ignore that, Map."

So he does.

"What are we going to do? Just drive a stolen car over the bridge? Won't someone notice?"

"Who?"

"Well, that was a good idea, technically, Tonya."

"On paper, yeah."

"Now what?"

"Let's just sit here and enjoy the scenery."

"Enjoy it?"

"Any better ideas?"

"..."

"Well?"

"No."

"If we wait just a little longer, we can watch the sunset over the ruined bridge."

Thump.

"There is it again. That thumping sound."

"Don't worry about that, Map. Don't worry, all is cool, or whatev."

"How many times are you going to say that?"

"How many times are you going to ask about that?"

"Okay, okay."

"Shut up, will ya? I'm trying to make the best of a ruined plan."

So he does. He shuts up. They are both quiet, with the exception of the occasional 'Thump' from the trunk of the med-car; at first he glances over towards Tonya, but after a while, he stops even that, they both stare ahead.

Thump.

They stare ahead of them at where the two bridges used to be, one with two lanes for traffic heading east from the mainland, the other one with two lanes for people leaving the once pristine beaches and heading back home; one a few decades older than the other, one at a slightly higher elevation that than other, power lines used to run on the north side of the higher bridge; gulls, ospreys and eagles would make nests there; fishermen would fish around the pilings; crab trap buoys would decorate the sound with their various colors.

Now, as Map and Tonya sit in the stolen, or liberated, med-car on the east side of the bridge, they can see where both bridges extend out over the sound, all four lanes, and where they rise to make room for larger boats to pass beneath, the lanes end, crumbled and destroyed.

"Waves?"

"Here? In the sound? Unlikely."

"Sabotage?"

"I don't know. Thom was always talking about how the infrastructure here was falling apart; I guess he meant literally."

"Hmm."

"Looks like one collapsed, finally, after years of neglect, and fell and took the other one down with it."

"Should we drive out there and check it out?"

She turns her head towards him in the passenger seat and smirks, raises an eyebrow. "..."

Map changes his mind: "Never mind. Pretty though, huh, the sun setting."

"Whatev."

Thump.

"..."

"Thom was right about so many things. The whole infrastructure of the county is falling apart: bridges, the grid, the antiquated power grid, the water system, the tax code, the ..."

"The tax code doesn't count as infrastructure."

"Shut up, Map. At least the war on drugs fell apart, but did you notice that as soon as the war on drugs OD'd that the next war was against us?"

"Patients?"

"The war against the sickies. The ultimate sickie solution. Sickiecide. Send them down here, forget about them, unemployment goes down, morale goes up, pills go down gullets, let them die down here, fall apart like the causeway bridge, crumble, let them drown in sand."

"Them?"

"Well - me, you, us. Let us all drown in sand. Sickiecide: the act of changing a sickie to a deadie."

"Nice, nice. How does this bridge play into all that?"

"This? Oh, out of sight, out of might, you know? There are other ways on and off, but no one wants to bother. Fuel is too expensive; the ferry fare is high and the schedules are followed as tightly as a young, drunk reggae band."

"Um?"

"The ferry schedule sucks, Map. Well, not the schedule, just following it is a problem. But, whatev."

"Maybe instead of falling down on its own, it was done on purpose; not sabotage, that word feels like a rebellion, but as a farce, a fake front. Maybe it was designed to look like an accident."

"Hmm."

"And if it was done right, and no one was hurt, no one would look too much into it. Old bridge; no deaths or injuries; no terrorist threats…"

"Wow. You might be onto something."

"Or, Thom could be right, no one cared to take care of the bridge, no one was paying attention, no one was checking it."

"Whatev. Look at that sunset, huh?"

"Yeah. Yeah, I haven't watched a sunset in a while."

Thump.

"I like the sunsets better than the sunrises."

"That's just because we can't see the trash in the sound, and we can't smell the ocean here. At home, crap did I just call the old unit home?, but at the units, we see the trashline, smell the rot. No good, nope, no good."

Thump.

Map glances over at Tonya.

"I'm glad you didn't say anything; I might have had to slap you."

They stare out the windshield in front of them, towards the setting sun, the remains of the toppled bridge, towards the bastard blue and radical red warning lights on the other side of the sound. Map says, "Hey, why is it that there are police cars on the other side of the bridge warning people not to proceed, but none over here?"

"Think about that a sec, Map."

"Ah."

"Yeah: what do they care if some of us, say, stole a car and drove off the bridge? Except for the loss of a medi-car no real loss, right? I mean, I think the preferred method is for a wave to come in and take us away that way only nature can be blamed, not man, or rather man's lack of maintenance."

"The houses. The units. They are bound to be worth more than the med-cars."

"Maybe. Older houses, newer cars with technology … I don't know. Good point. But I still think it all comes down to blame."

"Blame nature."

"Less bother in election years."

Thump.

"Yeah, I guess you are right. Well, they'll be fixing this soon enough, or starting to, anyway."

"Map, I'm not so sure that this is going to be any type of priority. This would be worse than a bridge to nowhere … this is a bridge to an island, okay, technically a peninsula, whatev, but a bridge to a peninsula full of sick patients, dying people, contagious people, and worse, there is less and less land mass here every day. The Barrier Islands have become the Burial Islands."

"The row of houses across the street from our unit will be waterfront soon."

"Soon? Our old unit is gone, bozo – the houses behind it are waterfront now."

"If they are even still there."

"Yep. Worse and worse every day."

Thump.

"Okay, okay, Map, I admit: that's getting to be a bit annoying now."

"…"

"Flock it. I'm going to have to take care of that, aren't I?"

Tonya reaches over and opens the door; Map stares ahead at the remains of the toppled bridge; the driver door slams shut; Thump!; Map wipes his eyes; the trunk opens; the car shifts from side to side; the trunk Slams!

CHAPTER THIRTEEN

the Tide and the Tied

This is the talk on the Barrier Islands near the expanding trashline:
"Wait. Really?"

"What's that, Map? Dang, I think I broke a nail. And I'm getting hungry; this is usually when I get ready to eat breakfast. My twilight breakfast. You hungry?"

"Well, a little, but, we can't just leave her there."

"Why not?"

"I don't know, it just doesn't feel right."

" ... "

"It's not right."

" ... "

"Really."

"Then go untie her."

" ... "

"I didn't think so."

" ... "

"Come on, Map, she was basically reverse raping you."

"Is that a thing?"

"I mean, I heard her, she was refusing to give you the meds or your shot or whatev until you went down on her herpied what-where. Screw her. She's a flocking psychopath. She's sickicidal."

Map laughs. "You gotta admit, it's a little funny that you are calling her a psychopath."

"I think she is one."

"That's not what I mean. I'm talking about how you just left her tied up, naked, under a street light."

"She's not naked; she's wearing her belt."

"Not around her waist!"

"Ready to go?"

"No, wait. Can we just leave her there? What is someone finds her and hurts her? Rapes her?"

"First of all: so what? She's a twisted, lazy psycho. I heard her. I don't need to tell you – you know. Also, who is going to find her? The bridge is down, so no one is coming from the mainland. It's just about dark, so no fellow sickies are going to be out and about. There's no crime here, except what's done by the authorities. It's one of the safest places to be these days, if you work for the system. And if you don't, the cops and nurses are all you have to be worried about."

"Then what if a cop comes by and decides to take advantage of her?"

"Judging by the amount of flashing lights on the other side of the sound, all the cops are over there. I haven't seen one out here on Sickie Shoals all day, have you?"

"No, I haven't now that you mention it."

"Most likely some nurse running late is still here and will drive to try to cross the bridge and find her."

"Then she'll tell the authorities we did that to her."

"First of all, I did this, all me, not you. Secondly, then we tell what she was doing to you. Lastly, where are they going to look for us?"

"Hmm. Okay."

"Good. Let's get one more look at her and get out of here. Go ahead, I know you want to. She's hot. Heck, I want to take one last look at her."

They both look at Princess, naked and tied to the light post, struggling a little, but not much.

"Tonya, let's just get out of here."

"That's what I've been saying…"

She slowly does a U-turn in the deserted street and drives away. Map watches out of the rearview mirror as the naked nurse gets smaller and smaller under the electric light post as the sun sets over the ruined bridge.

"So, what now?"

"Yes, that's the million dollar question, isn't it: What now?"

"…"

"Any thoughts?"

"No. You?"

"Let's just go find a place to crash for the night … you're looking exhausted and I could use a break or whatev."

"Okay."

"…"

"Let's go."

"Okay. Let's go."

"So, what do you think ever happened to Pist?"

"I'm not sure, Map, I'm not sure at all. But I wish I knew. I feel bad, you know, I always told Ms. Nevershe that I'd look after Pistachio if anything ever happened to her, to Ms. Nevershe, and I've lost her. That's not how I meant for my promise to pan out."

"It's not your fault."

"Well, I don't know, maybe not, maybe so. Even so, I feel responsible."

"She was old anyway."

"That doesn't make me feel any less guilty."

"…"

"But I don't know. I guess she got lost, got turned around. She could have wandered out to the beach and gotten washed out by a wave. She could have gotten attacked by some of those dirty, flockin' gulls. Wouldn't that be a nasty way to go?"

"I've seen a lot of nasty-nasty ways to go since I came down here."

"Imagine me: I've been here even longer."

"Yeah, yeah, I guess so."

He wakes up in the passenger seat; it feels like a couple hours later since he drifted off.

The night has turned lousy; they don't even need to see the water to know that the ocean is fierce tonight.

"Hey." She's looking over towards him.

"Sorry about that." The wind whips, shaking the car just like those stilted units during a nor' eastern.

"Whatev." Her hands are on the steering wheel; there is sweat, or rain, on her forehead, perhaps both.

"What's going on?"

It's raining, windy, and dark. The windows are fogged, the headlights are off.

"I just couldn't do it."

"What's that now?"

"I just couldn't do it."

"…"

"I got so gung-ho."

"It happens. We all do, sometimes."

"No, no. Hear me out. Just shut up for a sec, okay?"

"…"

"After Thom, and all. I mean, he was one of my only real friends down here in this blank canvas of a life. A bit like a big brother and a mentor all in one, you know?"

"I can see that."

"Trust me. He was. And I never had many. You're not one."

"Okay."

"Because you're a friend, but I wouldn't say that you are a mentor. No disrespect or whatev."

"I wasn't thinking that I was."

"Good then, we're on the same page."

"But you should be getting back to that page."

"Right. Okay. So, I guess I've just gotten so angry. Recently. Just so angry, at what I can't control, and about things that control me, or try to at least. I don't know. It's not something I'm used to. I'm just mad, sad, depressed, pissed, tired, bored, hurting, suffering, alone and worn out all rolled into one word."

"…"

"But it manifests itself as sweltering anger sometimes, inside, screaming inside."

"I don't understand. That's not how I see you."

"I've been keeping it in check, so to say. It stays deep down; I let it out occasionally."

"Okay."

"I just didn't want to be the one. The one with the anger; the one causing the anger."

She pauses; he has nothing to say: "…"

She switches on the car's headlights; they switch on silently, emitting a bright, synthetic light, bits of trash and rain race through the beams.

She clicks on the windshield wipers, to wipe away the gray blots of rain, and the sandy griminess which occurs whenever one stays in one place too long, say, just long enough to sneeze and it starts.

With the lights on, and the windshield cleaner, Map turns his head, looks out ahead of him, and sees the pole where earlier Tonya had tied up the near-naked nurse Princess.

The empty pole. Empty of nurses, at least.

"Oh." That's him.

"…"

"What do you think happened to her? Was she gone when we got back here?" He's looking out the side and rear windows now, not seeing anything in the stormy darkness.

"Let me go on."

"With what?"

"My story, Map. My story."

"Oh, okay."

"I just didn't want to be the one to cause pain."

"…"

"I know this is going to sound weird, but not too long ago, well, years ago, but not too many years ago, I had a job. Worked for an apartment building landlord. The guy owned houses, too. Rentals, cheap ones. I basically worked the desk at night at his office; you know, in case there were any emergency issues that come up with one of the places. Whatev. A boring job, for the most part, which is why I took it, and at night, to boot. Well, actually, I was only looking for night jobs."

"No surprise there."

"Right? So, boring, boring, boring for the most part, alone at night, in this office. Read some, watched the television, online stuff, not much real work. Not much pay, either, but enough, I'm not a girl with too fancy of tastes."

"Sounds like a good career job."

"Oh, no, it was a total dead end job. Totally. Busted pipes in the basement in the winter. Drunk neighbors being loud on the porch in summer. Drunk tenants calling to say they couldn't find their dog, the dog that they weren't supposed to have there anyway. Things like that. Good times. Well, there was that one time at night where I'm there eating a snack, applesauce most likely, right?, and I'm watching the local news on the television. The reporter, who was a woman just a little older than me, was standing in front of a building, an apartment building with four units in it. I remember having a spoon of applesauce in my mouth and just leaving it there for the whole report, which was just maybe a minute, I mean, it wasn't big time news. But, ha, I do remember thinking, 'This is going to make my quiet night a little rougher.'"

"Ha."

"So, there were four units. One lady, 2-B let's call her, stabbed the guy in the unit diagonally down from her. Let's call him 1-A."

"Got it."

"So, quick recap, and quick story, as this isn't actually the story-story, okay? 2-B stabs 1-A, something about 1-A broke 2-B's vacuum cleaner, or stole it, something like that, it was never made clear; 1-A is stabbed pretty badly, he dies from it, but not quickly, and he suffered for a while. All the while 2-B starts screaming and wailing herself, like she's been stabbed, that's when other people, namely 2-A and 1-B, call the police. Meanwhile, 2-B has thrown the knife on the roof of the place, just above her unit, too, in fact, and she's huffing and puffing and dragging the vacuum, her vacuum, perhaps broken, perhaps liberated, when the police arrive. They take her away. She's still away today, I guess. I don't know. I haven't thought about 2-B and 1-A in a while, a long while."

"..."

"So, now we have two apartments to fill, because they, 2-B and 1-A, were the only tenants in each. Each night I come into the office after dark, and turn on the computer, and there's a to-do list for me, from my manager: do this, do that, fix this, find someone to fix that, and on and on and on. So, now, or then, add to that list: find tenants for these two units.

"So the search is on. I actually have something to do for a few nights. I fill one of them rather quickly, if I remember right. Pull credit, verify employment, quick background check, blah blah blah, nothing too invasive, but enough to turn down some people. One down, one to go. In fact, I had quickly leased out 2-B again, leaving only 1-A."

"The one where the guy got stabbed."

"You're bloody right. The one and only, yeah. Cleaned up, of course, but it wasn't that bad, he was stabbed at the back door and staggered out. As convenient as it gets, from my perspective, from my position at the time."

"So, you need to fill 1-A."

"I do. And it's just not working out for some reason. One guy has good credit, but an arson charge. One girl has good credit and a good background, but can't prove employment to save her life, and I don't want that going on in one of my places, whatever that happens to be... And, finally, I get an application from a guy, a nice guy, nice looking guy too, I happened to be there when he was dropping his application off at the office one Thursday night, looked like he was on his way home from work, or maybe on his way to work, turns out, it was a little of both.

"After a little of doing nothing, I thought I should probably do a little something, just to pass the time or whatnot. So, I started on his application. The first thing I did was pull a background check, because the boss did not want any people with destructive pasts, I can't blame him, I guess. This guy passed. Then I checked his employment section. Seemed he was working two jobs; I verified them both that night easily. Also saw that he was an ex-soldier. Had been deployed overseas for one of those recent wars we had gotten ourselves in. But he was out of the service now, and working two jobs. So, I pulled his credit, and I can't remember the details, but it wasn't good, so I wrote him an email and sent it to him, just basically saying thanks but no thanks, he didn't pass the lease application. And I went on my way, doing as little work as possible, and didn't think much about it for a while."

"Okay."

"..."

"Go on."

"So, the next week, I'm going through the mail, and there's a letter. From this guy. An actual letter, not an email or a text. So, I open it, and I end up crying."

"Crying?"

"Oh, yes. Crying. Bawling. Like a baby. Totally."

"Ha."

"No, it was no joke, no. This was like a Shakespearean tragedy rolled into a lease application. It was crazy. Crazy well written and crazy disturbing. It caused a fit in me, for sure."

"A fit?"

"Like recently. Fit to be tied; fit to tie up."

"I see."

"So, the letter. An actual letter, one of the last I've seen, or at least the last I've looked at."

She pauses.

The car rocks from side to side in the wind. Not too far away, over the remaining natural dune, over the artificial dunes, over the dunes made from the bodies of former patients, the storm ravages the ocean. Row after row of white-capped and trash-capped foamy waves crash ashore, dragging out old buckets, roofing materials, clothes, shoes, hats, glasses, and bodies. Tonya and Map have been on the Burial Island long enough to know they are missing a show at the shoreline in this weather.

After a moment, he says, "Go on. The letter."

"He had been a veteran, or I guess, that's not right. He was a veteran; he had been a soldier. Overseas. To one of those wars. I honestly forget which, perhaps more than one. That would make sense. A year here, a year there."

"Yeah."

"And, so, somewhere along the way, from desert to mountains, his wife back here takes his credit cards and maxes them out, takes all the money from the bank account, takes the good stuff out of the house, takes the kid, they had a son I believe, and takes the dog, and just takes off. With some random guy."

"Of course."

"And he at first finds out about this from his wages being garnished."

"That would piss me off."

"And then, I guess he somehow got home sooner from overseas, or whatev, or maybe not, I don't recall, but when he got home, home home, to his apartment, the locks were changed for lack of rent."

"Oh, huh."

"So, here he is, his credit cards are maxed out, late fees, penalties, all that crud, and his paychecks are being garnished, and his son has been taken from him, and his dog is gone, the dog he's had since before he even met his wife, and the locks on his apartment are changed."

"..."

There's a massive thunder clap loud enough to wake a deadie.

"And he's writing all of this to me in a letter."

"To explain why he's got no money and why he's credit is all flocked up."

"Exactly."

"I see."

"And all this happened while he was being shot at during a war, too, to boot."

"Ugh."

"Right? But, still here's the deal, I'm totally on this guy's team now, karma wise or whatev, but, boom, a fact's a fact, this guy can't pass the test to rent from my company."

"So, you do what you have to do, and you change things around, and make it happen, quietly the whole time, right?"

"Exactly."

"Of course."

"And that's no problem."

"Smooth." The car shakes.

"Smooth sailing, so to say. Month one, fine. Month two, fine. Months three and four, yeah, fine. Check always arrives; no complaints for maintenance. Perfect. Not stabbing any other residents, not getting drunk and cursing out the cops, who then call me at four in the morning to go secure the property as the tenant is in the drunk tank."

"But then?"

"But then. But then, the next month. Check is late. I let it slide. No late charge, but come on, I leave him a message saying, I need that rent check. I don't want to have to fine you or report this to the credit bureaus."

"Because of policy. Company policy?"

"Right, it is what it is. I mean, I had pulled a quick one in the system to get him in this place; he needed to do his part by staying under the radar, and I mean by just once a month getting a check in on time."

"Sounds fair."

"I thought so, too. So, that month a check finally rolls in towards the end of the month. Not early for the next month, just almost a month late."

"At least he paid you in the same month."

"At least. But then, same thing the next month."

"..."

"Week one, no check. Week two, no check. Week three, a phone message, saying it would be soon."

"Soon."

"Soon. Two days later, and one of the neighbors swears she hears a gunshot. She calls me. She calls the neighbors. The neighbors, having gone through the whole 2-B and 1-A thing prior, were not strangers to this type of thing. Whatever this type of thing might be."

"And?"

"I got a call a little while later, still in the middle of the night, mind you, but I got a call that I should come down and secure the property."

"..."

"Was someone being taken to jail? Or being taken to the hospital?, I asked the man on the other end of the phone call. 'No, no jail.' Then I asked where the tenant was. The man said, 'They're taking what's left of him to the morgue, I guess.' And then he hung up."

"Oh."

"And I went over there. It wasn't too close to the office, but not too far. Fifteen minutes, I guess. Especially at that time of night. Only people around are the drunks and the cops looking for the drunks, and I wasn't a drunk or anything, so that didn't bother me."

"They were looking for me, back then."

"Ha! Right, right. But, yeah, so I get there, and the body is gone, this guy is gone, but the sun is coming up, soon, it is getting light, and there is, uh, parts, bloody bits around. That's all I want to say about that."

"I get it."

"..."

"..."

"I mean bits and blood everywhere. On the picture of his son on the mantle. On a nearby book. The wall. The floor. The ceiling. I'd never seen anything like it, not even since, not even down here. It was like a war, I guess, a mini war, in a way. Like one that he been in, over there, wherever it was that he was. Shooting people, trained to, and he's just a person, so he was just doing what he was trained to do."

"To shoot a person, is that what you mean?"

"Yes."

"I see."

"And, it took a little while to sink in, I mean, after I first got sick, there. Sick right then and there. Barely made it outside."

"Bleh."

"You don't know the half of it. I found a pack of ciggies and lit one and left it burning in an ash tray just to change the smell of death in the air. It was the only thing I could think of doing."

"Hmm."

"So, the cops left, the body left, the ambulance left, the neighbors left, the smoke left, and everything and everyone left, except me. I was still there."

"Why?"

"I was waiting for cleanup. You can't just paint over something like this, and legally, we had to take care of this right away, or we couldn't rent out the unit, I mean the apartment, here I am so used to using the term units, ha. But I waited and I waited."

"Did you see a note?"

"No, no, that's what I'm getting at. It's like, I was looking for one at first, without even knowing about it. But then, after a little while, I realized that there was no note."

"No note."

"Because, there didn't need to be one. Or, at least, there didn't need to be another one. I mean, I had read it, months ago."

"The letter he wrote to you?"

"Right, the letter he wrote to me."

"I see."

"I knew why. He knew why. I later told the detective on the case. I remember he said that he had already figured that one out, but thanks, thanks anyway."

They smile, they exchange glances, the car shakes, and extra buckets of gray rainwater seemingly are dumped onto the windshield of their stolen car.

"But?"

"Sorry?"

"Or, and? I mean, I feel like there's something more to this story."

"..."

"I feel like you have a little more to say, and that's why you brought it up, not just over 1-A..."

"...which, as a unit, remained vacant the rest of my time there, by the way..."

"...but something else?"

"No, yes. No, you're right, I mean."

"..."

"I just never wanted to be that woman."

"Which woman?"

"The ex-wife."

"Ah."

"Yeah, I decided then and there that I never was going to be that type of woman, ever, to anyone. The type to cause pain and suffering."

"Gotcha."

"But, you see, after months and months of isolation and percolating hatred, and then with Thom being killed..."

"... or just dying ..."

"...okay, with Thom gone, how's that?, with Thom gone without warning, I just got so flocking angry. And after those cops and that video, that one Damn was jacking off to. I was angry. So, so angry."

"Rightfully so, too."

"Maybe. But anger is still poison."

"..."

"It poisons us, Map. It's bad, for us and those around us."

"Agreed. Agreed."

"Ha, when I first got down here, I was assigned to a 1-A, and I said, 'Oh, no, please, something else.' And then, they assigned me to a 2-B, and again, I begged out. I think they wrote me off as some kind of crazy woman in the files on the first day."

"Ha. Yeah, I can see that, ha."

"But, see, the whole reason that I brought this up, the whole point, was that recently I saw myself becoming like that ex-wife, but even worse, instead of aimed at one person, just aimed outward. Outwardly projected anger."

"That's never good."

"Never good."

"..."

"And, you've actually taught me that, to a degree, Map."

"Me?"

"Yeah, just by the way you are."

"Ah."

"..."

"And, what's that, exactly?"

"Calm."

"I see it as resigned, as a negative."

"I know you do."

"..."

"But, I didn't want to be like that. Correction, I might have wanted to a little at some point, but I don't now. I don't now, for sure."

"Good."

"And so, we need to go. We need to go find someplace to ride out this storm; we can't live in this car forever."

"You have somewhere in mind yet?"

"Not specifically. But there's another handy trick I picked up from back in my days working for the leasing agent."

"Oh, yeah? What's that?"

"I can get us into any unit we decide we want to get into."

"Let's find one that looks like it's been empty for a while and go there; one off the recent rotation."

"Exactly what I was thinking, Map."

The car shakes again; the windshield wipers can't keep up.

Him: "Oh, hey."

"Yeah, what's that?"

"What about the girl?"

Her: "Come again?"

"The nurse?"

" ... "

"The one you tied up there earlier?"

"Oh, her?"

" ... "

"Whatev."

" ... "

"Just take some more sand, Map, and take a nap; I'll wake you later."

And outside the stolen car, a freed hub cap races across the road pushed on by the trashy gale. She turns the car around; chunks of sand land on the wet windshield, making the wipers virtually useless. The road is wet, the car is wet, the bridge is out, the street lights are blinking, blinking, then staying off, then coming back on as she drives in the middle of the night down the empty road, with no destination in mind, and the wind shifts the small car from one lane to another, and then back again, and puddles are deeper than she anticipates, and the car shakes and rattles, and she can smell smoke, and it reminds her of being in the apartment of 1-A after the incident, after the call, and now she can't be sure if the smell is from her engine, or from the ships burning out in the polluted sea, or if perhaps the entire Sickie Shoals has started burning, a final sickie solution. Sickiecide.

And then, as she needs to decide at a fork in the road, the streetlights blink off, and they stay off, and they stay off, and they stay off, and after a minute, then two, she realizes that the street lights are not going to be coming back on again.

The bridge is down and the power's out, and she flips an invisible coin and turns left and drives on, with Map out from the Sandman beside her, and the car shaking in the storm, and the sea air smelling like burning ships, she drives on.

The waves are getting closer and closer, but she doesn't need to see them (see the rat rot by the sea, sickie; now it is his fate, but soon it will be me), she feels them.

She's gotten used to it by now.

CHAPTER FOURTEEN

the Forever Floaters

This is it, a little later behind the eroded dune line, and this is what she's saying: "The lights are out, but nobody's home."

"Hmm?"

"The lights are out, but nobody's home."

He opens his eyes and looks over towards her voice; his neck hurts from how he slept up against the car door. "I don't think that's how that saying goes." She's leaning into the driver's side door, speaking to him across the seat; she's left the headlights on, they illuminate the carport in which she's parked the stolen medi-car.

She smiles. "I know. But it fits so well, and when the fit gloves, uh..."

"Again: that's not how it goes." He is dizzy, feels ill.

The smile stops. Outside of the car, the storm still rages, but Tonya has pulled them up under a unit, into the underneath carport, partially surrounding by wooden slats on three sides, a dune nearby, sand being blown by the crazy gales. When they stop talking, all they can hear is the wind whipping through the wooden slats, and just over the dunes they hear the raging manic fit of the tortured Atlantic.

"Come on, I just unlocked it. The bottom level..."

"What?"

"Crud. I just realized I have to carry you upstairs; I would have chosen a one floor place to crash, if there was one, I guess there isn't though, is there?"

"I can stay here."

"In the car? You're not thinking right. You can't just stay here."

"Why not?"

"In a stolen car, in this crazy storm?"

"..."

"No. No, Map, no. Stupid."

"Okay, I'll come inside."

"Of course you will, fool. It's not that I don't want you staying out here by yourself, but that I'd rather not go in there by myself."

"..."

"And be careful for the dead pelican over there." She motions with her head to her left.

"Oh."

"I guess it came in here to get out of the wind at some point, and never made it back out. Maybe gulls came in and had a little feast, those flockin' poxed ratholes."

"Maybe, maybe."

And then as sudden as a debilitating stroke, as sudden as cracked-up methed-up lightning, he lurches towards his right, leans on the passenger door, his hand grabs the interior door handle. The door of the med-car swings open, he falls towards the concrete, and now he's getting sick on himself, again, and getting sick on the carpet in the car, getting vomit on the salt-air rusted hinges, getting puke on the cracked vinyl on the door, getting stomach trash on the trash between the seat and the door, spitting bile at the random feathers flowing in the rancid breeze, and then he falls all the way out of the stolen medical-car, and then he lands on his elbow in the orange hued sickness, he cusses, he cringes, and he closes his eyes, maybe, maybe rather his eyes close themselves, his mind shuts itself down, the car's headlights dim, his ...

Clank clank clank.

...

Clank clank clank.

...

Whirl, hum, whirl, hum.

...

Clank clank clank. Whirl, hum.

...

He's passed out in his own vomit, under the house, within spitting distance of the dead, rotting pelican, but his mind is working as in a dream, but he doesn't know it, and to his mind he's back in an MRI machine again. Clank clank clank. Silence. Whirl. Clank clank clank. Silence. Map is dreaming of being in that loud plastic coffin.

The cream colored plastic is just inches from his nose; the tube surrounds him, it's not dark but not light, and there is no silence, even when there's no noise there is no silence; there's a cool breeze, odorless, blowing through the confined tube; it is a breeze that he is not used to anymore, one that is cool and odorless as opposed to smoky, ashy, trashy and unpleasant. Clank clank clank. In his hand he thinks he has the button to signal to the technician that he wants out; he squeezes it, there is no voice in the earphones that they have on him. Sometimes there was music being piped in, classical, but today in the MRI they are piping in the crazed screeches of those poxed feather flying rats, which he finds weird but he has no control over.

He squeezes the button again. He would like to be out of here; he's miffed of the MRIs, of the CT Scans, of the PT Myleos, of the EMGs, of the facet joint injections, tired of the radio frequency nerve ablations, mind-numbingly tired of the medial branch blocks, endlessly tired of the epidural steroid injections, too tired of trying things which don't work, which make him feel worse, which give him false hope, tired of the medications that make him sick when he takes them and makes him sick when he doesn't take them, sickly tired of the sweats, the shakes, the shivers, the confusion, the constipation, the mood swings, the exhaustion, the falling and the tripping, the co-pays, the waiting rooms, the surgical rooms, the recovery rooms, the IVs, the steroids, the anti-inflammatories, the anti-spasm meds, the narcotics, the non-narcotics, the generics and the brand name pills, the experimental sand pills, the placebos, the ghost smells, the phantom sounds, the nausea, the vomiting, the dry mouth, the hurting hair follicles, the boredom, that lack of inspiration caused by the sand, that damned sand, the bottles and bottles of pills, the piss stench of the units, the ammonia smells, the lingering deaths, the clanking of the machine is driving him nutty...

He presses the bottom in his hand again and again and again and again and finally:

"Map?"

"..."

"Map?"

"…"

"Flocking damn it, Map, wake the hell up!"

The clanking stops. The whirls stop. The humming stops. The cool odorless breeze in the tube disappears.

His eyes remained closed and he hears his name again, but now his nose works, and now his brain registers the persistent rot smell in the breeze from the trashline, and a faint odor of oil from the stolen med-car. "Map?" The wind's screams increase; he might be able to hear the waves, he can smell the burning ships, that combo of plastics and public hair and flesh all burning and combined into a fragrance of death and rot. He's gotten used to it by now: the burnt and the blistered, the sick and the dead.

He spits, swallows vile bile. His red-streaked eyes sting. He answers, "Yeah?"

"Map? Can you hear me?"

"Yeah." One ear feels like it is head butting the other; one eye feels like it is stabbing its twin; his hair hurts, his tongue feels swollen.

"Jesus, Map, I thought you were dead for a sec there or whatev…"

"Where am I? Where are we?"

"That's two different questions with two different answers."

"Hmm?"

"I'm under a unit, in a carport."

"…"

"You're passed out in a puddle of puke about to use a rotting pelican as a down pillow. Nasty."

"Ugh."

"Can you get up?"

"Right now?"

"Well, uh, yeah."

"Give me a few…"

"No, no. Come on. Let me help you up and get you inside of this place."

"Let me just close my eyes for a second."

"No way, Map, after hitting your head like that on the concrete, regardless of the padding your puke might have provided, I don't think that's a wise idea."

"…"

"Seriously. I'm either helping you up or kicking you in the nuts on the count of three, your choice."

"…"

"One."

"…"

"Two."

"…"

"Thr…"

"Hey, fine, help me up."

"Whatev."

He extends a hand; she reaches out to help him.

She pulls him up, he's lost weight in his time in the unit, she pulls him up, and slowly lowers him onto the car's warm hood. The ruffled feathers from the dead pelican flutter in the trashed breeze. She looks into his dilated eyes, feels his forehead and wipes off beads of sandy sweat, and then she uses her sleeve and wipes away the liquid gunk from his stubbly face.

"I feel like hell."

"You look like it, too, man."

"Thanks."

"Whatev."

"Are we going in there now?"

"Let's just take it easy for a minute, Map."

"…"

"Want me to make animals in the car headlights?"

"What?"

"Like, maybe, dead gulls?"

He smiles; his teeth hurt.

"Or boobs?"

He laughs; it hurts deep down inside. "Stop, it hurts to laugh. I think I might have hurt myself."

"What's new, huh?"

"…"

"Let's just sit here. I like it outside tonight, despite the rage out there. I like hearing the rain and the ocean so close together, like an orgy of wetness, but here we are, pretty dry, for the most part, except what blows in between the slats."

"…"

"So, when you were sleeping in the car and I was driving around, looking for a unit, this one as it turns out, I got to thinking."

"Okay."

"..."

"What were you thinking about?"

"Well, actually, about Ms. Nevershe."

"Oh, yeah?"

"Yeah. And more about what she said to me once, that time when she was talking to me about God. About what she'd say? To God. About what she'd say to God when she got there ... and I don't know, I guess she's either nowhere or somewhere with God now, you know? I mean, her body might have been washed out, into the trashline with the rest of the old unit, and she might be floating or she might have sunk ... and that's kinda of how I see it, the big picture. Make sense? No. I'm no deep thinker, I know; I'm not seminary student, let alone a candidate to be one. But, and I know this is simplifying things, but I guess she's either floating or sunk. You see?"

"Not really, no. But go on."

"I guess if she's wrong, her fat shell just sunk to the bottom, to be food for the leftover crabs, the ones that can live in that putrid salt water. Or, maybe she's floating. I'm trying to make allusions here, Map, is that the word? I don't know, and you can't think straight now, but hear me out, as I try to think this out. She said that she knew she'd see God, because she believed. Then she'd be floating. But if there's nothing, she'd be sunk. See?"

"Uh, okay."

"But, I think it doesn't matter."

"Oh? How's that?"

"Because, in the end, I think she lived her life with the aim that it did matter, and that's all that matters, mattered."

"..."

"I guess it all comes back to 1-A and 2-B."

"Those were the tenants, from the story you told me earlier."

"See, now we're synching, right on."

"Sinking?"

"Synching, right, Map." She wipes sand from her eyes; she fiddles with a tooth; some feather fly off the dead pelican and become lodged in her hair; she resembles a native warrior to Map, in his dizziness, as he looks up at her from the hood of the liberated medi-car. "And it has nothing to do with them, 1-A and 2-B, and nothing to do with Ms. Nevershe, but it does, I know I'm not making a lot of sense, but I think you'll follow."

"Go on, please."

So she does: "See, the end result doesn't matter: she, and here we'll continue to use Ms. Nevershe as our example, she might be up in Heaven, talking to God with his Son at his right hand, and she might be explaining how the last few painful years don't matter because she was just jubilant to experience all the beauty in life, she can see beauty even in the sun rise over the trashline... Or, she could be, just nothing, because that's the opposite of Heaven, nothing, not Hell, because if Heaven exists then Hell must exist, might exist, should exist, but if Heaven doesn't exist, then nothing exists afterwards, right?"

"Okay."

"But you never know. Or, we don't know now. Now being the key. And I guess we might know later, but not now. And I'm no scholar, Biblical or otherwise; I never even applied to college. But I think it's the journey, not the destination, and I know that seems naïve like a bumper sticker, but I think it is all about the journey, and not just the destination, you see, Map?"

"..."

"And I think it all comes down to two words, just two words, and whether the end is Heaven and Hell, or trashlines and nothingness, it comes down to two simple, but heavy, and hard words, Map, and nothing else matters after all the other crap, nothing at all, nothing at all..."

"..."

"..."

"Well?"

"..."

"Well, what are those two words?"

"..."

"..."

"You don't know?"

"I'm not sure."

"Ready?"

"..."

"Mercy."

"..."

"Forgiveness."

"..."

"Mercy and forgiveness."

They exchange glances; he smiles and it hurts; she smiles and a tooth almost falls out; gulls cry in the distance; the stench of the burning ships increases; the pelican feathers that were in her hair fly out in a new gust of wind; he repeats what she said to him, "Mercy and forgiveness."

"Right."

"..."

"That's why I have that naked cunt of a nurse back in the trunk of the medi-car; I couldn't let her die out there; I could never get it off of my conscience. That would be neither mercy nor forgiveness."

"Oh."

"I mean, she might die a slow, painful death. But I don't want to be the cause of it. I don't want to be that person, no matter what happens after I croak, I want to know, now while I'm here and alive, that while maybe these people, her especially, showed no mercy or forgiveness, I want to go knowing that at least I tried, and sometimes I failed, because I'm not perfect, hell no, but at least I tried, at least I tried, and from this point on, no matter how long or how short my sickie life turns out to be, I want to try, no matter if I float in the giant trashline in the sky, or sink into the crab fodder of nothingness."

"..."

"..."

"Well, are you going to let her out of the trunk? She can help you carry me upstairs."

"Let her out of the trunk? Are you flocking crazy? No way. I'm letting her live; I'm not going to let her try to kill us. Come on, Map, let's get inside. She'll be fine there."

"What about forgiveness?"

"Oh, I forgive her."

"..."

"I just don't trust her."

"Fair enough."

She leans over towards him, about to help him up, and then she stops, straightens up again, shuffles her feet in the sand, kicks the car, wipes sand from her eye, and says, "And another thing I've been thinking about recently ... while you were asleep earlier. Well, I noticed that you sleep a lot at night, I thought I changed that? Oh, well. But I was thinking about Thom, missing Thom, and then I got to thinking about how fragile it all is, all of this, all of us, even in this sandy flocking hell. I know that sounds stupid, because, heck, we're all sickies, down here, sickies here, sickies there, sickies everywhere, right? But, I, maybe we, we get so used to it. So stuck in our ways, stuck in ourselves, stuck in our own self-imposed ruts, right? Not quite digging our own graves, but definitely not noticing the six foot deep hole in the ground near us..."

"If we'd be so lucky; so lucky not to be gull fodder."

"I don't mean literally, Map, I mean, come on, whatev. But, we're so blind down here, worrying about ourselves, and I guess I'm talking about me, but I think we all feel it."

"..."

"I guess I was thinking about T.G."

"T.G.? Who is that?"

"I'm about to tell you." She pauses and spits out sand, gulls shriek outside of the carport, wind blows in rain drops so Map can't tell if her eyes are full of tears or rainwater or seawater or a combination, "T.G. was this guy I knew a little all my life. We went to school a little bit, you know, middle school, high school, and then we'd run into each other back at home, in the store, in a parking lot, in a random party, that sort of thing. And we were never intimate, but never strangers, see?" Map nods; Tonya continues: "So nice. So pleasant and nice every time I saw him, but not in a hitting on me way, right?, not trying to get into my pants, no, just genuinely nice. At a party, if he came over and said, 'Tonya, I haven't seen you in a year and a half, what have you been up to?', I felt like not only did he remember the last time he saw me, but he was interested in my answer."

"Okay."

"In a store, I'd be trying to reach a jar of applesauce, top shelf of course, only the best smashed apples for me, ha, and I be on my tippy toes, and all of a sudden a hand would appear, and it was a larger, taller person, a man, and he'd hand me the applesauce, smile, and go on, and it was T.G. Or, I'd go into a bar, once in a while, and he'd be behind the bar working, and give me two beers and only charge me for one. I mean, we weren't the type of friends who would call each other on the phone, or send letters to one another, nothing quite as tight as that, but just who would always be there. I mean, I've probably gotten closer to you, but unit-mates and all, well, living and dying in close quarters will make you know a person, you know?"

"Right, right, I know."

"So, that was then: that was on the mainland, healthy or whatnot, pre-Sickie Shoals, okay? Fast forward some, time jump in the story to this is here, this is now: Sickies in Sickie Shoals. One day, or, that's a phrase, it was night, of course, but one night I'm stressed out, one of our unit mates died, this was early on, before I got so flocking used to it, death, dead roomies, whatev, and I might have taken a little extra sand, because that's what it is there for, that's how I see it, to make you not feel, because it doesn't make you feel better, it makes you not feel, or not feel as bad, or not feel as sick, I don't know, I was stressed, I was a little upset, I was a little buzzed and stupid from the pills, and I went down to Thom's store, as much for human companionship as for applesauce, but Thom wasn't there, someone else was there that night, which was weird and threw me off a little more, and I was already unbalanced. What's new? Crap. Ugh. Sorry. I'm getting lost in myself; I hate that, this. Anyway, I did some shopping, bought more than I thought, popped some more sand, kept some under my tongue, and checked out, gave them my plastic card, they gave me back my plastic bags, great for the beach, right?, and my hands were full, and I wasn't paying attention, and I go to the door and realize I have too much in my hands to open the doors. But then they open up for me, the doors."

"Automatic doors?"

"Might as well have been for all I was paying attention. But, no, no. It wasn't. It was a man going to the store at night, and he opened the door, and I barely looked up, afraid I would drop something, or some of the flocking beach bugs would get in my eyes, or I don't even know what I was thinking about, but I wasn't thinking about whoever opened the door, that's for sure, and if it sounds bad, it just is how it is, okay?"

"Okay, I understand."

"And I walk on out, and I hear the man say, 'Hey, Tonya, how are you doing?'"

"Oh, let me guess, it was your friend?"

"Right. It was T.G., right there opening the door, and holding it for me like a gentlemen. Ha. I don't know why I just laughed right now, maybe so I don't cry. But, I'll be drowned if it wasn't him. T.G. And I was so caught off guard, and so distracted, that all I did was smile, make the briefest of eye contact, and all I said to him was, 'Oh, hey, hi.'"

"..."

"Can you believe it, just 'Oh, hey, hi.' I mean, barely words, more like sounds. And then I turned and I left and went on home to wallow in whatever problems were my own."

"I'm sure he understood."

"No, no, Map, maybe you don't understand. I sure didn't at the time. It took me til the next night, after a day's sleep, and I finally woke up and was looking at the hazy moon, and it was like Bam!, it was like a kick in the puss, I realized, once I got over thinking about me me me me me, that, oh crap, if T.G. was opening the door for me at Thom's store, which he clearly was, I mean, I may be a sickie but I'm no crazy, then he was down here, down here like the rest of us."

"Convalescing by the sea?"

"You know that's just pussy government double speak for dying next to the crapped out ocean."

"Oh, I know, I know."

"Right, T.G. was a no-hoper. A sickie. A soon to be deadie. And probably like most of us down here, all of us down here, he was sick, so sick and lonely, and hurting inside, and confused, and low on hope, and low on options, and low on funds and low on friends..."

"..."

He can tell the tears from the rain on her cheeks now; she goes on: "If there was a time in my life where I should have put on my big girl pants and kicked my problems to the side and put down my stupid plastic bags full of whatev it was that I was buying, it was then, it was then and there, but I didn't. And I regret that."

"I'm sorry."

"Yeah, you and me both, Map, you and me both..."

"..."

"I tried to find him, and, ha, it all comes full circle, but I found out where he was from our little nude wench in the trunk here."

"Princess?"

"I won't call her by a name, she doesn't deserve it."

"How?"

"How did I find him? Through the nastiest of ways. I had told her his name, or actually I think I had mentioned it to that other nurse, the one who never makes eye contact, and she must have told Princess, and a few days later, they are in the unit, doing as little as they possibly can, as usual, and she drops a photograph onto my floor, under my door actually, slides it under, and she laughs and she slams the front door to the unit, and gets in her car, this one you are sitting on, I guess, and she leaves."

"What was in the picture?"

"T.G."

"Good, right?"

"No, it was a picture of him dead."

"..."

"I just never got the chance to make up that mistake of that night. It can never be undone."

"I'm so sorry."

"I just felt so bad about it then, and I still do now. I think I'm going to barf just talking about this."

"You need to talk about it to someone; thank you for talking to me."

"Hold on..." She turns around, goes back a few feet, and Map can hear her getting sick on the pavement. She's gone a few minutes, and she comes back, crying, wiping her mouth, and she extends her hand towards his, he takes it, and she says, "This time, this time I'm ready to help you inside. Let's go, Map."

"Hey, T?'"

"Yeah?"

"If it helps you sleep at night -"

"I don't sleep at night..."

"That's just a figure of, never mind. Anyway, if it helps you sleep better (how's that?), maybe your friend, T.G., had come to the same conclusion as you have."

"What's that, Map?"

"Mercy and forgiveness. But, I guess in this case, specifically forgiveness."

Tonya is silent, listening to the wind screaming through the wooden planks, and the waves, seemingly closer and closer, and the ever-present poxed gulls screaming and fighting and crying and laughing at her pain, at her confusion, at her sickness, at her alienation, at her isolation.

Map goes on, "I mean, think about it, and consider this: you and he had the same background, came from the same place and ended up at the same place, right? Started in Richmond, ended up in Sickie Shoals; hundreds of miles apart, but so close at the same time. Right?"

"Whatev."

"No, no, not your 'whatev' gull crap. Seriously. You are great and all, but you're not the first person to believe in forgiveness. Everyone gets to the same ends sometimes through different means, right? Think about it, you would have understood if the roles were reversed. You'd forgive him; let yourself believe that he would've, no, that he did, that he definitely did, forgive you."

"..."

"Okay?"

"Okay. Okay, alright, let's go inside."

She looks down, something's rubbed against her ankle, it reminds her of a pet from childhood, a charcoal kitten, rubbing against her shin. She looks down, and it's the rotting corpse of the pelican, with the wet feathers tricking Tonya's distracted mind into thoughts from yesteryear.

"Ah, flocking gross." They both look down. She continues: "Uh, we need to be getting upstairs soon. The power is gone, keep the headlights on so we can see; we'll find a flashlight or something once we get in."

As she moves her feet, her shoes are wet and there is a sloshing sound. Map's been on the hood of the liberated medi-car, unaware. He looks down; concern comes over his face: "Oh. Crap. This can't be good."

The wicked, wild waves, not all of them, just some forward scouts, have penetrated the dune line like drunk seniors on prom night, and have washed on down, past the remaining sick-sea-front convo units, washed across the street, and have turned the carport into a kiddie pool, which, instead of smelling like piss, smells like death and dismay.

"Let's go, we need to go upstairs."

She turns around; she signals for Map to crawl onto her back, "Piggy back ride time, Map-o," she tries to smile, but even in the dim light he can see her frown, her concern.

He climbs on, he's lost weight over the last year, and more and more down here, while seaside, while convalescing by the sea.

She walks to the unlocked door, which she broke into earlier; the first floor is simply a utility room with a couple of closets and stairs leading to the main living floor, but it is a few steps up from the sandy ground, and is currently still dry.

The headlights of the medi-car penetrate enough of the darkness to see a little. She lowers Map off her back, and leaves him leaning against the wall, next to the door.

He says, "Hey, Tonya?"

"Yeah?"

"Notice anything?"

"What?"

"Odor-wise. Scents. Smells."

She's rummaging through a closet, she comes back with two flashlights, she turns both on, holds one in her hand, and turns the other up facing the ceiling so it illuminates the room.

"Well," she inhales, looks around, shines the flashlight up the stairs into the dark emptiness, "well, I guess I don't smell anything."

"Right. No ammonia. No chemicals. No sickness smells, or, I guess I should, as the nurses would, no sickie smells."

"Hmm, yeah. I guess not. This one must not have been used as a convo unit yet, or not for a while recently. And it's not waterfront, so who'd have thought it would wash away quickly and easily, which is what they want to happen here, of course."

Map sniffs the air in the unit. "But I'm a little confused." He sniffs again.

"About what?"

"About what I smell."

"What is that?"

"It smells like a combination of ... of ... a reggae concert? And dog piss? I must be tired. Am I going nuts? No, don't answer that..."

"Yeah, yeah, I smell it, too. Both. Like a pissy, dreadlocked dog."

She starts shining the flashlight around the room, at the ceiling, at the walls, and then to the floor, and she bends down close, examining the floor, and she wipes her fingers on the sandy floor, then licks them and she wipes them on the floor again and raises her fingers under the flashlight's beam, which reveal short pink hairs and longer red hairs.

"What the flock? No, no flocking way..." And she turns and she starts going up the stairs, skipping every other stair, and she ends up at the top and she disappears around the corner, and she's out of sight when Map thinks he hears an engine of a car close by, and then he hears tires parting the sheet of sickly sea water on the carport, and then he's certain that he hears a car door slam shut, and by the time he's seen the shadows pass in front of the liberated medical-car, he wishes that he had the other flashlight in his hand, as opposed to it sitting on the floor in front of him, just out of reach.

By the time she comes back down the stairs, smiling and snuggling with an un-bloated, half-shaven and band-aided ancient pink poodle, she has no time to react. The dog pisses, Tonya drops her flashlight which then shuts off, leaving only the other flashlight pointed at the ceiling. The porky doctor laughs and his beard's dreadlocks shake, dancing with his laughter, looking like warriors chanting around a fire in the fading flashlight's beam.

De Gouge's browned teeth are illuminated in the dim light; Tonya can see specks of dust and sand falling from the dreadlocks, she can hear water washing under the carport. Tonya briefly thinks about the naked and bound nurse in the trunk of the stolen car, but a flash of light gets her attention again, her arms are warm as the ancient poodle empties her bladder involuntarily.

"Whoa ... what's going on?" Then she notices the syringe that is already stuck into Map's neck, but still being held gingerly in de Gouge's fattened fingers, his dirty, sandy thumbnail reflecting light, as his fingers are poised to inject whatever it is that the mad doc has in the tube.

His dreadlocks seemingly ask, "Hey, Tanya or whatever your sickie name is, how'd you like your gimp friend here to go the way of that pink bitch there, not to mention her croaked whale of a mistress, eh?"

Map is silent and still; salty sweat rolls over his eyebrows and into his eyes. The waves outside are coming over the dune line; the trashline is rolling in. Piss drips down Tonya's leg, dripping from the confused, exhausted, bandaged bitch. The bulb in the remaining flashlight dims and then goes black, the headlights are the only light for a moment; the waves echo in the carport, overwhelming the gulls' shrieked choruses.

"Put the bitch down, you infected twat, or I'll turn this sickie into a bloated medicine ball." He briefly removes his hand from the syringe, it dangles down, stuck in Map's neck; a trail of bloods starts to drip, mixing with the sweat. The flashlight turns back on; a gale comes in, blowing Tonya off her balance, the obese de Gouge isn't budged.

Tonya slowly steps back, hesitates and steps forward to where she had been, and then she takes one more step forward. "Hey, hey, now." She takes one more step back, to where she was, hesitates for a moment, feels like she might get sick again. Cradling the now-found poodle in the crook of her right arm, she reaches up and feels a tooth with her left hand. The dog tries to wag her tail, tries to move her phantom rear limb, thinks about licking Tonya, but ends up doing nothing. She lays cradled like an ancient child in Tonya's arms. "Hey, come on, what are you doing?"

"What do you think, huh, vamp?"

"I tell you what: I won't kick your old ass if you back away from Map."

"Ha!" Dreadlocks dangle and dance. "Fat chance you can hurt me." He grips the syringe again, his thumb is on the plunger. "I don't seem especially concerned now, do I?" There is drool on the side of his mouth; she sees spit shoot into the air.

"Here." She shifts Pistachio's weight from being cradled and holds her with both hands, then holds the dog's tender frame in front of her.

"I don't need that thing anymore; I got some of her ready to go right here." He's moving the syringe in Map's skin; Map closes his eyes for a moment, holds his breath. The demented doc goes on, "You don't know how to play this game, do you, sickie?"

Tonya takes a step forward, with the dog face level, towards her left; de Gouge takes a smaller step backwards, and a bit to his right, dragging Map with him. The doctor is standing now in the doorway; Tonya can't tell if he is trying to block the door or back out of the door. The wind whips in, sand and toxic smelling fumes, a few feathers fly in, the waning and waxing sound of the waves echoes under the house, into the small entry room.

She goes on, but stands still, "Okay, I've got something else for you. In the trunk of the car."

"I don't know what you possib-," then the doctor's huge head is flung away from Map, like he was hit in the head by a baseball bat from behind.

The doctor stumbles to his left and as Map drops to the floor, eyes opening, mouth shouting in pain from falling on his hurt leg, Tonya notices an extra shadow in the medi-car's headlight beams.

The doctor slumps onto the floor, dazed but awake; his hand no longer grips the Pist-blood loaded syringe, which dangles from Map's neck.

A man, boots soaking wet from the invading water, hair and face wet from the buckets of rain, is standing in the doorway. Now blocking most of the headlight's beams, he is standing with a piece of driftwood in his hand, held like a tennis racket.

Northern Wrecks doesn't look over at Tonya, she is frozen like a statue, Pist also is a statue; Tonya's not even sure if he knows she and the pink poodle are in the room, just a few feet away.

The crazed man ignores Map also, but stares at the fat doc, and starts to speak:

"There once was a sea,"

He raises the driftwood over his head.

233

"Beloved by the likes of me,"

He slams the driftwood down into the doctor's plump side with all his might.

"Before it became known as Sickie Shoals."

The doctor moans; his dreadlocks try to retreat.

The man raises a booted foot into the air, water dripping off, sandy.

"But now we have this beach,"

He kicks the doctor in the knee.

"For which beauty is now out of reach,"

The doctor grabs at his knee; Tonya drops the dog.

"And its sand is used only for burial holes."

Tonya drops to her knee and bends over Map. She yanks the syringe from his neck and holds it like a knife.

Northern Wrecks rears his foot back again, kicks it roughly into the small of the doctor's back; the doctor winces in pain.

"See those waves, once so fine,"

She grabs onto Map; hoists him upwards.

"Be pillaged by the trashline,"

The man goes down on one knee; then leans over the doctor's face.

"And the crap of a million poxed gull."

He thrusts his forehead into the doctor's nose; a sick cracking sound is heard over the echo of the wind and waves.

Tonya moves towards the door, partially dragging the stumbling Map.

"I'd do anything to fix it, to turn it back,"

Northern Wrecks pulls down his ever-present face mask, stained teeth scream, and he slaps the doctor's fleshy face.

"I only just started with that smack,"

While Northern Wrecks is distracted with beating the doctor, Tonya and Map sneak behind him out the door and into the flooded carport.

"And I'm not going to stop until the trashline gets your skull!"

Northern Wrecks opens his mouth, and thrusts his teeth down onto the doctor's left ear, biting and tearing and smiling throughout.

The three-legged dog trots undetected behind Northern Wrecks, tries to take a quick rest, and then follows Tonya and Map outside.

In the carport the whipping wind and the marauding waves are making it almost impossible to hear the doctor's painful shrieks.

The waves in the carport are up to the small landing that they stand on, covering the few stairs; the seawater gets halfway to the doors of the car, then backs out, rushes back in; the carport has become almost a tidal pool, a unique ecosystem. The dog empties her ancient bladder in confusion again.

Wooden slats start popping from the force of incoming waves; the trashline is making progress over the dunes and into the convalescent community.

Northern Wrecks, not wanting to end the blood games quite yet, grabs and pulls Map back into the hellish fracas.

Pist, seeing the madman's violence next to her, plumps up in size, back to her medicine ball proportions; a perturbed look crosses her face.

A banging sounds starts under the house, adding to the symphony of wind blasts and wave shouts and the yelps of pain from the downed doctor, and random poetry is shouted into the gales by Northern Wrecks, the dog whimpers, Map goes silent again. Welcome to the shoals.

Tonya bends over and once again yanks Map up, falling backwards off the wooden landing into the two or three feet of seawater which has now made itself at home in this carport and all around the war zone of a unit.

The dog jumps into the water to follow Tonya, who drags Map towards the two medi-cars in the driveway; the current under the house as she tries to walk is surprisingly swift.

Parts of the house start to float by, slats that once provided some privacy, are now washing into Map and Tonya as they struggle towards the parked and swamped medi-cars.

They struggle past the car they stole, as it is blocked in by de Gouge's car. Tonya forces Map onto the hood of the car which is barely above the water level. He struggles up the slight incline of the windshield and then slides up onto the roof, which is perhaps now two feet above the water line, which is starting the contain more pieces of discarded items and dead animals. The trashline is crossing the once sandy, now flooded streets of Sickie Shoals.

Map turns around reaches out his hand towards Tonya; she says, into the wind, "No!"

Pist, bloated and soaking, is struggling to get onto the hood, out from the current. Tonya pushes the old dog up, it scrambles as best that it can: old claws slipping on the slick hood.

"I can't leave her there."

"Who? Pist? She's fine, come on!" His hand is still extended towards Tonya; he looks around them into the dark, wishing for the moon to throw just a little more light on their dark situation.

"No. The nurse. In the trunk."

Map looks at the car in front of them; the water level is half way past the trunk entrance.

"Don't worry about her; she might not even be alive in there anymore, look at the water line."

"No, Map, no."

"..."

Tonya walks back towards the drowning car, and then yells back to him: "Mercy and forgiveness!"

Map pulls the bloated pink bitch up onto the roof with him; Tonya struggles to find the trunk latch on the flooded medi-car.

After a struggle, she opens the trunk, engulfed with water; the nurse's face was above the waterline, barely, but she's coughing and bobbing in the deep trunk.

Map notices the house moving, no, wait, no yet, that's not right, and he realizes that the car he and Pist are perched upon is drifting, drifting away from the house.

Under the house, Tonya is pulling the soaked and still naked nurse Princess out of the trunk, and the current is pulling and yanking her, and she wonders about sharks and trash and then up splashing towards her comes Northern Wrecks, his face bloody and sandy, and smiling.

Tonya half swims and half yanks the bound nurse through the current and the trash, towards the drifting car. She gets to it, it seems to be running from her, but the current is pushing her towards it at the same time. She grabs Princess's hair, and starts to climb onto the hood; Map slides down and helps her. They yank the nurse close enough, some hair comes out, and then they pull her onboard.

First they smell it, even in this gale, then the next second the trashline surrounds them (he's gotten used to it by now), the water comes faster, gets deeper. The car spins, its tires are no longer on terra firma.

Too many feet deep now, what was once a sandy street is now a trashline canal; the house they were just in is now halfway to submersion.

The car moves with the water; the occupants struggle onto the roof.

One minute the car is pulled towards the remaining dune line, where there are still minimal dues, and the next minute the rushing waters push the car back towards the shallow sound and the mainland, still so far away, so far away.

The hood is now submerged; the car will sink sooner than it will become a life boat, a death boat, a death buoy, a sandy and rusty crypt.

From the darkness all around them, cracking noises, pops, as pilings sway and snap, houses dance and bend in the rushing and rising invading waters.

Rain falls, currents ebb and flow, the trashline is up to the windshield, and the nurse is throwing up and gagging, the bloated dog is trying to empty an already emptied bladder.

Tonya grabs hold of Map's hand, and holds on tightly. They look at each other and then back at the black trash-filled waters surrounding them.

"You know, right?"

"..."

"I'm not sure, either, but it's either going to takes us out there," a nod east towards the wrathful sea, "or eventually way over there," a nod west, towards the mainland. "But either way we're going to be getting out of Sickie Shoals."

"I hope it takes us that way." A nod towards the east.

"Into the ocean? We'll drown for sure."

"No."

"What?"

"Towards the floaters."

"The forever floaters?"

A nod. Eye contact. Another nod.

A pause.

A wave.

"But, you know what?"

"I think."

"..."

"..."

"I'd rather drown in salt water than drown in sand."

"..."

"..."

"Yeah. Yeah."

And it seems that the waves thus far have been only a test, as out of the east, from the darkness under the rain clouds, the waves pound and push and rape and pillage and the water comes up to the medi-car's rusty roof (he's gotten used to it by now), and nurse is the first to go off, she slides off almost like a child in a water park into the cold dark trashline, and then the dog slides off, she's bloated again like a medicine ball and she floats nearby, and then the next wave takes Tonya and Map, hand in hand, into the cold water, the Barrier Islands have become the Burial Islands, and Tonya's hand grabs onto Pist's remaining rear leg, and the floating dog acts as a buoy, and Tonya kicks with all her might, and Map moves his good leg, but is weighted down by his bad left leg, and then the currents go back out, and floating out, being pulled back out, the Barrier Islands have become the Burial Islands, Tonya starts to swim, the dog uses her worn out front arms, and the currents pull them towards the Forever Floaters out there, seemingly so close, but actually far, and they kick and they float and Map has a thunderbolt of pain, and his vision goes black, and as a wave comes over his face, he forgets about the sea (see the rat rot by the sea), and forgets about the sickies, forgets about the sand and forgets about the units, the rot race, the Burial Islands, and the cold is salty but he's gotten used to it by now, craps of fate he has, but try as he might to stay in the watery movement, the salty moment, he starts to dream, to daydream, to drown-dream about recovery and the bubbles float towards the trashline.

But still they kick, they try to swim, they struggle under the trash and the currents and the violent waves. But they kick, they try to swim, they try, they try, they try.

This is it: Sickies sink in the nasty ocean tide, sickies that were dying or just along for the ride. Up on shore, the sand blowing against hollow crab shells combined with the sea oats beating each other are a percussive hypnotic; the stench of death is enough to bring you down from any prescribed narcotic.

The Barrier Islands have become the Burial Islands; one always feels fine drowning under the trashline.

There once was a sea,
Beloved by the likes of me,
Before it became known as Sickie Shoals.

But now we have this beach,
For which beauty is now out of reach,
And its sand is used only for burial holes.

See those waves, once so fine,
Be pillaged by the trashline,
And the crap of a million poxed gull.

I'd do anything to fix it, to turn it back,
I only just started with that smack,
And I'm not going to stop until the trashline gets your skull.

Handsome Kelly (a.k.a "Northern Wrecks")
Sickie Shoals, NC

Stalwart Supporters:
(or, *thanks for the encouragement and editorial assistance*)

Heather C. Harding
R. Devon Porter
Brian C. Ring
B. Jacob Campbell